The Missing Ink

"Karen E. Olson has launched a delightful new series with *The Missing Ink*, featuring tattooist Brett Kavanaugh. Brett is proud that she makes grown men cry. She also makes grown women laugh. I look forward to more adventures for this Las Vegas needle artist."
—Elaine Viets, author of the Dead-End Job Mysteries

"In *The Missing Ink*, Karen E. Olson has penned a winner, full of crisp dialogue, a red-hot setting, and a smart, sassy, tattooed protagonist. Viva Las Vegas!"
—Susan McBride, author of the Debutante Dropout Mysteries

"[A] pleasantly jargon-free themed mystery. . . . Readers need not be conversant with 'street flash' or other industry terms to enjoy the setting and follow Brett down a trail of needles and gloves to the dramatic finale." —*Publishers Weekly*

"A fun read. . . . The characters are as quirky as Las Vegas itself. . . . [Brett] is both likable and down-to-earth, and will have readers returning for more." —The Mystery Reader

"Olson uses the fresh setting of an upscale Las Vegas tattoo shop . . . for a fast-moving tale with quirky but affectionately portrayed characters. Although stubborn, Brett never becomes too stupid to live in her determination to solve the mystery. The tension is kept at a high pitch." —*Romantic Times*

"Fun. . . . The setup is pure, the setting is flashy . . . and I expect that Brett Kavanaugh will find a devoted following."
—Gumshoe

"This one has it all with edgy characters and a tight plot."
—*Mystery Scene*

"Ms. Olson walks readers through a multiple-murder mystery, supplying clues at a steady pace. *The Missing Ink* is suspenseful, entertaining from the start, and has a touch of romance that nicely rounds out the story." —Darque Reviews

continued . . .

The Annie Seymour Mysteries

Shot Girl

Dead of the Day

"Like an alchemist, Karen E. Olson blends together wildly disparate elements into pure gold. *Dead of the Day* is a delightful dance with the devil—dangerous, dark, and romantic."
—Reed Farrel Coleman, Shamus Award–winning
author of *Soul Patch*

Secondhand Smoke

"Annie Seymour, a New Haven journalist who's not quite as cynical as she thinks she is, is the real thing, an engaging and memorable character with the kind of complicated loyalties that make a series worth reading. Karen E. Olson is the real thing, too, a natural storyteller with a lucid style and a wonderful sense of place."
—*New York Times* bestselling author Laura Lippman

"Authentic urban atmosphere, generous wit, and winning characters lift Olson's second outing for Annie Seymour.... Readers are sure to look forward to Annie's further adventures."
—*Publishers Weekly*

"Annie is a believable heroine whose sassy exploits and muddled love life should make for more exciting adventures."
—*Kirkus Reviews*

"[Olson's] fast-paced plot and great ending make it a perfect read for patrons who like a bit of humor in their mysteries."
—*Library Journal*

"Olson knows exactly how to blend an appealing heroine, an intricate plot, and inventive humor. Annie's is a story worth pursuing and a story well worth reading."
—*Richmond Times-Dispatch*

Sacred Cows

"A sharply written and beautifully plotted story."
—*Chicago Tribune*

"Olson writes with a light touch that is the perfect complement for this charming mystery." —*Chicago Sun-Times*

"Karen E. Olson plunges readers into the salty-tongued world of cynical reporter sleuth Annie Seymour.... Spins from sinister to slapstick and back in the breadth of a page. Engaging."
—Denise Hamilton, bestselling author of *Trials to Treasure*

"A boilermaker of a first novel.... Olson writes with great good humor, but *Sacred Cows* is also a roughhouse tale. Her appealing and intrepid protagonist and well-constructed plot make this book one of the best debut novels of the year."
—*The Cleveland Plain Dealer*

Driven to Ink

A TATTOO SHOP MYSTERY

Karen E. Olson

AN OBSIDIAN MYSTERY

OBSIDIAN
Published by New American Library, a division of
Penguin Group (USA) Inc., 375 Hudson Street,
New York, New York 10014, USA
Penguin Group (Canada), 90 Eglinton Avenue East, Suite 700, Toronto,
Ontario M4P 2Y3, Canada (a division of Pearson Penguin Canada Inc.)
Penguin Books Ltd., 80 Strand, London WC2R 0RL, England
Penguin Ireland, 25 St. Stephen's Green, Dublin 2,
Ireland (a division of Penguin Books Ltd.)
Penguin Group (Australia), 250 Camberwell Road, Camberwell, Victoria 3124,
Australia (a division of Pearson Australia Group Pty. Ltd.)
Penguin Books India Pvt. Ltd., 11 Community Centre, Panchsheel Park,
New Delhi - 110 017, India
Penguin Group (NZ), 67 Apollo Drive, Rosedale, North Shore 0632,
New Zealand (a division of Pearson New Zealand Ltd.)
Penguin Books (South Africa) (Pty.) Ltd., 24 Sturdee Avenue,
Rosebank, Johannesburg 2196, South Africa

Penguin Books Ltd., Registered Offices:
80 Strand, London WC2R 0RL, England

First published by Obsidian, an imprint of New American Library,
a division of Penguin Group (USA) Inc.

First Printing, September 2010
10 9 8 7 6 5 4 3 2 1

Copyright © Karen E. Olson, 2010
All rights reserved

OBSIDIAN and logo are trademarks of Penguin Group (USA) Inc.

Printed in the United States of America

To my sister, Sandy

ACKNOWLEDGMENTS

I have to thank Clair Lamb and Cheryl Violante for their help with the manuscript and for not letting our friendship get in the way of a firm critique. The First Offenders (Alison Gaylin, Jeff Shelby, Lori Armstrong, and Anthony Neil Smith) are, as usual, a wonderful sounding board and great friends. Thanks to my favorite book bloggers (Wendy, Christina, Alice, and Iliana) for being so supportive, and to Ania, who helped me see beyond the tattoos. Special thanks to Molly Weston, who went above and beyond to make me, Julie Hyzy, and Hank Phillippi Ryan feel like celebrities. Thanks to Rachel Kristina Jones for her generosity and such a great name. My agent, Jack Scovil, continues to be enthusiastic and always puts things in perspective. My editor, Sandy Harding, and publicist, Megan Swartz, are a pleasure to work with. Thanks to all my readers who e-mail me to tell me they love Brett and her world. It keeps a writer going to know you're out there. And a final shout out to my husband, Chris, and daughter, Julia, who are everything to me.

Chapter 1

When Sylvia and Bernie came back from That's Amore Drive-Through Wedding Chapel with my car, it would've been nice if they'd taken the body out of the trunk.

As it was, I didn't discover it until a day later, when I hit a bump and heard a thump that made me curious about what I might have forgotten to unload on my last trip to the grocery store. By that time, the newly married Sylvia Coleman and Bernie Applebaum—Sylvia said at her age she wasn't about to take on any new names—were at the Grand Canyon on their honeymoon, and I was in my driveway staring at the corpse of a man in a tuxedo—as if he'd expected death would be a black-tie affair.

Being both the daughter and sister of police officers, I did the first thing that came to mind: I called Sylvia's son, Jeff Coleman, to find out whether he knew anything about this.

"Murder Ink." Jeff's voice bellowed through my ear. Murder Ink was his business, a tattoo shop up near Fremont Street, next door to Goodfellas Bail Bonds. He specialized in flash, the stock tattoos that lined the walls of his shop, even though I knew firsthand that he was an amazing artist when he put his mind to it.

Despite the flash, Jeff was one of my main competitors in Vegas. I own The Painted Lady, where we do only custom designs. We cater to a classier client, and my shop is in the Venetian Grand Canal Shoppes on the Strip, a high-end themed mall that would never have allowed a tattoo shop to sully its image without a little blackmail by the shop's former owner.

"It's Brett."

"Kavanaugh?"

"Your mother seems to have left me a little something for the use of my car yesterday." Sylvia had asked me nicely if she and Bernie could use my red Mustang Bullitt convertible for their drive-through wedding. She said it was preferable to Bernie's blue 1989 Buick and her thirty-five-year-old purple Gremlin, which looked like a lizard with its tail cut off.

"What about Jeff's Pontiac?" I'd asked her.

"It's bright yellow. It looks like a pimp's car."

I couldn't argue with that. It did look like a pimp's car. I told Sylvia that she was welcome to use my Mustang, but she had to drive. Bernie's cataract surgery wasn't scheduled for another six weeks, and even though Sylvia said she "watched the road" for him, it didn't inspire much confidence.

"What are you talking about, Kavanaugh?" Jeff was asking.

"There's a man in my trunk."

A low chuckle told me that perhaps I hadn't described the situation properly.

"A dead man. In a tuxedo."

"And you're sure my mother left it there for you?"

"I certainly don't remember it being there before she borrowed my car."

"So let me play devil's advocate a minute. Maybe he climbed into your trunk and died *after* my mother and Bernie returned the car."

Hmm. I hadn't thought of that. I recounted where the car had been since they dropped it off for me at the Venetian, and it had only been there and here, in my driveway overnight, and then at Red Rock Canyon this morning when I went for a hike. I leaned farther in toward the body. On the right breast pocket I could see something stitched in red thread: "That's Amore."

"He's from the wedding chapel, Jeff. His tux is an advertisement. It's got the name sewn on it."

"Is your brother home? Has he seen the body?"

My brother, Detective Tim Kavanaugh, hadn't been home all night. I could only surmise that either he was catching bad guys or he'd had a late date that spilled over into morning.

"No."

"Have you called the cops, then?"

"Doing it now." I punched END on my cell and sent Jeff Coleman into oblivion as I now entered 911. But as I was about to hit SEND, I realized I should try to reach Tim first, before he came home to a driveway full of police cruisers and the coroner's van.

He answered on the first ring.

"What do you want, Brett?"

His tone was cold, but the fact that he'd actually answered his phone meant that he was probably doing police stuff and not with a woman. A good thing for me, but perhaps not for him.

"You remember how I let Sylvia and Bernie borrow my car? For their wedding the other day?"

A heavy sigh told me he wasn't into tripping down memory lane and I should get on with it.

"Well, they left me a body. In the trunk."

A second of silence, then, "What are you talking about?"

I told him about Mr. That's Amore. "He's from the chapel. The drive-through." I explained about the stitching on his pocket.

"Brett, how do you get yourself into these messes?" He was referring to a couple of other incidence in the last six months, incidence that were completely out of my control, thank you very much.

"I told you not to let that wacko borrow your car," he said.

"She's not a wacko," I said, although not with much confidence. Sylvia had her moments. I didn't know exactly how old she was, but I guessed she was in her seventies or possibly early eighties. She and her former husband had owned Murder Ink before he died and she retired, handing over the business to Jeff. She spent a lot of time at the tattoo shop and had actually inked my calf: Napoleon going up the Alps. It was one of my favorite Jacques-Louis David paintings, and I did the stencil. Sylvia, as far as I knew, didn't do any original designs—and sometimes I wondered whether she hadn't a touch of dementia. But I was happy she and Bernie had hooked up. They started swimming together at the Henderson pool a few months back, and it developed into a late-in-life romance.

"So you don't recognize this man?" Tim asked, completely reversing the conversation and throwing me off balance for a second.

"You mean the guy in the trunk?"

"Yes, Brett, the guy in the trunk." Exasperation had seeped into Tim's tone, and I totally didn't need that right now.

I counted to ten as I leaned a little farther into the trunk and peered at Mr. That's Amore. His face was whiter than that zinc stuff you put on your nose so you won't get sunburn. His eyes were closed, but his mouth hung open slackly, as if he didn't have the energy to close it. With only a few spots of dust and dirt, the tux was remarkably neat, considering he was stuffed in my trunk.

He looked uncannily like Dean Martin.

I didn't have time to ponder that further, because I could also see the side of his neck, below his ear.

He had a tattoo of a spiderweb.

I told Tim, who made a sort of *mmm* sound. I knew what he was thinking: Spiderweb tattoos were popular in prison. And from the looks of this ink, it could've been a prison tat: a sort of blue-black with rough edges that bled into the skin.

And what was that? I leaned in even farther, my finger precariously close to pulling back the white shirt collar.

Tim was warning me not to touch anything.

I yanked my hand back.

"No kidding," I said, eager not to give myself away. "Although I did open the trunk, so my fingerprints are on that."

"I should be there shortly," he said, then added, "The forensics team and a cruiser are on their way. Stay where you are and wait for them."

Where I was, was in the driveway. I was just back from Red Rock. I wanted to change out of my grubby jeans, long-sleeved T-shirt, and hiking boots, and, most of all, I wanted something to eat. I'd had some toast before I left at seven, but that was four hours ago. I also needed to get to the shop by noon, because I had a client scheduled.

"Do I have time for a shower?" I asked hopefully.

"No." Tim hung up.

Without thinking, I leaned against the back of the car. Immediately I felt it bounce a little—not that I'm that heavy; I'm actually pretty skinny—and Mr. That's Amore shifted slightly with the movement. I jumped away from the Mustang as I stared at the body, which rocked for a second and then rested again.

There it was. Poking out slightly through the collar of the shirt.

I couldn't help myself. I reached in and moved the fabric so I could see it better.

It was the end of a cord.

A clip cord.

I'd recognize it anywhere.

A clip cord is used to attach a tattoo machine to its power source.

Chapter 2

My eyes strayed from the cord back to the spiderweb, noticing now a dark line running across the base of Mr. That's Amore's neck. A dark line that had nothing to do with tattoos but probably everything to do with that cord.

A clip cord can be six feet long. The part that attaches to the tattoo machine has L-shaped ends that clip onto the binding posts, and the other end sticks into the power source, which looks sort of like an amplifier because it's got dials with numbers on them that show how high the power can go. Although it doesn't go up to eleven.

There's another cord that goes from the power source to the foot pedal. A tattoo machine runs like a sewing machine, in that I put pressure on the pedal with my foot, sending power to the source, which sends power to the machine, causing the needles to puncture the skin and push the ink into the skin's second layer, where it stays forever.

It's a pretty simple process and one that hasn't needed to be improved upon much since the late 1800s, when it was first invented.

The tattoo machine can't run without the clip cord.

I hadn't really been aware that I was holding my breath until I let it out.

A look around told me the police were not considering my situation an emergency.

I kept my eye on the end of the cord as I punched a few numbers into my phone and heard Bitsy's voice.

"Hey, there," I said to my shop manager. "I'm going to be a little late."

"What? Did you fall off some mountain or cliff or something?" Bitsy didn't understand why anyone would want to go hiking. She's a city girl. Her idea of wilderness is the buffet bar at Caesars.

"No, I'm waiting for the police to arrive—"

"What did you do now?"

"Why do you assume that *I* did something?"

"You're always getting into trouble."

Okay, so maybe my reputation has preceded me.

"There's a body in my car trunk," I said, explaining about Mr. That's Amore and the clip cord.

Bitsy made a sort of snorting sound.

"That Sylvia Coleman's a whackjob."

"Why does everyone think that?"

"Because she is. Do you think she killed him?"

For a split second, I wondered whether she had. I wouldn't put it past Sylvia. If this guy had crossed her in some way, who knew what she'd do to him. I pushed the thought out of my head.

"Just because the body's from the place where she and Bernie got married, it doesn't mean she killed him," I said.

"But she does have access to clip cords."

"So do you."

"You tell me how I'd get a guy in someone's trunk." Bitsy's tone was matter-of-fact, and she was right. Bitsy is a little person. Unless the body was only four feet tall, it would be pretty tough for her to hoist it into a car trunk. "So who do you think put him there?" she asked.

"Maybe he climbed in there himself," I suggested.

Bitsy snorted. "Like a cat who knows it's going to die, so it crawls into some dark corner somewhere? Give me a break."

Okay, she had a point.

I told her I'd give her a call as soon as I could get on the road. She mumbled something about rescheduling my first client before she hung up.

I stuck the phone in my jeans pocket and again leaned

into the trunk. I wanted to take another look at that cord and the guy's neck.

My hand was hovering over him when the cruiser careened into my driveway. I pulled back faster than you could say "That's Amore" and straightened up some, slamming the back of my head into the lid of the trunk.

Sister Mary Eucharista, my teacher at Our Lady of Perpetual Mercy School, would have said I deserved that.

The uniformed cop who stepped out of the cruiser looked like a fireplug. I recognized him immediately. His name was Willis, and I'd had a couple of brief encounters with him a few months earlier when he was looking for a missing woman.

Let's just say that we hadn't gotten off on the right foot.

And from the way his mouth was set in a grim line, I figured I could easily bet that hadn't changed.

In Vegas, sure things are hard to come by.

Willis took a couple steps toward me, but before either of us could say anything, another car swung into the street behind the cruiser. Tim. And then a big black SUV pulled up to the curb. Two burly guys got out from either side. One held a big case, the other, a camera.

If I'd known they were going to take pictures, I would have washed my car on the way back from Red Rock.

A third car, one that looked identical to Tim's Impala, drove up and parked behind the SUV. An older man with salt-and-pepper hair cropped close and wearing a charcoal pin-striped suit climbed out.

It was like a party. Mr. That's Amore was even dressed for the occasion.

Me, on the other hand, well, I was sweating bullets in my long-sleeved T-shirt and jeans. Not because it was hot outside. It was December in Vegas, when the temperatures actually meant a sweater or even a jacket at night.

The nattily dressed man walked around his car and met up with Tim. They both stopped a second to greet Willis before coming over to my car. Willis forced a smile, but it didn't extend to his eyes. The two guys with the equipment gave curt nods to everyone.

"Brett, this is Detective Flanigan," Tim said, introducing me to his companion. "Kevin, this is my sister, Brett."

Even though I sensed he must be another detective, he didn't dress like any of the cops I knew. He was too neat, and that suit must have set him back about five hundred bucks, if not more. But I'm not a fashionista—preferring jeans and cotton skirts and T-shirts—so I don't know much about men's suits.

I held out my hand and said, "Nice to meet you," because it's what my mother would've expected from me.

Detective Flanigan didn't care about introductions. He stared past me at my Mustang Bullitt, its trunk gaping open. I stepped aside so he'd have a better view.

"So here he is," I said, waving my hand over the trunk like Vanna White on *Wheel of Fortune*. Too bad Mr. That's Amore didn't win the washer and dryer.

Flanigan was already pulling on a pair of latex gloves. Willis was standing sentry, scowling at me. Tim had his hands on his hips as Flanigan started poking around inside the trunk. I stepped closer to Tim and asked in a low voice, "You're not going to check it out?"

"Brett, this is my driveway. You're my sister. Kevin's in charge."

As if on cue, Flanigan turned to me, taking only a second to indicate the two burly guys should start documenting the scene. One of them pulled out a little flashlight like they've got on those TV shows so he could see farther into the back of the dark trunk.

"Miss Kavanaugh? When did you discover the body?"

I took a deep breath and told my story: getting home from Red Rock, feeling something thump in the trunk, opening it to find Mr. That's Amore. Flanigan opened his mouth at that point, and I knew what he was going to say, so I launched into the story about Sylvia and Bernie and That's Amore Drive-Through Wedding Chapel, and how I'd lent them my car and they'd returned it a few hours later, before leaving for the Grand Canyon.

"So you don't know this gentleman at all?" Flanigan asked, his eyes boring into mine. Even though he was younger than my dad, the way he looked at me made me wonder if he had teenage daughters who were into tattoos.

"I have no idea who he is," I said.

He studied my face for a second before apparently deciding I was telling the truth, because he said, "Is there any way I can get in touch with this Sylvia Coleman and Bernie Applebaum?"

I was impressed. He had a little notebook out, but he hadn't scribbled much of anything. Maybe he had some sort of weird mnemonic thing that helped him remember names so well.

"I'm not sure where they're staying, but they're at the Grand Canyon. I think there's only a couple of hotels there, so they should be easy to find. I can give you Sylvia's son's phone number, and maybe he can tell you," I said, rattling off Jeff's name and number. Flanigan did write those down.

"So do you think he was strangled with the clip cord?" I asked, glancing over at the car, where Tim was chatting up one of the forensics guys.

"With what?" Detective Flanigan had been flipping through his notes, and now his head snapped up with surprise.

I probably shouldn't have said anything, but it was too late now.

"It looks like a clip cord around his neck." I explained how the cord attaches to the tattoo machine on one end and the power source on the other, providing the electromagnetic charge that causes the machine to run.

It was too much information.

I knew that the minute I started, but for some reason I couldn't stop. As though I was trying to impress him or something.

Right.

I was trying not to give him the opportunity to ask how I came to ascertain that there actually was a clip cord around his neck. Because I wouldn't have seen it or the bruise without peeking under his collar.

I didn't tell him that the one around Mr. That's Amore's

neck was pretty basic. It could've been from anywhere.
Someone could've bought it off the Internet. You can get a
custom cord made, just as you can get custom coils for the
machines. Joel's machine's coils have skulls on them. Mine
are plain. And all the cords at my shop are standard, nothing special.

Like this one.

"Miss Kavanaugh, did you touch the body?" His voice
brought me out of my thoughts.

Flanigan had my number like Sister Mary Eucharista
used to. It was a little disconcerting.

I shrugged and gave him a little smile. "Well, I may
have moved his collar a little, you know, because I thought
it was a clip cord, but I couldn't be exactly sure without
checking."

"And you felt compelled to check?"

"Wouldn't you?"

"I'm a detective. It's my job."

And I'm a tattooist who should just shut up already.
Okay, I got it.

"Kevin?"

I'd forgotten about Tim. I could only hope he hadn't
heard our exchange, although he was the only person I
knew who could hear those whistles that only dogs are supposed to hear. At least that was what he told me when we
were kids.

Tim was gesturing now, indicating that there was something enthralling going on in my trunk. As if we didn't
know that already.

Flanigan joined him over at my car. Not wanting to be
left out, I sidled up next to them and hoped they wouldn't
notice.

But when I peered over Tim's shoulder, I let out a loud
gasp. I couldn't help it.

Mr. That's Amore's wasn't the only body in my trunk.

Chapter 3

They had rolled Mr. That's Amore over, and apparently the rat had been squished underneath his body. The guy with the camera was busy shooting pictures from all angles, obviously terribly excited that there was something new to the composition.

The rat had been dead longer than the man. The bits of fur that still clung to the carcass were matted with dried blood.

Needless to say, it was a bit gross.

I stepped back a little. Tim and Flanigan were mumbling to each other. I picked up a couple of words, but nothing useful.

Finally, Tim turned to me.

"Brett, we're going to have to take your car."

"What?"

"It's evidence in a crime. You can use my Jeep." He looked sorry. Although it was probably more because I was going to drive his beloved Jeep for an indeterminate period of time than that my car was being confiscated.

I looked from Tim to Flanigan, who was staring at me as if daring me to oppose this turn of events. It was the good cop–bad cop thing.

The coroner's van eased against the curb next to the driveway. Maybe I should've made hors d'oeuvres.

"How much longer is this going to take?" I asked. All I wanted to do was take a shower and go to work.

Tim was surprised, probably because he thought I'd argue

the car issue. But honestly, now that they'd found the rat, the whole thing was giving me the willies. I didn't know why a dead guy was less creepy than a dead rat, but it was. So there.

"You can go in and get changed if you want," Tim said.

I smiled my thanks and started toward the door, but Flanigan's voice stopped me.

"We're going to need your clothes."

Not again. I'd had to give up my clothes once before after finding a dead body. If this was going to be a habit, I'd have to keep two separate wardrobes.

"I'll put them in a plastic bag," I promised.

But that wasn't good enough. Flanigan told Tim to go in the house with me. I glared at him. As if I'd substitute this outfit for another one. As if I'd have some sort of crime evidence on me.

And now the forensics guys were looking at me the same way Sarah Palin looks at a moose in the woods.

I went into the house, Tim on my heels. Once inside, I turned to my brother.

"Can I go to work after this?"

He took a deep breath. "Flanigan's in charge."

"Does he think I had something to do with this guy and the rat?" I asked.

"I don't think so." But his tone wasn't exactly reassuring. He started to say something else, then stopped himself.

"What?" I asked.

Tim shrugged. "Wondering about that clip cord."

I frowned. "Wondering how?"

"Wondering whose it is."

"It's not mine. I don't keep my equipment in the car."

"But he wasn't killed in the car," Tim said softly.

"How do you know that?"

Tim rolled his eyes. "Brett, do you really think that the guy crawled into the trunk on his own, and then someone decided, *Hey, why don't I strangle him with a clip cord while he's in there?*"

"Maybe he did it himself."

"Did what himself?"

"Strangled himself with the cord. You know, all that autoerotic-stimulation stuff. Aren't some guys into that? You start to strangle yourself while you're—um—well—servicing yourself so it feels even better? Maybe he did that, and he couldn't stop. Maybe he strangled himself by mistake." As I spoke, I began to wonder whether that wasn't what had happened.

"With a dead rat?"

Okay, so I'd forgotten that tiny detail.

Tim started scratching his chin in that way he does when he's deep in thought. "Although it's an interesting theory."

I left him with that as I went into the bedroom, plastic garbage bag in hand for my clothes. I filled the bag and stuck it in the hall, shutting my door before heading to the shower.

It felt really good standing under the stream of water, the heat soaking into the Celtic cross across my upper back, the dragon that curved around my torso from my breast to my hip, Monet's garden on one arm and a Japanese koi on the other, and the tiger lily stretching along my side. Not to mention Napoleon on my calf.

I knew I wasn't done yet, though. Getting tattooed, I mean. Every time a client came in, I wondered what my next one would be. The last was the koi, designed and inked by Jeff Coleman himself.

As I pulled my tank top on over my favorite denim skirt, I heard Bruce Springsteen singing "Born to Run." My phone had fallen off the bed when I was getting changed. I picked it up and heard, "Kavanaugh?"

Speak of the devil. Jeff Coleman was the only person who ever called me by my last name and only my last name. I couldn't remember him ever calling me Brett.

"Yeah?"

"The cops called."

"I gave them your number. I didn't know where Sylvia and Bernie were staying."

"Why do you think they're involved with this?"

"Jeff, they had my car at the wedding chapel. This guy is from the wedding chapel. I'm sorry if it seems clear to me that perhaps Sylvia and Bernie might know something. They may even have met this guy before he was killed."

A loud knock resonated through the room.

"Hold on," I said to Jeff as I tugged the door open.

Tim was holding the bag with my clothes. "Is this it?" he asked.

I nodded. "Everything."

He strutted down the hall and out of sight.

"Kavanaugh?" I heard Jeff asking.

"Yeah, I'm here." I wasn't going to tell him that I had to strip down. There were things Jeff Coleman didn't need to know. "There wasn't only a dead body in the car."

"What?"

I told him about the rat.

"How do you get yourself into situations like this, Kavanaugh?"

"I didn't get myself into this situation, Jeff. It was your mother. By the way, did you reach her?"

He was quiet long enough so I thought maybe the call had been dropped.

"Hello? Hello?" I asked.

"I'm here." But then it got quiet again.

"Hello?"

"Yeah, yeah, I hear you. There's just a little problem."

I didn't like his tone.

"Problem? What kind of problem?"

"My mother and Bernie never checked into their hotel at the Grand Canyon. I have no idea where they are."

Chapter 4

Now this wasn't exactly a surprise. Sylvia Coleman didn't always do what anyone expected of her. Which was probably why she'd gotten her first ink when she was fourteen and didn't stop until most of her body had been covered.

"I called Bernie's daughter, Rosalie," Jeff was saying. "She had the same information I did. Now she's worried."

Something about the way he said it made me ask, "But you're not?"

Jeff chuckled. "You know my mother. She moves to a different drummer."

As I said.

"If they stopped somewhere else that she might have liked better, then plans would change," Jeff continued. "My mother is the queen of spontaneity. She told me the one thing that irritated her about Bernie was how he had to plan everything months in advance." He paused. "She said she was going to change all that."

Seemed as though she'd already started.

"So you don't think something happened to them. Something bad," I added.

"My mother can take care of herself."

Well, I had to agree with that.

"Did you tell Flanigan they're not at their hotel?" I asked.

"Who?"

"The cop who called."

"I talked to someone named Willis."

Right. "Did you tell him?"

"Not yet."

"Why not?"

More silence. Uh-oh.

"You're not going to, are you?"

"You're not my mother, Kavanaugh. I'll tell them when I'm ready. I figure I'll do a little hunting around in the next couple hours and see if I can't locate them first. I know if I tell the cops my mother isn't where she said she'd be, then they might think she had something to do with what's in your trunk."

As if no one was already thinking that. But I let him have his little fantasy.

"So don't tell anyone yet, okay?"

I bristled. "Why would you think I would?"

He laughed. "You're one of the most law-abiding people I know, Kavanaugh."

I almost told him I'd touched the guy's collar, but he'd probably think I was lying, so I bit my tongue.

"I have to get to my shop," I said. "I have to take Tim's Jeep."

"You could borrow my mother's car."

I'd driven the antique purple Gremlin a few months ago, and I totally didn't want to get behind that wheel again.

"No, thanks. The Jeep's fine."

"I'll let you know what I find out," he said before the call ended.

As I combed my fingers through my short red hair and changed out a couple of the silver earrings that hung in rows outlining my ears, I wondered where Sylvia and Bernie could've gotten to.

I itched to tell Tim, but I'd promised Jeff. I hoped nothing had happened to them. Since Jeff wasn't worried, I shouldn't have been, but I couldn't help it. They were an elderly couple who'd decided to drive an old Buick to the Grand Canyon instead of taking one of the bus tours that ran regularly. Granted, when Sylvia had hinted she wanted to take my car not only to the wedding chapel but also on their honeymoon, I did say no with no reservations.

Maybe I should've lent them the car.

I shrugged off the thought and went back outside. Nothing I could do about it now.

Flanigan let me go to work an hour later, after he had me run through each moment of the previous day, before and after Sylvia and Bernie had dropped off the car. I struggled to come up with exact times for everything, although I said if he called my shop later, I could double-check my appointments with Bitsy, who kept track of every minute. It seemed that he didn't think I had anything to do with Mr. That's Amore, although he did spend a bit of time questioning me about Sylvia and Bernie.

When he finally felt satisfied, or at least sated for the moment, I left the cops and the coroner in my driveway, the banana yuccas fanning the crime scene, and headed out through Henderson and onto Route 215 toward the Strip.

The good thing about leaving late was there was no traffic. When I turned off the highway, I went up Koval Lane, behind all the resorts and casinos, so I could miss all the lights on the Strip. I was convinced that some deranged traffic administrator got a lot of pleasure out of knowing that timing the lights the way they did would mean an extra fifteen minutes on my drive up to the Venetian.

I parked on the sixth level of the parking garage and took the elevator to the level for the Grand Canal Shoppes. Once the doors opened, I turned to the left and then to the left again and through the sliding doors that led into the mall.

The developers probably would take issue with me calling it a mall, but that's what it was. Granted, there wasn't a Sears or JCPenney like at home in New Jersey, but the high-end stores, like Barneys New York, Shooz, Kenneth Cole, and others, that lined the walkway running along the fake Venice canal and surrounding St. Mark's Square did constitute a mall, in my opinion. So what if it had ornate gold trim and paintings of cherubs on the ceiling with fake sky and clouds, and musicians and dancers dressed in Renaissance garb who entertained the tourists and shoppers, rather than a hokey North Pole setup with cotton-ball snow and Santa at Christmastime?

I sidestepped a couple of the aforementioned tourists as I reached the end of the canal, where gondolas were waiting to pick up their next fares, and pushed open the door to The Painted Lady.

Because it was a high-end mall, we weren't allowed to advertise that it was a tattoo shop. We looked more like an art gallery. Ace van Nes, one of my tattooists, paints comic book versions of famous works of art. Today we had da Vinci's *The Last Supper*, Ingres's *The Valpinçon Bather*, and David's *The Lictors Bring to Brutus the Bodies of His Sons* hanging on the walls. The blond laminate flooring clashed in a good way with the dark mahogany desk at our entryway. Four individual workrooms were divided and closed off to the public. In the back, a sleek black leather sofa and glass-top coffee table served as our waiting area. We also had a staff room with a refrigerator, microwave, and light table, as well as a small office.

Bitsy kept everything in order. That was why I kept her on when I bought the business two and a half years ago. And while we had four rooms, we had only three artists at the moment: Ace, Joel Sloane, and me.

Ace was in Bitsy's usual seat at the front desk.

"Hey, boss lady," he drawled. He'd been calling me that for the last month or so, and even though I kept asking him not to, he persisted.

"Where's Bitsy?" I asked.

"I'm fine. How are you?" One of Ace's eyebrows rose higher than the other. It gave his handsome face a comedic look, and I couldn't help but smile.

"Fine, fine."

"Heard you had some excitement this morning."

I bet he did. Bitsy couldn't keep her mouth shut about anything.

"I'm not sure I'd call it exciting," I said. "Where's Bitsy?"

"She's in with Joel." Ace cocked his head toward Joel's room. The door was closed. Something was up. Joel never closed his door unless a client specifically asked for privacy or he was tattooing a particularly private body part. Before working here, he'd tattooed in street shops, where most of the stations are all out in the open. He doesn't like being closed in if he doesn't have to be.

I took a step toward the room, but Ace's voice stopped me.

"They'd hoped they'd find it before you came in."

My heart had jumped up into my throat, and it took me a second to ask, "Find what?"

Ace sighed. "Joel's clip cord. It's missing."

Chapter 5

It couldn't possibly be the same cord. Mr. That's Amore had been in my trunk since yesterday, and Joel was working yesterday, so it couldn't be. As I'd told Tim earlier, I hadn't taken any equipment home with me and didn't keep anything in my car. But it did seem odd that I'd discovered a body with a clip cord around its neck, and now we had a clip cord that had gone missing.

"I used the extra one yesterday," Joel was saying. "I don't know what I did with it."

Bitsy was riffling underneath Joel's shelves, where he kept extra baby wipes, boxes of latex gloves, and inks. Her face was bright red, her breath ragged. I'd never seen her so undone. She was obviously making the connection, too, between what had happened this morning and Joel's missing cord.

"I knew it was here," she kept saying. "I put it right down here. I know I did."

Joel and I shook our heads at each other and shrugged.

"Who was in here yesterday?" I asked Joel.

"Well, besides me and Bitsy, I did a couple of tattoos in the morning and three, I think, after lunch. It was a busy day."

Bitsy stood up with her hands on her hips, staring at the space where she insisted she'd put the clip cord, as if it would miraculously appear telekinetically.

"So Ace didn't borrow it?"

"Why would he?" Joel asked. "He's got a couple in his room."

I knew that, but I had to ask. I had two clip cords in my room, too, so would have no need to borrow anyone else's.

"A client wouldn't take it," Joel said. "Would they?"

"It's got to be here somewhere," Bitsy muttered, shoving between me and Joel as she left the room.

"It probably got put somewhere, and we'll find it later," I said. "She's jumping to conclusions."

"You have to admit it's a little weird," Joel said, going over to his shelves and taking another look.

I didn't help. I really was beginning to think this was just hysteria. There was absolutely no reason why anyone would take a clip cord from our shop.

Bitsy was scouring the appointment book when I came back out, leaving Joel to his own search. Ace was nowhere to be seen.

"He went out to that oxygen bar for his fix," Bitsy said, referring to Breathe just down the walkway from the shop. Ace was addicted to the aromatherapy oxygen pumped through his nostrils at the trendy "bar." He said the pretty Asian girl who massaged his back while he was hooked up wasn't bad, either.

Joel lumbered past, his hefty frame looking—dare I say it—maybe a little less hefty.

I forgot about the clip cord for a second and asked, "Joel, have you lost weight?"

He grinned. "I'm on the Atkins diet. I've lost twenty-five pounds. You noticed?"

While I was pleased he was losing weight, I was dubious about Atkins. "You mean you're only eating meat?"

"Haven't you noticed he's not eating the buns with the burgers?" Bitsy asked without looking up from the appointment book. She was the queen of multitasking.

I guess I'd been remiss. But Joel wasn't holding it against me.

"I'm eating salads, too."

"How long?"

"About two weeks."

"No, I mean, how long are you going to be on it?"

"Brett"—he scowled—"there's no time limit." He reached for the door.

"Where are you going?" Bitsy looked up from the book. "You've got a client coming in ten minutes."

"I want to take a walk around the canal. I'll be back."

As the door closed slowly behind him, Bitsy and I looked at each other.

"Exercise?" I asked.

"It won't last," Bitsy said. "You know how many times he tried that Weight Watchers." She went back to her book. "His clients yesterday were a Ronald Haugen, Jessica Storey, Mark Wilkinson, Dan Franklin, and Tony Perez. But not in that order. Franklin was first. Then Perez, then Storey, Haugen, and Wilkinson."

"Why does it matter what order?" I asked.

Her head shot up, and she stared at me, her bright blue eyes flashing. "Maybe because it makes me feel good to think there's some sort of order in this chaos."

I wasn't quite sure how to respond to that, so I asked, "When's my first client?"

"Not until three o'clock." Her head was buried in the book again. "I rescheduled you."

I figured I'd get some stencils done in the meantime, so I went into the staff room and sat at the light table. I'd been working on a portrait of a woman's daughter who'd passed away earlier in the year. A pile of manila folders sat perched on the edge of the table, and I picked them up and leafed through them, looking for mine.

One of the folders slipped out of my hand and fell to the floor, its contents spilling everywhere.

It was one of Joel's. I recognized his bold lines. As I stuffed the drawings and stencil back into the folder, one caught my eye.

I picked it out from the rest.

It was merely an Old English script, but what it said made my heart start to pound.

"That's Amore."

Chapter 6

The name on the folder was Dan Franklin. Joel's first client of the day yesterday. The day the clip cord went missing. The day Mr. That's Amore ended up in my trunk.

It couldn't be a coincidence.

I was faced with a dilemma now, though. Did I call Tim and tell him about this? Maybe one thing didn't have anything to do with the other. Maybe this Dan Franklin had come in wanting the title of a Dean Martin song embedded on him somewhere because he was a Rat Pack fan.

Rat Pack. Dino, Frank Sinatra, Sammy Davis Jr., Peter Lawford, Joey Bishop. Vegas and the Rat Pack were interchangeable in the fifties and sixties. One of my favorite movies is *Ocean's Eleven*, not the George Clooney version, but the Rat Pack original.

Had someone been sending a message with that rat in the trunk?

If I did call Tim, that Detective Flanigan might get suspicious of Joel. After all, Franklin was his client, and it was his clip cord that was missing.

On the other hand, if I told Tim, he could look for this Dan Franklin to find out whether he had any connection to the guy in my trunk. And we couldn't be sure that the cord around Mr. That's Amore's neck was Joel's.

I looked through the file folder but saw only the sketches Joel had done. I took it out to the front desk, where Bitsy was sitting with her head tucked in her arms.

"Dan Franklin," I said loudly, startling her.

She jumped up and stared at me with wide eyes. "What?"

"Where's the paperwork for Dan Franklin? Joel's first client yesterday." While I spoke, I waved the "That's Amore" sketch at her.

Bitsy's mouth formed a perfect "O" as she pulled out the drawer in the bottom of the desk and retrieved yet another file folder. This one, however, held the copy of the receipt and the release form Dan Franklin had filled out before his appointment.

"He paid cash," Bitsy said as I scanned the form.

The release form included the client's name, address, phone number, and a statement the client had to sign, claiming he was over eighteen years old. We made photocopies of the client's driver's license to prove he was of age. It was similar to the form you'd fill out at the doctor's office, because it asked about health issues. We needed to know whether the client had any condition that might mean the tattoo would be dangerous to him or to us. The documents also included a waiver we asked clients to sign, saying we weren't responsible for infection or aftercare.

Even Jeff Coleman, in his street shop up near Fremont and next to Goodfellas Bail Bonds, had client forms like this. Any reputable shop does.

Dan Franklin's form said he lived in Henderson. Not too far from where I lived, actually. I picked up the phone, but I stopped before dialing. What would I ask him? *Hey, you got a tattoo at my shop. Did you just happen to pocket one of our clip cords when you left? And if you did, did you use it to kill Mr. That's Amore?*

It all sounded so ridiculous. And I didn't even know Mr. That's Amore's name.

Bitsy scowled as I hesitated, and she leaned over and snatched the phone out of my hand. She punched in Dan Franklin's phone number.

After a few seconds, she said, "Mr. Franklin, this is Bitsy Hendricks at The Painted Lady. We're checking up to make sure everything's all right with your new tattoo. Could you please call back at your earliest convenience? We need to

make a report to the health department, so we'd appreciate your call. Thank you." And she rattled off our number
before hanging up.

Smooth. Very smooth.

"That's why you work for me," I said proudly.

Bitsy was beaming. "Thank you, thank you, to the Acad-
emy," she said, bowing slightly at the waist, her short blond
bob bouncing against her face.

I looked out the glass door toward the canal and spotted
Joel lumbering back toward the shop. It was all I could do
not to rush out and pull him in. I waited as patiently as I
could until he pushed the door in, stopping short when he
saw Bitsy and me staring at him.

"What? What did I do?"

"Dan Franklin. Why didn't you tell me you tattooed
'That's Amore' on him?"

Joel shrugged. "What of it? He wanted the tat around
his biceps. Easy. Why does this matter?"

"The guy in my trunk was from the That's Amore Drive-
Through Wedding Chapel."

"Really?" He looked from me to Bitsy and back to me.
"I didn't know that."

Bitsy slapped him on the forearm with Dan Franklin's
file. "You did so. I told you that's where Sylvia and Bernie
got married."

"But you didn't tell me the dead guy was from there."

The folder, which was about to come down again,
stopped midair. "Hmm," Bitsy said thoughtfully. "Maybe in
all the excitement I did leave that little tidbit out."

"*You?*" I teased. "You left out a *tidbit*? What else have
you left out? Don't you know we rely on your reporting to
know what's going on?"

The folder changed direction and came down on my
arm this time.

"Don't get smart with me." She frowned, but I could tell
she didn't mind.

"So do you think this Dan Franklin has something to do
with that guy in your trunk?" Joel asked. God bless him, but
he was slow on the uptake today. Maybe it was all that meat

he was eating. Give the man a doughnut, and the sugar rush would spark his brain.

"Could be," I said.

"Maybe you should go over there, to that wedding chapel," Bitsy said. "See if anyone there knows this Dan Franklin."

Now that was an idea. Although I could hear Tim now, telling me I shouldn't get involved in police business.

But I was still on the fence about that. Franklin might not have anything to do with Mr. That's Amore. It could be a coincidence.

If it turned out not to be, then I could share what I found out with Tim.

At least that was the way I was justifying it.

Problem was, if I went over to the wedding chapel, would they tell me anything?

I didn't have time to play detective. I had a client coming in. And speak of the devil, but didn't the door open right at that very moment.

Carla Higgins had a Dr. Seuss fetish. She already had the Cat in the Hat on her right shoulder and the Lorax on her left, and today she was in for Yertle the Turtle in the center to balance them all out. She'd expressed a desire for Thing 1 and Thing 2, one on each biceps, but decided Yertle was more pressing.

I took her into my room with a little shrug in Bitsy and Joel's direction. Work before pleasure. Or at least before any snooping around.

I put the stencil on Carla's back and gave her a mirror to make sure it was in the right place.

"It's perfect," she said as I pulled a disposable needle and needle bar out of their respective packages.

As I pressed my foot on the pedal that turned on the machine, causing its familiar whine, and started to draw, I thought about Joel's clip cord and why Dan Franklin might have thought to pocket it on his way out of here yesterday. Had he seen it and thought it would make a good murder weapon? Something that couldn't be traced back to him directly?

Who thought like that? Who went through their day looking for unusual murder weapons?

I obviously was not in tune with the mind of a murderer.

Which was a good thing.

Yertle the Turtle was done in no time. Carla was thrilled as she went out to pay Bitsy. I started cleaning up my inks, throwing away the small containers. Everything had to be disposable or sterilized. Usually Bitsy cleaned up, but I wanted the busy work, something to keep my mind occupied, because I was still going over how I would talk to Tim about Dan Franklin. Halfway through Yertle, I'd realized I had to tell him, even if it was way off the mark.

My gut told me it wasn't, though.

Bitsy stuck her head through my door, waving the phone. "Phone for you, Brett." She put her hand over the mouthpiece.

"It's your brother," she said in a stage whisper.

I took the phone from her and said, "What's up, Tim?"

"We have an ID on your body. His name's Ray Lucci. He's a Dean Martin impersonator over at that wedding chapel."

So the resemblance was earning the guy a living. Who knew?

"Lucci was an ex-con, like we thought. Remember the spiderweb tattoo?"

I did. But I knew Tim wasn't done yet. And when he spoke again, I suppose I should've been surprised, but I wasn't.

"He's got a new tattoo, too, Brett. It says 'That's Amore' around his biceps. And he's got Joel's business card in his wallet."

Chapter 7

Mr. That's Amore was Dan Franklin? Hadn't Tim said the guy's name was Ray Lucci? I was trying to wrap my head around this.

"Brett?" Tim said when I took too long to respond.

"Yeah, I'm here. I've got something to tell you." I launched into the story about Dan Franklin and Joel's missing clip cord.

Now it was Tim's turn to be quiet.

Finally, he said, "I appreciate you telling me this, Brett. Sounds like this guy was using an alias. I'm going to have to tell Flanigan about the clip cord, and he's going to have to talk to Joel and Bitsy."

"Bitsy?"

"She must have met Lucci yesterday, too, right?"

"They're not suspects or anything, are they?" I asked.

It was a second of hesitation, but I noticed. "No, I don't think so," Tim said.

"But you're not in charge on this one. You told me it's Flanigan. He doesn't like me," I added.

"He doesn't like anyone," Tim said as he hung up.

Joel was in his room with a client. I poked my head in the doorway.

"A minute?"

The machine stopped whirring, and he set it down, telling his client he'd be back in a second. He came out into the hall.

I told him how Flanigan would be contacting him because my dead guy was someone named Ray Lucci, who'd called himself Dan Franklin here yesterday.

Joel stared at me. "What's up with that?"

I rolled my eyes. "Obviously the man didn't want anyone here to know his real name."

"But you'd think then that he'd be the one doing the killing, not the one being killed."

There was an odd logic to that.

I shrugged. "What do I know?"

Joel went back in with his client, and I went out to talk to Bitsy.

"So this detective might think that a person of my stature might actually have stuffed that man in your trunk?" she asked.

"He doesn't know that you're a little person," I said, although I wasn't sure why I was defending Flanigan. "And I'm sure he won't think you killed him. He just wants to talk to you about Dan Franklin."

Bitsy tossed her blond hair to one side and said, "You know, Brett, when Flip owned the shop we never had the cops around asking about anything."

Great. I didn't want to get into it, so I went into the staff room to finish up the portrait. I wondered how long it would take Flanigan to get in touch with us.

As I drew, I thought again about Sylvia and Bernie and wondered whether Jeff was having any luck finding them. Because I was a little bored, I pulled my cell out of my bag and punched in his number.

"Kavanaugh, to what do I owe this honor?" Jeff asked before I could even say hello. He must have my number queued in. I wasn't quite sure how I felt about that.

"Just wondering if you've found your mother."

"Not yet."

I could hear a radio playing in the background.

"Are you in your shop?" I asked.

"No. I'm out near Hoover Dam."

"You're going to the Grand Canyon?"

"Seems to be the only way. I called the hotels there, but no one's seen my mother."

"So you're going out there? You don't believe them?"

"Well, it's not as though my mother is the typical white-haired little old lady in a housecoat." That was true. Sylvia's ink would make her stand out anywhere. "So I do believe them. I'm going to check out all the hotels and motels on the way there, in case they decided to stop somewhere else instead."

"But what if they went off the beaten path and in the total opposite direction, like L.A. or something?" I wasn't really meaning to play devil's advocate, but I had nothing better to do.

"My mother hates L.A. No, if they went anywhere, they stopped in the desert."

"So you *are* worried about them?" I teased, remembering how he'd insisted he wasn't.

"Maybe a little." But from his tone it sounded like a lot more than that.

I decided to let it slide. "You know, it would be easier if you told the cops about this, and they could put out one of those APBs on them."

"I thought I explained why I didn't want to do that right now."

Sure he had, but that was before my entire shop was going to be questioned by the police. I said as much, telling him about Dan Franklin, aka Ray Lucci.

I heard a low whistle when I finished.

"Sounds pretty weird," he said. "Listen, Kavanaugh, I'll give you a call later. If I haven't found them by tomorrow morning, then I'll go with you to the cops and we can report my mother missing. And if I do find her, then I'll take her to headquarters, so she can talk to that detective. How's that?"

It was the best I would get, and I agreed, even though I knew tomorrow morning was the latest I could give him.

I closed the phone and threw it back in my bag, turning back to my stencil. It was nearly done. I spent the next half hour working on it and then started another one I'd need the next day. I kept looking at the clock, expecting Flanigan to show up any moment.

It was dinnertime when he finally came through the
door. He looked as neat in his suit as he had this morning—
surprising, since he'd spent all day in it. I tried to see whether
he was rumpled in any way, but he caught me staring, and
I felt my face flush.

"I'm here to talk to a Joel Sloane and a Bitsy Hendricks," he said.

Problem was, both had gone down to the Mexican res-
taurant for dinner a few minutes before. They'd been on
edge all day after I'd talked to Tim, and when it looked as
though Flanigan wasn't going to show, I said they should
take a break and go have something to eat. I could hold
down the fort.

"It's too bad you did that," Flanigan said when I explained. "Because now I have to interrupt their dinner."

Okay, so I was the villain.

"And I'd appreciate it if you stick around. I've got a few
more questions for you, too," he said as he went out the
door.

Great. Not that I was going anywhere, but now, because
I couldn't, I had an incredible desire to take off. Nowhere
in particular. Just somewhere other than here.

As I pondered my imaginary escape, the phone rang. I
picked it up.

"The Painted Lady."

"Is this a tattoo shop?" The voice on the other end was
gruff.

"Yes." There were times when I regretted the name of
the shop. Especially when we got the occasional call thinking we were an escort service. "May I help you?"

"I got a message on my machine."

"Yes?" I prompted when he didn't continue right away.

"From this number. This shop. Saying you were checking up on a tattoo I got there." He paused. "I've never been
in your tattoo shop, so I don't know what this is all about."

"I'm sorry, Mr.—"

"Franklin. Dan Franklin."

Chapter 8

I froze for a second, letting this new information seep in.

"Excuse me? Are you there?" Dan Franklin asked.

"Oh, yes, I'm here. I'm sorry about the confusion, but we had a gentleman in here yesterday who gave us your phone number and name. That's why we thought it was you." That was easy to explain. Ray Lucci stuffed in my car trunk wasn't.

"Who?"

He did have a right to know.

"Well, since we left you that message, we found out the gentleman who was in here was really someone named Ray Lucci."

The second I said the name, I heard him take a breath.

"Lucci? Really? What's he up to now?" Sounded like he knew him.

"He's dead," I said before I thought.

Silence, then, "Dead?"

"Murdered. I'm sorry to be the one to tell you."

"Don't be sorry. He wasn't a friend. In fact, the opposite."

"Do you know why he would use your name here?" I asked.

"He's been using my name all over the place. Thinks it's funny or something. We sort of look alike." His tone was laced with bitterness.

"How do you know him?" I wasn't totally sure I wanted

to know. Lucci was an ex-con, and it was possible they'd met in prison.

"We work together."

A lightbulb went off. "At That's Amore wedding chapel?" I asked.

"That's right. We're both Dean Martin impersonators."

"Really?" They probably did look alike, then.

"There are five of us. We sing 'That's Amore' at the end of each ceremony."

I could picture it, and it sounded ridiculous but sort of cool at the same time.

"How long have you worked there?"

"A year."

"How about Ray Lucci?"

"About three months."

"So did you know Lucci had been in prison?"

"Six years. He stole cars. Liked the flashy ones. Not sure he was done with that, either. He told me he had his eye on a red Mustang Bullitt convertible."

I stopped breathing for a second. He'd described my car. The one Lucci was found dead in. Had Lucci been planning on stealing my car when he ended up strangled and dead inside the trunk? Had he first seen it at That's Amore, or had he been tracking me? Was it maybe not a coincidence that it was *my* trunk he ended up in?

"You know," I said, struggling to get back to Dan Franklin, "the police may want to talk to you."

"The police?" His voice went up an octave.

"Well, Lucci was found strangled, so I'm sure anything you can tell them could help figure out what happened."

"I'm not sure about that," he said slowly, making me wonder whether he didn't have something to hide.

"Can I give them your number?" I asked. "It might be really helpful."

He sighed in resignation. "Well, maybe. Sure, I guess so." He probably figured that I already knew where he worked, so the cops could find him anyway.

"I really appreciate this," I said. "Thanks."

"Okay, sure," he said and hung up.

I put the phone back in its cradle and stared out at the canal. A gondola was sailing past, the gondolier smoothly pushing it along the water, a couple of tourists smiling at each other as they fed into the illusion. I heard the faint strains of a harpsichord and knew the dancing was about to start in St. Mark's Square, the men dressed in hose and ornate coats, the women in corsets and long, flouncy gowns. I spotted a mime scurrying past on the other side of the canal, not bothering to stop for the camera flashes. His shift must be up.

Joel and Bitsy and Flanigan were nowhere to be seen. Maybe they had invited Flanigan for a margarita.

I could so use one myself right now.

I pondered what Dan Franklin had told me, wondered about his reaction to the police contacting him, his obvious dislike of Lucci.

And then there was my car. Maybe I shouldn't drive such a flashy car, but *Bullitt* was one of my favorite movies and I had a crush on Steve McQueen. When I'd first seen the red Mustang, I fell in love with it and the idea that I was living my own movie.

I'd driven all the way out here from New Jersey in that car, leaving my parents' house for only the second time in my thirty years. The first time I'd gone to Philadelphia, to the University of the Arts. I moved back in with my parents afterward, wondering what I'd do with my life. That was when I hooked up with Mickey at the Ink Spot and began my tattooing career.

My mother still had issues with my choice. My father, a former Jersey cop, not so much. He encouraged me to be creative in any way I could. If I couldn't set up an easel along the Seine in Paris, then I'd tattoo body parts in northern New Jersey.

Owning my own shop had been only a dream, but when Tim called me to tell me about his friend Flip Armstrong, who wanted to sell his business in Vegas, I jumped at the chance.

I'd gotten a little stagnant with Mickey, not that we weren't having fun, but I was ready to move on. Both from the Ink Spot and from my fiancé, Paul, who felt that, as his new wife, I shouldn't have a career, but only support his. *So* wasn't going to happen.

Tim's girlfriend, Shawna, had moved out, too, and he needed a roommate to help pay his mortgage. It was win-win all around.

Joel's big frame came around the corner, interrupting my thoughts. Bitsy after him, and Flanigan at the rear.

Showtime.

I met them at the door, opening it as they all came in the shop.

Flanigan gave me a nod, Bitsy rolled her eyes, and Joel looked as if he was about to cry.

This should be fun. Not.

"Do you have a place where I can speak with Mr. Sloane alone?" Flanigan asked.

Joel's eyes grew wide, and I gave him a pat on the arm to try to reassure him.

"You can use the office," I said. "It's in the back there."

Flanigan allowed Joel to lead the way, and Bitsy and I stared after them until we heard the door shut. I turned to her.

"What has he said?"

She shook her head. "Not much. Just that he wants to talk to Joel about the clip cord and this Dan Franklin guy."

"I just got off the phone with the real Dan Franklin," I said softly, not wanting Flanigan to hear. I told her about the conversation.

"You need to tell him," she said, tossing her head toward the back of the shop. "You know, maybe Dan Franklin really killed that guy and is trying to throw you off the trail by pretending to cooperate."

The thought had crossed my mind.

"Should I interrupt?"

Bitsy shrugged. "Depends how important you think it is."

I thought about my car again. It was pretty important.

I went to the back of the shop and tapped on the office door.

Flanigan opened it as if he owned the place. Did not endear me to him.

"Yes?" he asked, his tone frosty.

"I talked to Dan Franklin," I said, launching into the phone conversation before Flanigan could stop me.

When I was done, he scratched his chin and frowned. "Thank you for this information. I appreciate you sharing it with me." He said it as though he didn't think I'd share anything. I hoped Willis wasn't dissing me behind my back.

I started to close the door, but Flanigan moved toward me, holding up a finger to Joel to indicate he'd be but a second. A few steps outside the office, Flanigan stopped.

"Miss Kavanaugh, I understand you're friends with Jeff Coleman, Sylvia Coleman's son?"

I nodded, unsure where this was going.

"I spoke with Mr. Coleman earlier, and he wasn't forthcoming with any information about his mother and her new husband. I did, however, speak to Mr. Applebaum's daughter, who is very concerned, as she should be. She was very helpful in giving us the make and model and license plate number of the car her father was driving."

He paused for a second, and I had a feeling I wasn't going to like what he was going to say.

"We found Mr. Applebaum's car. Outside the Grand Canyon entrance. It was abandoned."

Chapter 9

It took a few minutes to sink in. Sylvia and Bernie's car? Abandoned? That wasn't good. I thought about Jeff, on his mission to find them.

Flanigan was looking at me as if he could read my mind.

"Do you have another number where I could reach Mr. Coleman?" he asked, and from the way he said it, he knew I did.

"I might be able to find out," I said.

Flanigan gave me a smile, as if I were a puppy that had passed obedience training. "Thank you." And then he turned and went back into the office. In the second before he closed the door, I caught Joel's eye and gave him a small smile. He smiled back, although I could see how nervous he was.

I ducked into the staff room and got my phone. I punched in Jeff's number.

"What's up, Kavanaugh?" he asked.

"Where are you?"

"Some little hole in the wall. No sign of them."

"Well, the police found their car."

Silence, then, "Where?"

I told him what Flanigan had said.

More silence.

"Jeff?"

"Yeah, I'm here."

"He wants to talk to you."

"I bet he does."

"Listen, Jeff, now is not the time to be some sort of renegade. Your mother might be in trouble."

"She might be."

"So call Flanigan."

"I'm not far from the canyon. I'll get in touch with the rangers. They'll tell me what's going on."

"Why don't you want to talk to this cop?"

"Because he thinks my mother had something to do with that guy in your trunk."

I suppressed a chuckle. "I doubt that."

"He sure as hell indicated that when I talked to him before."

"That's his job."

"Trust my instincts on this, Kavanaugh. I'll be back tonight. I'll let you know what I find out."

And the call ended.

I heard a small cough.

Flanigan was standing in the doorway.

"Was that Mr. Coleman?"

I put my phone back in my bag. "Yes."

"Is he going to take my call?"

"No."

We stared each other down.

"There's just so much I can do," I finally said. "I told him you needed to talk to him. I told him about finding their car. He said he's going to see the rangers at the canyon."

"They won't be able to help." Flanigan started picking at imaginary lint on his suit. "The state police have already taken the car away."

"Well, then he'll find that out, and he'll come home."

"Did Mr. Coleman know Mr. Lucci?"

The question came out from left field.

"I—uh—I don't know," I sputtered.

"His mother knew him," Flanigan said. "She requested he sing a solo at their wedding."

"Maybe she just liked the way he sang."

"She requested him by phone before she and Mr. Applebaum arrived. She requested him by name."

I sighed. "So because of that, you suspect a little old lady who's got to be pushing eighty of killing him and stuffing him in my trunk?"

"She had access to clip cords, too."

True enough.

"What about the rat?" I asked, suddenly remembering it. "Why the rat?"

Flanigan's eyebrows rose slightly. "We need to talk to her."

"But she's missing. Maybe whoever killed Lucci did something to her, too." As I said it, I saw something cross his face, and I couldn't breathe for a second. He thought that, too. He wasn't trying to find Sylvia because he thought she and Bernie killed Lucci. He wanted to find them because he thought something had happened to them.

"You think they saw something, don't you?" I asked softly. "You think they're witnesses and that's why they're missing."

From his expression, I could tell I was right.

"Mr. Sloane has identified a picture of Mr. Lucci as the person who posed as Dan Franklin," Flanigan said. "And Miss Hendricks concurred. Miss Hendricks also gave me Mr. Franklin's phone number. If you hear from Mr. Coleman again, I'd appreciate you emphasizing to him how important it is that he contact me."

I nodded, and he stood there, staring at me.

"Is there something else?" I asked, his gaze unnerving me, as if he thought I was holding back on something. Which now, I really wasn't.

"According to the time line you gave me yesterday, the Applebaums returned your car at three o'clock, and it was in the parking garage here until you left work. What time did you leave?"

We'd been over this, but I made a point to look at the appointment book so I could tell him the exact times of my clients and that I'd left an hour after my last one, at midnight.

"Were Miss Hendricks and Mr. Sloane still here?"

I'd cleaned up myself because they'd both left early. I told him so. "Ace left about half an hour before I did."

"Ace?"

"Ace van Nes, my other tattooist."

"And when you left, you took your car right home?"

I nodded.

"Can you show me where it was parked?"

I frowned. This seemed a bit odd. But who was I to tell the detective how to do his job? Bitsy was in the staff room, and I told her where I was going. She seemed curious, too, but didn't say anything.

I usually parked on the sixth level, and that's where Sylvia and Bernie left the car. Three spaces away from where I had parked the Jeep today.

"You're sure about this location?" Flanigan asked, circling the Mercedes that was occupying the spot now.

I pointed to the row and level sign on the concrete post in front of the Mercedes. "This was it—I know from the sign," I said.

Flanigan took out his little notebook and began to make notations. He stooped down, checked the ground, stuck his finger in a spot of oil, and then wiped it off on a handkerchief he pulled from his pocket.

"Does anyone else have a key to your car?" he asked as he went around the front of the Mercedes, inspecting the concrete barrier in front of it.

"My brother has one," I said. "But no one else."

Finally, he closed the notebook and stuck it in his jacket pocket. He stood, facing me. "I appreciate your time, Miss Kavanaugh."

"Brett. You can call me Brett."

"Thank you, Miss Kavanaugh." So much for that. "I'll be in touch."

And he walked over to the elevator, which had just opened, got in, and disappeared as the doors closed on him. What was that all about?

Considering how the day had started, it ended on a quiet note. I tried Jeff again, but now he wasn't answering my calls, either. Joel brought back a huge burger from Johnny Rockets and ate it sans bun. I let Bitsy go home early and closed up the shop at eleven. The rest of the mall was shutting down, too—the gates pulled down over the store entrances, the gondolas docked and rocking slowly on the canal.

I didn't much like driving Tim's Jeep. The gearshift was stiff, and I had to press all the way down on the brakes to stop. The air-conditioning wasn't all that great, either, although tonight it was cool, and I hugged my jean jacket around me as I got out of the Jeep and scurried up the steps to the house.

It was dark; I didn't see any sign of Tim's Impala, so I figured he was off doing cop stuff. I wanted to pick his brain about Flanigan, but it would have to wait.

I stuck the key in the door and pushed it open. Tim had left the screen door open to the back porch and the air inside was cooler than out. I shed my jacket, threw it over one of the kitchen chairs, and opened the refrigerator, looking for some seltzer and maybe a late-night snack. The Johnny Rockets burger was hours ago now.

I leaned into the fridge to grab the seltzer off the bottom shelf. As I stood back up, a hand reached around me and shut the door, trapping me against the counter.

Chapter 10

I caught my breath and twisted around.

Jeff Coleman took the bottle from me.

"Nothing stronger, Kavanaugh?" he teased as he pulled a couple of glasses out of the cupboard.

"What are you doing in here? How did you get in?"

He handed me a glass of seltzer. "I have my ways."

A few months ago he was going to pick a lock, but we got interrupted so I never saw him actually do it. But because I lived with a cop, I wouldn't think it would be quite so easy for him to get into our house.

"What did you really do in the Marines?" I asked. "Were you some sort of covert operative?"

"You've been watching too many movies," he said, taking a long drink from his own glass. He put it on the counter, then said, "You really don't have anything stronger?"

"We've got some red wine."

He snorted and made a face. "I knew I should've brought my own bottle."

"What are you doing here? I thought you were going to the Grand Canyon. You couldn't have made it there and back in the time since I talked to you."

We walked over to the living room, where I plopped down on the leather couch and he settled into Tim's leather recliner.

"I didn't go after all," he said. "After I talked to you, I called the park, and they said the state cops had taken the car. I knew I wouldn't get anything from them, just some more grief about where I thought my mother was, so I came back."

"Why did you come here?"

"Maybe I wanted to pick your brain. And I knew you wouldn't come to me."

He had that right.

"Who's in your shop?" Jeff's shop, Murder Ink, was open 'til four a.m.

"I closed down. I didn't want the distraction of thinking about it."

I studied his face. If he'd closed his shop, then he was seriously concerned about his mother, but his expression didn't reveal his worry. Jeff Coleman was about ten years older than me, I guessed, in his early forties. He had close-cropped salt-and-pepper hair, and the lines in his face told me he'd lived hard. He was a little shorter than me, and wiry. Although in the last months I'd noticed he'd started to bulk up slightly, as if he had started working out. I wasn't going to ask, though. He'd probably give me grief for noticing.

So instead I leaned back and told him about Dan Franklin and that I suspected Flanigan thought Sylvia and Bernie might have been witnesses to Lucci's murder.

"He said Sylvia asked specifically for Lucci at the wedding chapel," I said. "Did she ever mention him?"

Jeff chuckled. "My mother knew a lot of people. She had that shop for a long time and met a lot of crazy characters. So maybe she did know him. Did he have any tattoos other than the spiderweb and the one Joel did?"

"I don't know." But it was worth asking Flanigan. I made a mental note to remember.

Jeff had closed his eyes, and for a second, I thought he was drifting off to sleep, but then he sat up straight and stared at me.

"I've got an idea, and I hope you'll keep an open mind."

Immediately, I knew I shouldn't agree to anything.

"Listen, Kavanaugh, it's a good idea. So hear me out, okay, before you make up your mind?"

I didn't have much choice, so I nodded.

"Tomorrow, you and I should go over to that wedding chapel."

On the surface, it didn't sound like a horrible idea. I'd toyed with the very same thing all day since talking to Dan Franklin. But I wasn't prepared for the next proposal.

"We can pretend we're getting married. We can ask specific questions, then, maybe meet this Dan Franklin. Find out more about Ray Lucci."

My brain was still two sentences behind. "Pretend we're getting married?" I asked. "What are you talking about?"

"They'd probably be more willing to talk if we pretend we're giving them business," he argued.

"And Dan Franklin? I already talked to him."

"But you never met him, right? He doesn't know what you look like."

I held out my arms, decorated with Monet's garden and a koi pond. "I'm the painted lady, remember? He may have heard about my tattoos. He may have seen the Web site."

Bitsy had set up a Web site for the shop in the last month. I hadn't been totally on board with it. I liked that we were more exclusive. Bitsy argued that we'd get more business, and since we were in a recession, it wouldn't hurt. Business hadn't slacked off at all, but she was hedging her bets. I told her she couldn't put an e-mail address on the site, just a phone number, because I didn't want to have to keep checking e-mail. She'd set up a page with some of our designs and photos of Ace, Joel, and me to "give the shop a face." I hated to admit it, though, Bitsy was right: We had gotten some clients who'd found us on the Internet.

"It's not the best picture of you," Jeff said flatly. "It doesn't show those glints of gold in your hair."

He was teasing me, and I rolled my eyes at him.

Jeff gave me a sly smile. "If Franklin figures out who you are, say you were intrigued by the idea of getting married there after you talked to him. I'll go along with it."

"So now it's *my* idea we're getting married?" I asked.

He snickered. "It doesn't matter whose idea it is, as long as it works."

Despite my better judgment, the idea was growing on

me. Not marrying Jeff Coleman, but going to That's Amore to poke around a little. I knew Tim was on the outside on this case, and Flanigan certainly wasn't going to be very forthcoming. I told myself I was helping a friend find his missing mother. Sylvia was my friend, too, and didn't I owe her that?

I stood up and took our empty glasses into the kitchen.

Jeff followed. "So, Kavanaugh, what do you think?"

"I think we'd better do this before I change my mind."

"You want to go tonight?"

I looked at the clock. It was one in the morning. While the chapel was probably still open, I figured I needed a good night's sleep before I took on this ruse.

"No. In the morning. I don't have to be at the shop until noon. Maybe we should meet at ten?" Now that I was on board, I was even organizing our adventure. Go figure.

Jeff opened his mouth to say something, but the door swung open, and Tim came in. The look of surprise on his face probably matched mine.

"Hey, well, what do you say?" he asked as he shook Jeff's hand. Tim looked at me, his eyes asking me what was going on.

"Jeff has been looking for his mother," I said. "He came by to see if I'd heard from her."

While I'm not usually a good liar, this lie slipped easily off my tongue. I figured I'd rather lie than have Tim think something was going on.

But from his expression, he knew we were up to no good.

"Don't mess in police business," he said sternly, his eyes moving from me to Jeff. "The best thing you can do for your mother is to let the cops take care of everything."

Jeff opened his mouth to say something, then had second thoughts and shut it again, nodding. I took his arm and started steering him toward the door.

"He was just leaving anyway," I said.

Standing in the doorway, Jeff leaned in, whispered, "My shop at ten," and shuffled out into the darkness.

I watched him a few seconds, wondering where he'd parked, when Tim came up behind me.

"Don't do it," he said.

"Do what?" I asked, stepping back and closing the door.

"Whatever it is he's planning and has asked you to do."

"It's nothing," I said, busying myself with putting the empty glasses in the dishwasher so I wouldn't have to look at him.

"He doesn't know where his mother is, does he, Brett?"

That one I could answer truthfully. I stood up straight and looked him in the eye. "No, he doesn't. And he's worried."

"He should be," Tim said, turning away. But I saw something in his face before he did.

"What do you know?" I asked his back. "You know something."

Tim turned around slowly. "You cannot tell Jeff Coleman."

"I won't."

"No, really, I mean it. You can't tell him. Because I don't think he knows."

"Doesn't know what?"

Tim sighed. "Ray Lucci was Sylvia Coleman's son. Jeff Coleman's half brother."

Chapter 11

As I drove toward Murder Ink the next morning, I thought about what Tim had told me. The police had found evidence of Lucci's relationship to Sylvia in his apartment. Letters she had written to him in prison.

When I asked Tim why he told me, he said that if I knew, maybe I'd keep more of an open mind. I could also keep an eye on Jeff Coleman, try to find out whether he knew about Lucci.

"But you said you didn't think he knows."

"He probably doesn't. But he's pretty good at covering stuff up."

No kidding. Even though he denied any sort of covert-operative job in the Marines, I wasn't too quick to believe him.

I was in the wrong lane. I missed my turn onto Koval, which meant I had to go up the Strip. Sitting at the intersection with the Statue of Liberty and the gold MGM lion hovering over me, I was again struck by the outrageousness of this part of Las Vegas. My neighborhood was a typical southwestern one, with stucco houses and faded red roofs and Home Depot and Target and strip malls interspersed among palm trees and banana yuccas. The mountains rose up in the distance, reminding me of my hike yesterday morning up at Red Rock, the hard red earth beneath my feet. The brownness of the desert was speckled with bits of green, and I couldn't wait until the flowers bloomed bright against their plain backdrop, spectacular for such a short time.

Being from New Jersey, I suppose I could say I missed the change of seasons, but we had it here, too, only in a different way. And I totally did not miss scraping ice and snow off my car. While I'm not that spiritual a person, despite Sister Mary Eucharista's best efforts, when I first saw Red Rock, I felt as if I'd come home in a way. I knew I probably would never go back east.

Tim felt the same way. Our sister, Cathleen, had moved to Southern California years before. Only my parents clung to the East, now in Florida in their retirement community, having cocktail parties and suffering the occasional hurricane.

The light changed, and I turned right onto the Strip. During the day it wasn't as glitzy, but the tall gold towers of Mandalay Bay, the Eiffel Tower at Paris, the dancing fountains at Bellagio, and the Roman columns at Caesars were proof that we weren't in Kansas anymore.

I passed the Venetian, wishing now that I'd gone to work instead of indulging Jeff Coleman's little adventure. The replica of the Doge's Palace might be realistic if there weren't valets out front and St. Mark's Square wasn't trapped inside its walls instead of being spread out in front.

Farther up, I went by Steve Wynn's newest behemoth: Encore. The economy really wasn't supporting these places, but Vegas is optimistic by nature; otherwise people wouldn't keep coming here and tossing their money on the tables.

Me, I didn't gamble. Well, I did once and won a nice bit of cash. But that was a fluke. No one really won in Vegas, despite their hopes. It would be healthier for everyone if they came here with no expectations; then if they won a little, they'd be happier, and if they lost, they could chalk it up to the fact that the house always wins. Almost always.

I was getting into a seedier part of town. The farther away from the Strip, the less glamour. Fremont Street, where Vegas started, sprouted up to my left, and I glanced over at the pedestrian mall and the Four Queens Casino.

Murder Ink was just north, tucked next door to Goodfellas Bail Bonds and across the street from the Bright

Lights Motel. The "B" was out on the sign, and it was flashing RIGHT LIGHTS, its neon barely discernible in the blast of sunlight that hit it.

I parked in the motel parking lot—I'd done that before, and no one ever said anything—and crossed the street to Murder Ink.

The door was locked, and the sign said it was closed.

I cupped my eyes and peered through the glass.

Suddenly, a figure moved in front of me, and I jumped back.

The door swung open, and Jeff Coleman grinned. "You wouldn't make a very good spy, Kavanaugh."

I stepped inside the shop. "I don't want to be a spy."

Jeff closed the door behind me and locked it again. When I turned to face him, he was looking me up and down.

"What?" I asked.

"You couldn't find something else to wear? I mean, it *is* your wedding day." He was teasing me, but I wasn't in the mood.

I was wearing a cotton skirt that touched my knees, a black T-shirt, and my usual Tevas. "What's wrong with this?" I asked.

"Well, it's more like you're heading off to work at the local homeless shelter. You'd fit right in in that outfit." The edges of his mouth twitched with amusement.

"I didn't think I should show off too much of my tattoos," I said.

"Oh, so it's a disguise," he said thoughtfully. "You don't really wear that outfit in public normally, do you?"

I wore this outfit every week or so, but the way he was trying not to laugh meant I was so not going to tell him that.

"You could've worn a pair of jeans," he added as he went toward the back of the shop and through a curtain of sixties beads into his office.

I sighed and followed him. This was not going to be fun at all. I tried to remind myself why I went along with this in the first place, but I honestly couldn't remember. Maybe it was because I was tired and he caught me off guard.

Jeff didn't stop in his office but went out a back door, his car keys jingling in his hand. He held the door open for me, and I saw the gold Pontiac parked in the alley.

"If we're supposed to be incognito, why are we going in that?" I asked.

"I don't think it's going to matter," he said as he opened the passenger door for me.

I sunk down into the seat and fastened my seat belt as he climbed in. He gave me a sideways glance.

"Sure you don't want to stop somewhere and get a pair of jeans or something?"

I took a deep breath. "Just drive, Jeff."

The smile tugged at the corner of his mouth, but he kept it at bay.

We were a block away when I realized something.

"Aren't you even going to try to have a cigarette with me in the car?" I asked.

Jeff did smile now, and he took his hand off the wheel for a second to pull up his short sleeve. A small beige patch was stuck to his bicep.

"I'm quitting," he said.

"That's great."

"I'm doing it for you, Kavanaugh."

"Yeah, right."

"I got tired of you telling me to put out my butts."

He couldn't be serious. Could he? The problem was, I really couldn't tell. And he knew it, too. He started to laugh.

"I had a doctor's appointment last week. The doc suggested it. Said I might not want to die of cancer or anything."

"I'm glad you're listening to him," I said, still not sure how he wanted me to respond.

"Are you really glad, Kavanaugh? Would you miss me if I kicked?" His eyes twinkled with amusement.

I turned my head and stared out the window. Would I miss him? Maybe. Jeff Coleman had grown on me since our first encounters, when we totally hated each other. He constantly teased me about my "upscale" shop and how I thought I was "too good" for a shop like Murder Ink. I knew my mother would tell me that he wouldn't tease me if he didn't like me, but the whole idea of girls suffering through boys' teasing just because the girls think the boys like them seemed to be a precursor for women getting into abusive relationships. *Oh, he verbally abuses you? He does it only because he likes you; so live with it.*

I'd like to think that women had advanced past that since it was the twenty-first century now, but unfortunately that sort of thing has never changed.

Jeff took a toothpick out of his front shirt pocket and stuck it in the corner of his mouth, chewing gently on it. His eyes were on the road, his fingers tapping the steering wheel as if to music.

The radio was off.

It didn't take too long to get to That's Amore Drive-Through Wedding Chapel. I knew it right away. The big white plastic heart sign hovered over the building, red and pink plastic ribbons weaving through the name of the chapel. And underneath, WEDDING CHAPEL flashed like a strobe. Below that, DRIVE-THROUGH, smaller. The building itself was long and squat, a long driveway, not unlike a bank drive-through, extending along the front of the building and out toward the side. The overhang dripped greenery and flowers, and as we pulled in, I could see they were fake. And not of very good quality, either. The stucco had been white at one point, but time had tinged it with gray.

It bothered me that Sylvia and Bernie had chosen this worn-out remnant as the place where they'd exchanged vows. Maybe they should've gone across the street to the chapel that had a bigger-than-life cutout of Elvis in a tux and doing a dance move over the entrance.

Surprisingly, however, there were three cars in line at That's Amore as we turned the corner. And then I saw the probable reason why: a sign advertising a special rate of twenty-five dollars if you had your own car.

Up ahead, I could see a Dean Martin impersonator singing in front of the first car parked at a small window. The bank analogy wasn't far off the mark. As we got closer, the impersonator's voice rang through the open car windows.

He wasn't half bad. Actually, it sounded pretty good. Not better than Dino, of course, but close enough to make someone's wedding day special. If they chose this particular type of nuptials.

Even if he had been awful, I wasn't one to judge. My voice was flat and lacking any sort of lyrical sound.

A white stretch limo was parked along the driveway, "That's Amore" in red cursive letters sliding across its side and the address of the chapel below, along with its phone number.

Looking ahead, I saw a couple on a motorcycle in the rear of the line, a big black SUV in front of it, and a sporty convertible at the window. That was the one being serenaded, and the bride had a long white veil over her head as she stood on the seat, waving something that acted as a bouquet but clearly wasn't. It was bulkier and very possibly yellow. I squinted to see what it was. I didn't want to ask Jeff to drive closer, or he'd think I was truly interested in this.

"What's that?" he asked, echoing my own thoughts.

"It's a bunch of bananas." We hadn't heard him approach. He wore a tuxedo identical to the one Ray Lucci had worn in my trunk.

"Bananas?" I asked.

"She's from one of those islands—Costa Rica, I think. It's a tribute to her heritage." The man spoke seriously, as if this were perfectly normal. "You here for a ceremony?"

Jeff nodded. "That's right."

"Pay here, and it's only a short wait," he said.

I figured Jeff would give him some song and dance about how we were just checking this out, but instead he pulled out his wallet, handing over a fifty-dollar bill. As if we really were going to get married after all.

Chapter 12

The fact that I started to hyperventilate did not escape the man in the tux as he handed Jeff his change. He leaned into the window and cocked his head at me as he asked Jeff, "Cold feet?"

I'd say freezing feet was more like it.

"Do you have a ladies' room or something where she might be able to freshen up?" Jeff asked, his voice perfectly normal. As any groom would be concerned about his bride.

At the thought, even more panic bubbled up in my chest, and I tried to catch my breath.

"Your head between your knees," Jeff said, his hand on the back of my neck, forcing me down. "Breathe deeply."

With my head down, I couldn't see him, but I heard him say, "I think we really do need a ladies' room."

"Park over there," the man said, "and go in the front door."

The car jerked around and then stopped again, and Jeff cut the engine.

"Kavanaugh, that was brilliant," he whispered.

I peeked up over my knee.

"You paid him," I said, barely able to hear myself over my pounding heart.

"Best way to get information," he whispered. "Now get out of the car and keep pretending like you're going to be sick."

"Who's pretending?" I hissed as I pushed open the car door.

I missed the glass doors in the front because potted palms practically covered them. I guess they didn't want just anyone wandering in and preferred that patrons stay in their cars.

The foyer was dingy white with a pink tinge, the color of underwear that got caught in the color wash. I could hear the strains of "That's Amore" coming from somewhere, probably the Dean Martin outside. I wondered whether it was Dan Franklin.

The man in the tux materialized suddenly next to me. He took my arm and led me to a door with a cutout image of a bride on it. "Here you go," he said.

I glanced back at Jeff, who nodded. I didn't want to go in there. I wanted to stay out here while Jeff asked this guy questions. But maybe this was Jeff's plan all along. I was only a pawn in his own investigation. He certainly couldn't come to a wedding chapel all by himself.

I went into the bathroom. I didn't have much choice.

This room was no more inviting than the foyer. The same dingy walls, old-fashioned sink and vanity. It was a one-seater, everything in one room. It was clean; had to give them that.

But it wasn't soundproof. I could hear Jeff outside.

"Heard that one of your singers got murdered."

Silence for a second, then, "Oh, yeah, Ray. He was an ex-con." He said it as though all ex-cons find themselves murdered at some point. "The cops were here all afternoon yesterday. Bad for business."

"Who owns this place? Seems like it would be a gold mine."

"It is. And I do. Own the place. Anthony DellaRocco."

"Great idea with the Dean Martins."

"A wig and a tux, and any guy can look like Dino."

"But they all can't sing, can they?"

"They can all act drunk."

I wished Jeff would get on with it. All this chitchat about

Dean Martins and who owns the place—who cared? We were here to find out about Lucci, weren't we?

"So Lucci was an ex-con?"

"Um, yeah." I could tell Jeff's change of subject threw DellaRocco for a second. "He stole cars. I got a little worried with him here because every now and then he'd talk about how great a car that came through was. Like that red Mustang Bullitt a couple days ago. I was sure he was going after that one."

I froze. That was what Dan Franklin had said, that Lucci was eyeing my car.

"That's the car he was found in," Jeff said casually.

"Really? How do you know that?"

"I've got a friend on the police force. He told me a few things off the record."

"Like what?" Everyone liked a bit of gossip.

"He and another guy named Dan Franklin had some sort of rift. Franklin works here, too, right?"

It dawned on me that if I could hear them, they could hear me, too. Or not hear me, since I wasn't doing anything. I turned on the water, which, unfortunately, drowned out the conversation.

Another glance around told me there was another door on the other side of the bathroom. Turning the water on a little higher to make more noise, I tiptoed over to the other door and tugged on it.

It swung open, and I peered around the corner. Seemed like it led into a sort of dressing room, although instead of a wide mirror across one wall, there was only a long vertical one stuck on the back of a door across the room, like you'd see in a store dressing room. A clothes rack was a sort of open closet; tuxedos hung side by side. Must have been ten of them. On a table that reminded me of those you see at a church craft fair, foam heads wore black wigs. Lockers lined the far side of the room. Must have been where the Dean Martins stashed their stuff while they were crooning to newlyweds.

A quick look around, and I stepped into the room, quietly closing the door behind me. Even though the cops had already been here, I wondered whether they missed something that Ray Lucci had left behind.

A rat's cage, maybe?

As I stepped closer, I saw masking tape with names stuck on the locker doors. WILL, ALAN, DAN, LOU, and RAY. Dan must have been Dan Franklin; Ray was Lucci. I didn't know whether I should care about the others, but I went over the names a few times in my head so I wouldn't forget them.

I paused, trying to hear whether anyone was coming. I couldn't hear Jeff and DellaRocco anymore, and the other door to the ladies' room must have been more soundproof because I couldn't hear the running water, either.

I didn't want to tarry too long, so I stepped up to Ray's locker and pulled it open.

Nothing inside. Not a scrap of paper or even a crumb. It was as though someone had vacuumed it. Like the cops. Who'd been here yesterday, interrupting business.

I shut the door.

Curiosity got the better of me, and I moved to the locker marked DAN. There were clothes in here: jeans, a T-shirt, a pair of running shoes. Because I'm almost six feet tall, I didn't even need to stand on my toes to see what was on the shelf.

A wallet.

Must have been pretty trusting.

I snatched it down and opened it. Credit cards, a few dollar bills, and a driver's license.

Dan Franklin should have had his picture taken again.

Because he was the spitting image of Ray Lucci, the guy in my trunk.

While I was always a fan of the Rat Pack, Dean Martin wasn't my favorite. I had a soft spot for Sammy. Maybe it's because I have two left feet and am tone-deaf, but Sammy's moves have always impressed me. Dino, on the other hand, was Frank's sidekick, the amusing drunk who seemed to be along for the ride.

It was interesting how That's Amore was breathing new life into him.

I stared at the picture of Dan Franklin and could totally

see how Ray Lucci could pass himself off as Franklin. Who would know?

I was about to put the wallet back when I noticed a plastic card that didn't look like a credit card. I slid it out. An ID card from the University of Nevada, Las Vegas. Laboratory Animal Care Services.

Dan Franklin was wearing a lab coat in the picture. He looked less like Ray Lucci here.

As I studied it, I flashed back to the rat found with Lucci in my trunk.

Rats are lab animals, aren't they?

A banging startled me. Tossing the wallet back in the locker and shutting it as quietly as I could, I tried to figure out where the banging was coming from.

It was the ladies' room. Jeff must have been wondering where I was.

In a few strides, I was at the door I'd come in from. I put my hand on the knob and turned it.

But nothing happened.

I shouldn't have let the door close. Because it was locked. From the inside.

Chapter 13

I twirled around and assessed my situation.

There were two other doors. One not far from the ladies' room door, and the one that wore the mirror across the room. I went to the closest one and opened it.

The men's room.

Figures.

How would I explain that I went into the ladies' room and came out the men's?

I had to see where the other door led.

But before I could reach it, it swung open by itself. Well, not really by itself—there was a person behind it.

He stepped around the door and his mouth formed a small "O" when he spotted me standing next to the lockers.

"Who are you?" he asked, his eyes skittering to the lockers and then back to me.

He was onto me. I thought quickly. "I came here to get married, but I got cold feet and went into the ladies' room, and I was trying sneak out so my fiancé wouldn't find me." Hey, sounded like a plan.

"Happens all the time," he said.

Really? Interesting.

I noticed now his resemblance to Dean Martin—and by extension Ray Lucci and Dan Franklin—but it could've been the wig and the tux. Maybe this was Franklin.

He looked from me to the lockers again, a frown etched

in his forehead. Being nosy wasn't a crime, although I hoped he didn't think I'd taken anything.

"This way," he said, crooking his finger at me so I'd follow.

He didn't believe my story. Best-case scenario: He'd kick me out and tell me never to come back. I could hear even more banging behind us as we went out into a dark hallway. I heard voices now, Jeff's and DellaRocco's.

"It's my fiancé," I whispered. Maybe now my story would seem more credible.

"This way," he repeated, and we moved down the hall and turned a corner.

The light blinded me for a second, and I blinked a few times before I realized we were going out into a back parking lot. He stopped in front of a blue Ford, unlocking it with a key fob and opening the door for me. I hesitated, and he looked at me quizzically.

"Don't you want to get away?" he asked.

My dad always told me not to get into a car with a stranger. "I don't even know you."

"My name's Will Parker." He tugged at the wig until it came off, and he tossed it into the backseat. He ran his hand through a mass of dark blond curls, and he unbuttoned the top button of his dress shirt. "I'll take you wherever you want to go."

He didn't look like Dean Martin anymore. He had a rakish look about him, sort of like the high school football quarterback who knew he'd get the head cheerleader in a compromising position at the prom.

I wasn't quite ready to be compromised, and I had a can of Mace in my bag along with my cell phone.

"I don't think so," I said. "I'm sorry, but I hope you understand." I paused a second before asking, "You probably have a girlfriend or something waiting for you anyway, right?" Might as well try to lighten up the mood—let him think I was more worried about his personal commitments than my own safety.

An expression that I couldn't read crossed his face, but

then he shut the door. He gave me a cautious smile. "Do you have a name, or will the media start calling you the runaway bride?"

"Brett Kavanaugh," I said without thinking. He hadn't answered my question.

He cocked his head, indicating the tattoo on my arm, the koi in a sea of blues and greens. "I like your tattoo." He shrugged off his jacket and shoved the sleeve of his shirt up. A skull with daggers through its eye sockets adorned his arm. It was faded with time, but it wasn't bad work.

"You should have that touched up," I said, reaching into my bag and producing a business card.

He studied it a second, then grinned and put it in his pocket. "I'll keep that in mind. Thanks." He paused. "Want me to call you a cab?"

I thought about Jeff Coleman and how he totally would not approve of what I was doing. But did I care?

"That would be nice," I said, "but I think by the time the cab gets here, my fiancé"—my voice caught on the word in a little cough—"will have found me out here with you."

And speak of the devil, but didn't Jeff Coleman bound right out of the door we'd come through. He didn't look too upset, though, maybe even slightly amused.

"There you are, sweetheart," he said, his arm snaking around my waist. "What's going on?" He looked at Will. "Who is this?"

I shrugged him off and stepped back. "Will Parker. He's one of the—um—performers here. I got locked out." I hoped he wouldn't press as to where I was locked out from.

"Thanks for taking care of her," Jeff said to Will. "I wouldn't want to lose her."

I was going to be sick. He didn't have to lay it on that thick. Especially since the longer I was looking at Will Parker, the longer I thought maybe I *would* like to take a ride in that car at some point.

"No problem, man," Will said, nodding, then turned to me with a concerned expression. "Are you going to be okay?" Now that I had a "real" fiancé, he seemed ready to forget about my snooping.

I nodded, although the thought of being engaged to Jeff Coleman still made me woozy.

"She wanted to get married in a church. This is all my fault," Jeff told Will before giving me a wink Will Parker couldn't see, then added, "We can go back home and talk about this."

"Hope to see you again," Will said, his eyes twinkling as he nodded at me.

I had a sudden urge to tell him to definitely call me. Jeff must have sensed my hesitation because again I felt his hand on my lower back, and he steered me back around to the front of the building. He gave Will a little finger waggle as we went.

"What was that all about?" he asked as we settled into the Pontiac. "Flirting with another man on our wedding day?" he teased.

"I was trying to get some information out of him," I said, strapping myself in with the seat belt.

"That wasn't all you were after," he said.

"You're not really my fiancé, so what do you care?"

He cocked his head at me and looked at me for a couple of seconds before saying, "You're right. Why should I care?"

And then he gunned the engine, and the tires screeched as the car slid out of the parking lot.

"So what did you find out from Mr. Studly?" Jeff asked when we stopped at a light. Neither of us had said a word to the other for the last five minutes.

"Nothing," I admitted, kicking myself that Will Parker now knew far more about me than I knew about him. "But there was this other door that led out from the bathroom into the Dean Martin changing room. There were lockers, and I found Dan Franklin's wallet. He looks exactly like

Ray Lucci. It was a little creepy, but it explains why Lucci might tell people he's Franklin."

"Interesting," Jeff said. "I'm surprised his wallet was in the locker."

"Why?"

"DellaRocco said he hasn't seen Franklin in two days."

Chapter 14

I thought about my conversation with Dan Franklin. How he'd said he and Lucci didn't get along.

"Franklin had an ID card in his wallet," I said. "He's some sort of lab-animal technician or something at UNLV."

Jeff immediately caught on. "That rat. You think Franklin offed Lucci and stuck that rat in there for some reason?"

"Crossed my mind."

"And now the guy's in hiding."

"Except that he did get Bitsy's phone message, so he must be at home."

"Or he has a cell phone. He could be anywhere."

Right. Cell phone. "But why would he leave his wallet in his locker?" And then I had another thought. Maybe he killed Lucci, stuck him in my trunk, and then took off without getting his stuff. Because maybe someone saw him. Like Sylvia and Bernie. Maybe he went after them next.

My imagination was getting the better of me. This was stuff that made a bad TV movie. Except it made sense. It would explain everything.

But then again, it probably wasn't that easy.

I could see Jeff's brain was working overtime, too.

"Where does this Franklin live?"

I flashed back on the file folder with Franklin's information. I remembered the address because it was only a couple of blocks away from my house in Henderson. I told Jeff as much.

"You want to go over there, don't you?" I asked.

Jeff didn't answer, but in seconds he was pulling into a parking lot and swerving around, putting the car in the opposite direction.

"We have no business going over there," I said.

"The man hasn't been to work. His wallet's in his locker."

"I talked to him yesterday, so he's not dead, like Lucci," I said.

"He wasn't dead as of yesterday," Jeff said. "Who knows about today?"

The Pontiac came to a stop at a light. A trail of Asian tourists following a man holding up a big orange flag moved across the intersection. A few heavyset couples wearing fanny packs got caught in the middle of the Asian group but managed to separate themselves on the other side.

Jeff shook his head sadly. "They're like sheep, aren't they?"

His question was rhetorical, and I merely nodded as the light changed and we started moving again.

The Strip was taking too long, so at the next block, Jeff hung a left and went down Koval. No scenery, only the backs of the resorts and casinos, but it moved faster.

"So did you get anything out of DellaRocco about Franklin?" I asked when we got onto 215 heading toward Henderson.

"I tried to find out if Lucci had any enemies, and that's when Franklin came up. Apparently there was no love lost between them. DellaRocco was pretty vague about it, though. We didn't get much further than that, because he got really suspicious as to why the water was running in the bathroom and you weren't coming out."

"So now it's my fault?"

"Has to be someone's," he said.

I was regretting this little adventure more and more.

We were quiet until Jeff reached my street. "Where to from here?" he asked.

I directed him a couple of blocks up and over.

The neighborhood was similar to mine: rows of stucco

houses, the occasional palm tree, banana yuccas. Some houses had lawns, real lawns that would need watering. Since Vegas was in the middle of a drought and Lake Mead was way lower than it should be, this upset me. We were in the desert, with beautiful desert flora that was perfectly fine as a yard. No need to drain the water system just because someone wanted to pretend he was living in another part of the country.

I opened my mouth to say something, but I guess I'd said it before because Jeff held up his hand and said, "I get it, Kavanaugh. Water shortage. You're a broken record, you know?"

I was thinking about a smart retort when I spotted the address we had for Dan Franklin. I pointed. "That one, there."

Jeff eased the Pontiac against the curb across the street and a couple of houses down. But it wasn't exactly as if we were incognito. It was a bright gold car. Sort of like how Starsky and Hutch were driving around undercover in that bright red Gran Torino with the white stripe. Stick out much?

An old blue Ford Taurus sat in the driveway.

"Looks like someone's home," Jeff said, indicating the car.

"I don't think so." The house was closed up: shutters drawn; the mailbox hanging open, leaking envelopes and advertisements; three newspapers on the front step.

I climbed out of the car and walked up to the driveway and around the Taurus, peering into the windows. It was immaculate inside, no litter of any sort. There was a university parking sticker stuck to the back bumper.

"Kavanaugh," Jeff hissed behind me. "What are you doing?"

I waved him off and went to the mailbox, reaching in and pulling out the mail. I leafed through it. Electric bill, a couple of credit card bills, junk mail. Jeff peered around my shoulder—I was a couple inches taller than him—and stuck out his hand, grabbing one of the envelopes.

"Hey," I said, twirling around, trying to get it back.

Jeff grinned and waved it around. "What? You're going to take the stolen mail from me?"

His words stopped me, and I realized what I was doing. Right. I was messing with the U.S. mail. I could get thrown in jail for this.

"Let's leave it," I said.

"Now you want to leave it," Jeff said. "You wouldn't want to if you saw what it was."

Against my better judgment, he'd piqued my interest. "Okay, I'll give. What is it?"

He stuffed it in his back pocket and took the rest of the mail from me, shoving it back into the mailbox. "This way," he said, going up to the front steps and actually ringing the doorbell.

"What are you doing?" I asked.

"Just in case the neighbors are watching."

Okay, that was a good idea.

We stood a few seconds, and Jeff punched at the doorbell a couple more times. He leaned around and tried to look in the windows, but the shutters were closed tight. "Let's go around back," he said.

I looked up and down the street, because now I worried we'd be perceived as burglars and the cops would show up any second. But nothing. Maybe the neighbors were all at work.

The back was as deserted as the front. A stone patio, a small grill perched at the corner, stuck off the back of the house as if it were unfinished. I thought about Dan Franklin, living alone and grilling his little piece of steak on it. And then I had a vision of myself doing the same thing. I shuddered as I checked out the steps that went up to a back door. A curtain hung over the window, but Jeff indicated a window to the left of it and just out of reach for him. "Can you see in there?" he asked me.

Nice to know he didn't have any sort of Napoleon issues when it came to my height.

I got on the top step, stood on my tiptoes, leaned over, and looked into a kitchen. No dirty dishes, nothing out of place, like that car. "It seems fine," I said.

"But what about this?"

Jeff was no longer standing right behind me. I spun around to see him bending over, picking something up.

When he stood and turned around to face me, I caught my breath.

He was holding what looked like an empty animal cage.

Chapter 15

"That doesn't prove anything," I said. "It's an empty cage. Could've been a cat or a small dog in there."

Jeff brought it over and we studied it a minute.

"You're right," he admitted, "but it does seem a little suspicious."

"The man works with lab animals," I said. "Of course he might have cages and critters around. We don't know for sure that the dead rat belonged to him."

"Who else would have a rat?" Jeff asked.

I sighed. He was probably right. It was possible that rat had lived in this very cage while he was alive. "I wonder why he put the cage out here," I said, stepping around Jeff and around the side of the house where he'd found it. A trash can was shoved up against the side of the garage.

"It was right next to the trash can," Jeff said, putting the cage back down. He leaned over and wiped the handle with the tail of his shirt. "Fingerprints," he said when he saw me watching.

Oh, right. We were trespassing. If Flanigan ever found out we were poking around Dan Franklin's rat cage, he might have issues with that.

"When you looked inside, did you see any sort of security keypad?" Jeff asked.

I shook my head. "No. What—" I stopped. "You want to get into the house, don't you? Like you got into my house last night?"

"You really need to talk to Tim about better security,"

he said as he walked past me and up the steps to the door. "You might not want to watch."

I turned my back and looked out over Dan Franklin's small patch of yard and into the backyard of the house on the next street over. A flutter in a window caught my eye.

"Jeff," I hissed. "Jeff!"

"It's open."

I swung around and saw Jeff in the doorway.

"We have to leave," I said as I hurried over to him. I indicated the house where I'd seen the curtain move. "Someone's watching us. The cops could be on their way."

Disappointment crossed Jeff's face, but he closed the door with his hand over the tail of his shirt to get rid of those pesky fingerprints, and we ran back around the house to the Pontiac. Jeff had just started the engine when I glimpsed a cruiser coming down the opposite street.

"Get going!" I said, and the car shot forward, the tires screeching across the pavement.

I caught the cop car in the side-view mirror as we turned the corner.

I took a deep breath and leaned back in my seat. "That was close."

Jeff grinned. "Don't you like living on the fast side, Kavanaugh?"

"I could live without it," I said.

"But you got your rocks off going through that guy's mail, all right, didn't you?"

I rolled my eyes and stared out the window.

"Hey, Kavanaugh, can you get it out?"

I turned back to see Jeff shifting up in his seat, his butt facing me, the white envelope he'd taken from Dan Franklin's mailbox flapping against the back of his seat.

I didn't really want to be that close to Jeff Coleman's butt, but I reached over and snatched it out.

It was a bank statement.

"We really shouldn't open this," I said, but my fingers were itching to.

Sister Mary Eucharista would have slapped those fingers with a ruler if she could.

What was wrong with me? Was being with Jeff Coleman turning me into a felon? We pretend to be getting married to get information; we steal mail; we almost break into a man's house. What else? Oh, right, I looked into a man's locker at That's Amore. But I couldn't exactly blame Jeff for that. I was alone at the time. But it was his influence, for sure.

Jeff Coleman wasn't good for me.

He was grinning. "Oh, go ahead," he egged me on. "Everyone does their banking online anyway now. Don't you throw those mailed statements in a box and not even look at them?"

How did he know what I did with my bank statements?

He was still talking. "Dan Franklin might not even realize that he didn't get a statement this month."

I sighed and tossed the envelope on the dashboard. "I can't do it," I said. "It's bad enough we took it."

We were stopped at a light at the Home Depot. Jeff grabbed the envelope, slid his finger into the crease, and opened it. He pulled out a couple of sheets of paper with Dan Franklin's personal business on them.

And he let out a low whistle.

"You ought to look at this, Kavanaugh," he said, throwing it into my lap as the light turned green and he hit the accelerator.

I jumped as if he'd thrown a snake at me.

"It's not going to bite," he teased.

I didn't even have to pick it up. It landed in such a way that I could see exactly what Jeff Coleman had seen.

Dan Franklin had made a withdrawal of ten thousand dollars two weeks ago.

Chapter 16

As with the cage, this might have not meant anything.

"Maybe he needed a new air-conditioning unit or something for his house," I said. "We don't know what he used that money for."

"It's a lot of money," Jeff said. "And maybe you're right. But he withdraws this kind of money and then disappears? After his coworker is murdered? With a dead rat underneath him in your trunk?"

"It still doesn't mean anything," I insisted. "And we committed a crime. We should bring this back."

Jeff indicated the torn envelope. "Don't think so. I wonder where he is."

"Well, it's clear he hasn't been home in a couple days at least."

"Three, if you count the newspapers. But why is the car there?"

I didn't answer as I stared out the window. Jeff had gotten onto the highway and was heading back downtown. The mountains spread out in the distance, their charcoal color clashing with the clear, light blue sky, clouds looking like cotton balls. A jet left a long white trail behind it as it sailed out of sight.

"Earth to Kavanaugh," Jeff was saying. "What is it about those mountains for you?"

I sighed. "It's peaceful up there. No worries. No schedules, no clients, nothing but me."

"Don't turn into one of those crunchy granola types."

I lifted my leg to show off my Teva sandals. "I already wear these."

"As long as they're not Birkenstocks."

"What's wrong with those?" I thought about the sandals in my closet at home.

He laughed. "You've got a pair, don't you?"

I felt my face flush hot, and I turned away from him so I could look out the side window. I heard him chuckling, then humming to himself as we took back roads all the way up to his shop.

He broke the silence as he pulled into the alley behind Murder Ink. "Maybe I should've let you hang a little longer with Mr. Studly," he said.

"What do you mean?"

"He liked you. Maybe he knows something. Something about Dan Franklin, why he's missing, or something about Ray Lucci."

"You think he'd tell me because he likes me?" I asked.

"Sure, why not? You should call him. Go out to dinner, wear something other than that skirt." He made a face as he glanced at it. "How he could be interested in you, looking like that? Well, there's no accounting for taste. Of course it could be worse. You could be wearing those Birkenstocks with it."

"So now you're Tim Gunn?" I asked. "You think you could dress me better than I can?"

He grinned. "Obviously you've got no fashion sense." He paused. "Except maybe for the tats. Especially that Japanese koi on your arm."

The one *he* tattooed.

The car eased against the curb, and Jeff cut the engine. I scurried out after him as he unlocked the back door to Murder Ink and followed him inside.

Jeff turned on the lights, and the fluorescent beams gave the room an unearthly glow. He dropped his keys on the desk that was already piled with scattered papers and folders. His filing system was an abomination. He said Sylvia had set it up, but the way Sylvia's mind worked made me wonder how he kept track of everything. I'd never told

Bitsy about it, because, knowing her, she'd be here in an hour reorganizing.

"So what now?" I asked as we went out into the front of the shop.

Jeff turned on the lights in here, too, and the one in the window lit up, advertising that the shop was open. I studied the flash on the walls, the stock tattoos that his shop specialized in.

"Wishing you had it this easy, Kavanaugh?" he teased.

I shook my head and rolled my eyes at him.

When Jeff had done my koi tattoo a few months back, I hadn't wanted him to do it here. I wasn't sure how clean this place was, and I knew you could practically eat off the floor in my shop, thanks to Bitsy. I'd made Jeff come to me.

What I hadn't told him was how much this place reminded me of the Ink Spot, where Mickey had first taken me in as a trainee and taught me all he knew. I was a twenty-two-year-old kid, fresh out of art school, still thinking about going to Paris and making my way. But I needed some cash to get there. I'd been mulling it over when I saw the shop. I'd given myself a crude heart tattoo on the inside of my wrist with a sewing needle and some ballpoint-pen ink when I was sixteen. I'd toyed with the idea of another tattoo, maybe one done more professionally, for a couple years, but even then I knew tattoos are permanent, and I wanted to be sure about the design.

Mickey *tsk-tsk*ed over the heart on my wrist and suggested a Celtic cross on my upper back, stretching between my shoulder blades. I liked the idea of something that would be covered up most of the time, like a secret only I would know about and that would be with me forever. I sketched it out for him, and his eyes showed surprise that I could visualize it so well.

Halfway through the tattoo, Mickey asked whether I'd be interested in learning the trade. He gave me an old tattoo machine and a grapefruit to practice on. I was hooked.

The Ink Spot smelled like Jeff's shop: ink and baby wipes and a little bit of sweat.

It was time to go. I took a step toward the door.

"Wait a sec," Jeff said.

I stopped.

"I'm not kidding about that guy back there at the chapel," Jeff said. "It wouldn't hurt to see if he knows anything. Tell him you broke up with me. Tell him we have an open relationship."

"So you want to pimp me out for information?" I couldn't believe what I was hearing.

"Call it what you will, Kavanaugh, but I thought you wanted to find my mother, too."

The worry laced his expression, and I saw that all the teasing was a cover-up for his concern about Sylvia.

"What do you think happened to your mother and Bernie?" I asked softly.

He took a deep breath and shook his head. "I'm not sure. I was hoping we'd find Dan Franklin. Maybe he knows. But since he's missing, too . . ."

He didn't need to finish his sentence. I was thinking the same thing. Something happened with Ray Lucci's murder that caused three people to go missing. One of them might even be a murderer. I didn't want to think about what could've happened to Sylvia and Bernie.

I nodded. "Okay, fine. I'll call the chapel and see if I can reach that guy." I didn't want to tell him that I'd given Parker my card. He'd probably give me a lot of grief over that.

"Thanks, Kavanaugh." Jeff's voice was soft, unlike him. It made me realize he really was human. Something that wasn't always so apparent.

"What about Dan Franklin?" I asked, not wanting to have an Oprah moment with Jeff Coleman. "Should I tell Tim about his wallet and that he works with animals like rats?" I had no intention of telling him about our little adventure over at Franklin's house. Although if I planted an idea about Franklin in Tim's head, maybe he'd start looking into Franklin's affairs and discover the empty house and the bank withdrawal. Despite what I'd said to Jeff, it did seem that the money could have something to do with all this.

"How are you going to explain to him how you saw the wallet?" Jeff asked.

That was a problem, definitely. I'd already told Tim about the phone conversation, so I couldn't now say, *Hey, Dan also dropped the fact that he works with rats; you might want to check that out.* I would need a better reason as to how I knew this, and not from messing around in the Dean Martin locker room at That's Amore.

"I'll figure something out," I said as I looked at my watch. It was almost noon. "Listen, I have to get to the shop. If you hear anything about Sylvia, call me. And I'll let you know how it goes with Parker."

"Who?"

I made a face at him. "Mr. Studly, as you insist on calling him."

A smile tugged at the corner of his mouth, and I wanted to leave before he thought of some other smart-aleck thing to say.

As I reached for the door, it opened, and a woman came in.

She wasn't as tall as me, but she was close. She had long dark hair pulled back in a ponytail, and she wore a pair of large sunglasses, dark jeans and a white button-down cotton shirt, buttoned almost too high, and a long strand of red beads bouncing against an ample chest.

She looked a little too high-class for Murder Ink.

Except when she took off the sunglasses to reveal a dark bruise circling her right eye.

When she saw me staring, her face went white, as if she'd seen a ghost.

I knew why.

I couldn't remember her name, but about a year before I'd tattooed two ribbons circling her left biceps. One ribbon was white, the other purple.

Both signified that she had been physically abused and survived.

I nodded at her, but before either of us could say anything, Jeff spoke up.

"Rosalie, what are you doing here? Did they find my mother and your father?"

Rosalie? As in Bernie Applebaum's daughter?

Chapter 17

Giving me an anxious look begging me not to reveal I knew who she was, Rosalie worried the edge of the sunglasses with long fingers tipped with short-clipped nails.

"I haven't heard a word," she said, her voice barely a whisper. "I was hoping you'd have some news."

Jeff went over to her and patted her on the forearm. "I went out to the canyon. Stopped everywhere I could between here and there, but I couldn't find them."

"Have you heard any more from the police about their car?"

"No, I'm sorry." And I could see in his face that he truly was. There was compassion there, and his own worry.

Hated to say it, but I liked Jeff Coleman better when he wasn't quite so human. Made him easier to deal with.

Rosalie was looking at me out of the corner of her eye, and Jeff noticed.

"Rosalie Marino, Brett Kavanaugh."

I smiled and held out my hand. "Nice to meet you," I said, hoping she'd see that I wasn't about to out her.

She took my hand limply with a couple of fingers. "Yes, nice to meet you, too."

"Brett's helping with trying to track down my mother and Bernie," Jeff explained.

Rosalie was still looking at me, and her eyes widened, but I shrugged and, before she could say anything, added, "So far, though, we're hitting a brick wall." I didn't want to get into the whole Dan Franklin thing. If we found out for sure he had something do with Sylvia and Bernie, then that would be the time to mention him.

Rosalie looked back at Jeff and gave him a sad smile. "I'm on my way to work. Can you give me a call if you hear anything?" She pulled a piece of paper and a pen from her bag and scribbled down a number, handing it to Jeff.

He took it and held her hand for a second. "We'll find them, Rosalie. Don't worry." His expression held a tenderness I'd never seen before, and her eyes filled with tears.

I shifted uncomfortably, uncertain what to do or say.

My cell phone made the decision for me as it warbled Bruce Springsteen from inside my bag.

It startled both Rosalie and Jeff, who seemed as though they had forgotten I was there.

I took the phone out of my bag, said, "I'll be outside," and flipped the phone open with one hand as I pressed the door with the other. Once on the sidewalk, I said, "What's up, Bitsy?"

"It's almost noon, and you've got a client coming in. Where are you?"

Who needed a mother with Bitsy around? The guilt started to seep in. Sister Mary Eucharista would make me write fifty times, *I will not exploit my employees while I go messing around in other people's business*. Although admittedly, I'd been asked to help, so I could be perceived as being a good friend. Somehow I'm not sure the sister would've seen it that way, though.

"I'll be there in a few," I said. "I'm up here at Murder Ink. Bernie's daughter just showed. She and Jeff are really worried."

That was the way to turn it around on the guilt, because Bitsy immediately said, "So there's still no word from them? Where do you think they might be?"

I quickly told her about our morning's activities—going to the chapel and then to Dan Franklin's house and finding it all closed up—and ended with my suspicion that Sylvia and Bernie had seen something they shouldn't have.

I didn't tell her what Tim had said about Ray Lucci

being Sylvia's son. Unlike Bitsy, I can keep a secret, and, anyway, I hadn't really thought that one through yet. How that could've played a role in all this.

Because I had started wondering whether it didn't play a role after all. It seemed as though it had to, but how, I wasn't sure.

Bitsy didn't notice I was holding back and latched on to the one thing I knew she probably would. "Are you going to call this Dean Martin guy? Are you going to see if he knows something?"

Before I got a chance to respond, she added, "You know, Brett, you've got the worst luck with men. Maybe this one will be different."

She was referring to the two men who'd been in my life in the last six months: a casino manager, who was too much of a ladies' man for my taste, and an emergency room doctor, whom I'd completely misread and, thus, had sabotaged something that might have been good.

"I met him for five seconds," I said, getting defensive. "I have no idea if we'd get along or anything."

"But you said he liked you." Bitsy is the ultimate romantic. She's been married a couple of times but never gotten bitter about it. She's dated her fair share of men and recently signed up for Match.com because, as she put it, "What else am I supposed to do with my time?"

Bitsy was a serial dater.

Not that there's anything wrong with that.

The fact that she's a little person was absolutely no deterrent for the men she dated, which I found fascinating. She dated little people *and* tall people.

She was still talking. "I think you should call him. Have lunch. Lunch is always good."

"Yeah, sure," I said, watching Jeff and Rosalie through the front window. Rosalie had sunk down into one of Jeff's chairs, and he was sitting across from her, his elbows on his knees, leaning over and talking. Her face was sagging with sadness.

"I'll be in shortly," I said again, hanging up on Bitsy.

I didn't know whether I should go back in or just leave

quietly. After a few seconds, I decided that leaving was the best thing. I didn't want to intrude on their conversation. So I made my way over to the Bright Lights Motel and climbed into the Jeep. The gearshift stuck as I tried to put it into first, and I could hear the clutch grind.

I wanted my car back.

I couldn't think about Jeff or Rosalie or Will Parker or any of it for the next couple hours. My client was already at the shop when I arrived, and I didn't have time to say anything but a quick hello to Bitsy and Ace when I walked through the door. Joel was already with a client, and I gave him a little finger waggle as I passed his room.

Carmella, my client, was older than me, maybe in her forties. She was here for her ninth tattoo: tribal ink on her left thigh, running from her hip to her knee. Carmella had found some designs, and I'd put together something that she was thrilled with, even though it was pretty simplistic overall and as an artist, not too challenging for me. It was time-consuming, however, and two hours later we were making arrangements to finish it up in a couple of weeks.

Joel was leaning against the front desk when Carmella finally took off, pleased with her half tattoo.

"Bitsy's been filling me in. Why did you pretend you were going to marry Jeff Coleman? I would've gone over there with you."

I appreciated the thought. But Joel's girth, his barbed-wire tattoos, the long braid that almost reached his waist now, and the chain that snaked into his pocket and held his keys all screamed biker, while his soft, lilting voice and almost girlish mannerisms revealed his true nature. No one would buy us getting married.

I smiled and thanked him. "I'm all done with that now."

"Are you? What about that impersonator?"

"I don't know."

"Does he really look like Dean Martin?" From the way he asked, I began to wonder whether Joel didn't have a Rat Pack crush, too. While we suspected his inclinations, we weren't positive which way Joel swung; he hadn't come out to us, and we never saw him with a date, girl or guy.

"Not without the wig, really," I said.

Bitsy pushed open the door. I hadn't realized she'd gone out. She was carrying a take-out bag from Johnny Rockets.

"Lunch," she announced.

It was two o'clock, but who was paying attention? It was always lunch in the shop, especially with Joel around. Although we had been eating way more burgers lately because of this Atkins thing. I wondered what it would be next. I couldn't see him turning vegetarian or vegan. Weight Watchers made a load of money off him, and he swore them off. Maybe that Jenny Craig thing I kept seeing on TV, where you have to buy their food.

None of it appealed to me, and fortunately, I was skinny enough and my metabolism obviously still worked well enough that I didn't have to worry about it.

We followed Bitsy to the staff room, and she handed out burgers. Joel's next client had arrived, though, so he downed his burger in two bites before taking his client into his room.

"Where's Ace?" I asked between bites.

"He's taking the afternoon off," Bitsy said. "He's working on some new paintings, and he wanted some time for that."

Of all my employees, I knew Ace the least. The things I did know were fairly superficial, like where he lived and how he got into this business. Ace was a frustrated artist, thus the comic-book paintings on our walls, but since he didn't make much money off those, he had to make money somehow. He'd fallen into tattooing by meeting up with Flip Armstrong, the guy who owned the shop before me, and training with him. I'd done the same thing back east with Mickey, but unlike Ace, I embraced my new career. Ace did great work, don't get me wrong, and was very conscientious about it, but he was always a little removed from it, as if he were too good for it.

A buzzer sounded. Someone had come into the shop.

Bitsy jumped up off her chair and went out front. I kept eating.

But the burger almost caught in my throat when Bitsy came back.

With Will Parker behind her.

Chapter 18

Will Parker grinned at me. Bitsy was smiling widely behind him, giving me the thumbs-up.

Great.

"Oh, hi, there," I said, standing awkwardly, acutely aware of some sort of burger dribble on my chin. I grabbed a napkin and wiped it across my face, hoping there wasn't anything else incriminating there.

When I gave him my card, I honestly didn't think I'd see him quite so soon. If at all. It had been only a few hours since I'd met him.

While I'd been worried about his intentions earlier, now I hoped he wasn't some sort of weird stalker.

Bitsy discreetly left the room. I was sure, however, that she hadn't gone far, since she probably wanted to hear every word. A good thing. Just in case.

Will Parker hadn't stopped grinning, but he was taking in the staff room: the lunch table, the fridge, the bulletin board with our favorite tattoo designs stuck to it, the light table with papers and file folders scattered on it.

He'd shed the tuxedo and was wearing a nice pair of beige slacks and a white button-down shirt under a navy blazer. He even wore a tie, baby blue with little yellow fleur-de-lis. I wondered what the occasion was.

Dressed the way he was and without the black Dean

Martin wig, I had to admit I was totally intrigued. Even if he turned out to be a stalker. Bitsy would be pleased.

"I didn't think I'd see you so soon," I said to break the ice.

His head bobbed up and down. "I know, lame, right? But I showed your card to one of the guys at the chapel, and he said your shop was over here at the Venetian, and I was headed over here anyway, so I figured I'd stop in. Maybe see if you could touch up my tat."

The red lights that had been flashing in my brain kicked up a notch. "Someone you work with knows my shop? Who?" I hoped I didn't sound too paranoid.

"Guy named Lou Marino."

I tried to place him but couldn't. Had he been a client? Something about his name was tugging at my brain.

Will was still talking, and I missed the first part of what he said, but his next words jolted me. "His wife's father got married the other day at the chapel. Lou said he married a woman who owns a tattoo shop."

"Sylvia Coleman? She used to own Murder Ink." Small world was suddenly an understatement.

He nodded, and it hit me. That was why the name was familiar. Rosalie Marino. Bernie's daughter.

"His wife is Rosalie?" I asked, thinking about Rosalie's tattoos. I wasn't sure Lou Marino was someone I wanted to cross paths with.

At the mention of Rosalie's name, Will Parker's grin vanished and he looked a little uncomfortable. I began to wonder whether Lou Marino's coworkers knew about the abuse.

"That's right," he said, "Rosalie."

"What does her husband do there?" I asked.

"He's another Dino."

I thought about Sylvia and how she'd requested Ray Lucci that day. Requested him because he was her son. It seemed too odd that Lucci worked with Bernie's son-in-law. Yet another coincidence. Perhaps.

"So what about my tattoo?" he asked, pulling me back

into the conversation. "Can you do it? Touch it up, I mean."

"Not now. You need to make an appointment."

"I can't stay now anyway," he admitted.

"You could've just called, then."

"I had to be over here at the Venetian. I've got a job interview. When Lou told me about your shop and I was heading over here anyway, I figured it might be karma that we met this morning." A smile crept back, and his eyes flashed with a distinct sexiness.

Karma. I liked the sound of that. And a job interview explained the outfit.

"Job doing what?" I asked, wondering in what capacity the Venetian would need a Dean Martin impersonator.

"They're looking for some performers."

"They're starting a Rat Pack routine?" I asked. It would definitely fit the Italian theme.

He shook his head. "No, no. I don't only do Dean. I'm a singer and a dancer. I can do pretty much anything."

I had visions of those Renaissance dancers who swirled around St. Mark's Square on a regular basis, and the idea of Will Parker putting that on his résumé bothered me for some reason.

Was I snooty enough to not date someone because he pranced around in tights and a big white wig?

Possibly.

He saw my hesitation.

"I know it's not Broadway, but it pays okay," he said. "And I've got to get out of that wedding chapel."

"Why?"

"Something's not right over there," he said, pausing.

"What's not right?" I prodded.

"Ray Lucci's murder, for one."

"But that didn't happen at the wedding chapel," I said before thinking. And a nanosecond later I realized I couldn't be certain it hadn't. He'd ended up in my car, which had been at That's Amore, and he had been dressed in his Dean Martin outfit.

But then I had a flash of that rat. That rat that came from somewhere, and even though I now knew Dan Franklin worked with lab animals, I didn't know how it would have ended up at the chapel, especially since there was an empty cage at Franklin's house.

Will Parker had started to notice that I wasn't giving him a hundred percent of my attention.

"Do you know where Lucci was killed?" he asked, his expression guarded now.

I flashed him an embarrassed smile. "No, no, I don't know about that," I said quickly and, eager to change the subject, added, "You said Ray Lucci's murder was one thing that's not right over at the chapel. What else is going on?"

"You're right—it wasn't just that. Although Ray was a crazy guy. Always talking about the cars that came through. We all knew he'd been inside for car theft, so we were never really sure if he was joking or not. He really liked that car Lou's father-in-law drove up in."

My Mustang Bullitt again. It didn't set right that a dead guy had been planning on stealing my car, or at least had thought about stealing it.

And then I realized something.

"Were you working that day?" I asked.

"Yeah, it was me and Lou and Ray."

"But not Dan Franklin?"

He seemed a little taken aback by my question.

"Do you know Dan?"

"I talked to him yesterday," I said, not lying. "So he wasn't working that day? He wasn't there at all?"

"I saw him come in, but he wasn't on shift. At least not when I was. This isn't his full-time job; it's something he does to make extra money. Tony lets him make his own schedule." He paused. "Why are you asking about Dan?"

I shrugged. "Just making conversation. So you saw the Mustang Bullitt, too."

The change of subject threw him a second; then he said, "Nice ride." His face clouded over. "That's one of the other things that's not right." He ran a hand through those golden locks of his. The grin was AWOL now.

He took a deep breath, and when he spoke, what he said was so unexpected I couldn't catch my breath. "That very same car tried to run me down two days ago, about four o'clock, over on Charleston."

Chapter 19

Will Parker said he was sure it was the same car, but he hadn't gotten the license plate number, which was why the cops hadn't tracked it down.

Until yesterday.

When Ray Lucci's body was found in it.

This could explain Flanigan's song and dance in the parking garage last night. He must have been alerted to Will Parker's report about the red Mustang convertible. So Flanigan showed up here to check out where it had been parked, to see whether there were any clues that it had been stolen. I guess someone could have taken it. I was in the shop, didn't leave until midnight. That meant there were nine hours during which my car was unattended.

I hadn't noticed anything unusual, though, when I'd gotten into it that night. There were no telltale signs that the car had been hot-wired. The seat was where I'd always left it; I hadn't had to adjust the rearview mirror.

This was why Flanigan asked me whether anyone else had a key.

Of course Sylvia and Bernie had borrowed mine. Did someone make a copy?

But that begged the question: If someone stole it, why bring it back? Maybe to make it look as though it was never gone in the first place.

Will Parker was looking at me funny. I'd been quiet too long. I didn't want to tell him it was my car. Somehow I had

a feeling that might not go over too well. And we were just
starting to get to know each other. If it went any further
and he ever saw my car, I'd deal with it then. Now was not
the time.

"You didn't see who was driving?" I asked.

"You sound like the cops," he said.

"My brother's a detective," I explained. "I think it's in
the DNA."

"Really? He's a cop?"

I chuckled. "Yeah, but he never takes anything I say seriously. So what happened with the car?"

"I didn't see who was driving," he admitted. "I was
coming from work, and I'd stopped at a Terrible's for
gas. For some reason my card wouldn't work in the
pump, so I had to go inside. When I was walking back,
the car came out of nowhere and plowed past me. I
jumped onto the hood of my car to get out of the way.
The Mustang just kept going. It was like watching something in a movie."

"You don't think that the guy driving just didn't see
you?" I had to play devil's advocate.

"The car was gunning for me. I swear it. It barely missed
me."

"Why would someone try to run you down?"

He knew what I was going for. "It's not me, I don't
think," he said softly. "I think it's all of us over at That's
Amore. First Ray, then me, then Lou."

"What? Lou? What happened with him?"

"He got mugged. Guy pulled a knife on him as he was
leaving work. In the parking lot. Cut his arm, but before
the guy could do anything else, some kids on skateboards
came by and scared the guy off. Lou's afraid to go anywhere now."

Was someone trying to kill all the Dean Martin impersonators? And why?

My brain was moving faster than a rat in a maze. Flanigan must have decided I hadn't been driving my car when
it jumped that curb at Terrible's; otherwise he would've

taken me in yesterday. I wondered whether he didn't already have a suspect who actually had a motive to knock off these Dean Martins.

Like maybe Dan Franklin.

"What about Dan Franklin? Do you think something happened to him, too?" I asked. "DellaRocco said he hadn't seen him in two days."

"He was in yesterday, but he took off pretty fast after he made a phone call, even before he could start his shift. Didn't even change out of his costume. You think maybe Dan had something to do with Ray, me, and Lou?" Will asked.

A phone call? Had he taken off after talking to me yesterday?

"I heard he didn't get along with Ray, but what about you and Lou?" I asked.

He thought a second, then said, "No, we got along fine. I don't really know about Lou and him, though. I'm not sure they work together all that much because of Dan's schedule. Dan mostly works nights and weekends. Lou, mostly days and never weekends. He's been there the longest. You watch a lot of cop shows on TV?" he asked. "Because you really sound like a cop."

"Maybe I watch a little too much TV," I admitted, "but like I said, my brother is a detective. My dad was one, too, before he retired to Florida." I gave him a small smile back. "I'm worried about you and the other Dean Martins. What did you do? Sing the wrong song or sing off key or something?"

Will shook his head. "I don't know. But ever since Ray came to work there, things have gotten weird."

"Weird how?"

"Ray brings out the worst in people. He and Lou have been on each other from the first day he started. Dan's gotten really quiet. It used to be really fun working there, but now . . ." His voice trailed off as he remembered the good old days.

Something flashed into my brain.

"There's a fifth impersonator, isn't there? Alan something? I saw his name on the locker in your dressing room."

His face changed, so slightly that if I wasn't looking carefully to see his reaction, I would have missed it.

After a second, he said, "Alan quit two weeks ago."

"Why? Did someone try to kill him, too?"

"No. At least not that I know of. He went over to that Elvis chapel across the street. Decided Elvis was more interesting than Dino. The boss won't even let us talk about him. DellaRocco and Sanderson, the guy over at the Elvis place, hate each other. They've been stealing each other's performers for years, hoping to put the other one out of business. Sanderson approached me a month ago, but DellaRocco gave me more money, so I stayed on. Guess Sanderson caught on and gave Alan an offer he couldn't refuse."

And possibly saved his life, I added to myself.

"So what about you?" I asked. "Do you know of any reason why anyone would try to kill you?"

The instant I asked, I regretted it. It implied that he'd done something to cause someone to try to run him down with my car. But he didn't seem to pick up on that because he thought for a second, then said, "I don't think so. I've stayed out of Ray's way, and I get along okay with the other guys."

As he spoke, his expression changed, as if remembering something. He frowned, then said, "Wait. I did have a problem with Dan about three weeks ago."

I waited.

"It was about that stupid rat he's got. He kept it in the dressing room. Creeped me out. I told him he had to get it out of there."

Rat?

"He got all pissy with me, said it wouldn't hurt a flea. But it was a *rat*."

My heart was pounding so loud, I could swear he had to have heard it.

"So did he get rid of it?" I prodded.

Will snorted. "Yeah, Tony agreed with me. Said he had to bring it home. And then last week Dan came in all sad and stuff, said I should be happy. The rat had died."

Chapter 20

While I could see motive in trying to run down Will Parker—I don't quite understand why some people think animals are worth more than humans—it was still unclear as to why Dan Franklin would kill Ray Lucci. And then there was Lou Marino's mugging.

Will had to leave for his interview, but he scheduled an appointment with Bitsy for a tattoo touch-up, and he even hinted that maybe he'd want more ink, too. I'd probably have to make sure to get the work done before he found out it was possibly my car that was used to run him down.

"Why don't we call Dan Franklin again?" Bitsy asked when I told her everything Will Parker had said. She was already tapping on the computer keyboard, pulling up Dan Franklin's information, the information Ray Lucci left for us.

"He's missing, remember?"

"But maybe this is a cell phone number. Maybe he's missing on purpose."

"Okay, so say I do call him," I said. "What am I going to ask him? *Why haven't you gone to the chapel in two days? Why is your wallet in your locker there?* Right. Like he's going to answer." I thought about that ten thousand dollars. Another thing Bitsy didn't need to know about.

Bitsy handed me the phone. "You'll think of something," she said.

But as it turned out, I didn't have to think of anything at all.

The recording told me that the number was no longer in service. A number that had been perfectly fine yesterday.

Something was definitely up with Dan Franklin, and I didn't know whether he was a good guy or a bad guy.

Even though my head was swirling, I couldn't spend too much time pondering the situation. My next client came in as I hung up the phone.

As I picked up my tattoo machine and it hovered over Rachel Kristina Jones's lower back, the clip cord got in the way a little, and I had to shift around slightly. I'd never looked at a cord as a murder weapon before, but now I could imagine it as one.

"Anything wrong?" Rachel's voice was muffled because her face was in the crook of her elbow as she lay on her stomach.

"No," I said, taking a deep breath and pushing away the thoughts. I dipped the needle into the ink and pressed on the foot pedal, the machine vibrating slightly in a familiar way against my hand.

Rachel was an English major at UNLV, and she was into quotations. So far I'd inked "Frailty, thy name is woman!" from *Hamlet* along her forearm and "We live as we dream— alone" from *Heart of Darkness* across her chest, just above her breasts. Today's quote was from *Crime and Punishment*: "To go wrong in one's own way is better than to go right in someone else's."

I vaguely remembered reading all three in school, but I spent my days with artists, not writers.

"So how's school going?" I asked casually as I worked, adjusting the light so I could see better.

"Pretty good," she said.

"I've never been over to the campus," I said. "But I know a guy who works with lab animals. Would you know where that might be?"

Smooth, Kavanaugh, smooth.

Now I was talking to myself like Jeff Coleman.

Rachel lifted her head a little. "That's probably over where all the science buildings are. I'm not really sure ex-

actly where, but you can access that part of campus over by
Flamingo Road."

Good to know.

I mentally slapped myself. What was I thinking? Was
I really considering going over there to check up on Dan
Franklin?

I paused a second, lifting the needle off Rachel's back.

Yes, I was considering it.

Tim would kill me.

"Is something wrong?" Rachel asked again.

"No." I went back to work.

If my next client hadn't canceled, I don't think I would've
found myself driving toward the university campus. And
if Bitsy hadn't pressured me into telling her where I was
going, she wouldn't have come with me.

But here we were, Bitsy and I, off to look for Dan Franklin, or at least see if anyone might know where he was.

"I should call Tim," I said for the umpteenth time.

"He's not even on the case," Bitsy said.

"Why are you encouraging this?" I asked, shifting the
Jeep into fourth, even though it really didn't want to. Tim
needed to get this Jeep serviced soon, or it would rebel on
him and stay in first gear forever.

"I'm curious," she said. "And it's not as though you
haven't already told that detective about Dan Franklin.
You did tell him about the phone conversation. But it
doesn't hurt to double-check things. Things they might have
missed."

"The police wouldn't miss anything," I said, although I
thought about Dan Franklin's empty house. Had the police
been over there? Did the cruiser that showed up on our
heels earlier check out the mail piling up in the mailbox,
the newspapers on the doorstep?

"They miss a lot," she was saying. "You've heard stories
about people being locked up in prison for years, and then
the police discover they're innocent and have to let them
go. What about that girl who was kidnapped and worked in
public and no one ever figured it out, even though the cops
knew the guy was a sex offender? Eighteen years and two

kids later they finally figure it out? Give me a break. And then there are all those crimes that are never solved."

She had a point.

"Unless you want to talk yourself out of this," Bitsy said.

We were halfway there already. Might as well do it and satisfy my curiosity. I could tell Tim about it later.

Bitsy had Googled the Laboratory Animal Care Services department and discovered it was in the life sciences building, surrounded by chemistry and physics buildings. These were all subjects I had no talent for. The sisters had tried to teach me chemistry, but after I set a trash can on fire by accident, we all agreed that my future would not include medical school.

I turned off Flamingo Road and took an access road into a large parking lot. Bitsy held up the map that she'd downloaded, then looked up at the buildings in front of her.

She pointed to one. "That's it."

I hated to admit that I needed the navigation help.

I parked the Jeep, and we climbed out. Bitsy came around the side of the Jeep, stuffing the map into her purse. We both looked up at the building.

"What if they don't let us in?" I asked.

She made a face at me. "You should stay in the car, then. I'll do it."

We started walking.

The life sciences building was boxy and concrete, with a green lawn and trees. In fact, there was a lot of green lawn around here, and it seemed an oxymoron in a desert city that was suffering a drought. Wouldn't any of these scientists see the contradiction in this? Wouldn't they make some noise and get the administration to revert to a natural desert environment?

Tim says I should work in city government so I can turn down all those permits for waterfalls and waterways.

A few people passed us on the walkway, both on foot and on bikes. Even though it wasn't the University of the Arts in Philadelphia, I felt somehow at home here. Maybe it was the whole college-campus atmosphere that trans-

lated from school to school. Maybe it was the green grass
and the trees. But I wasn't quite so uncomfortable anymore
as we made our way around to the entrance.

The security guard at the desk made us take pause.

"What do we do?" I asked.

Bitsy barely blinked. She flashed some sort of ID and
walked right by. I tried to act as confident as I followed her,
not making eye contact with the guard.

He didn't stop us.

We were on the perimeter of an atrium filled with flora
and fauna indigenous to the Southwest. Benches were
scattered throughout, and a few students were lounging
on them, some with laptops, some texting on their phones,
some wearing iPod earbuds.

Bitsy turned to the right, and I followed.

"Where to?" I whispered.

"Why are you asking me?"

"Because you're the one acting like you own the place.
What was that card you showed him?"

Bitsy grinned and pulled out her laminated supermar-
ket card.

I had to give her credit.

"But we need to keep moving," she said, stuffing it back
in her bag. "Otherwise they'll know we don't know where
we're going."

"But we don't."

"Ye of little faith."

When we turned the next corner into the next hallway,
even Bitsy had to admit we were going to have to ask
someone for directions. The building was too big to try to
find anything on our own.

A guy in a Nickelback T-shirt with a black backpack
slung over his shoulder started to skirt around us, and I said
loudly, "Excuse me?"

He stopped and turned. "Yes?"

"We've got an appointment in the Laboratory Animal
Care Services department," I said, "but we're lost. Can you
help us?"

He rolled his eyes. "You're kidding, right?" And he practically ran off.

I frowned at Bitsy. "What was that about?"

She shook her head. "Who knows? Let's keep wandering."

I didn't know how much wandering we could do without being found out, and as we passed classrooms and labs, I began to think this whole road trip was incredibly futile.

Until we turned another corner and ran into a familiar face.

Dr. Colin Bixby was as good-looking as I remembered. I just wished he'd stop looking at me as if I were a leper.

Chapter 21

"**W**hat are you doing here?" Colin Bixby demanded. As though I were stalking him or something. I hadn't even tried to reach him after thinking he was trying to kill me a few months back. I respected the fact that he wanted nothing else to do with me.

I hadn't forgotten, though, how hot he was. Long and lanky, with spiky dark hair, green eyes that flashed sexy all over the place.

He'd folded his arms across his chest, and those sexy eyes weren't quite so endearing today. I shifted from one foot to another, wondering how to talk to him.

Bitsy noticed the tension and spoke up. "We're looking for the Laboratory Animal Care Services department."

He noticed her then. "Oh, you."

"Excuse me, Dr. Bixby," Bitsy said, and I recognized her tone. Uh-oh. "We are merely looking for directions. We would appreciate it if you could help us, and then we'll leave you alone."

His eyes slid from Bitsy back to me.

"Are you on some sort of wild-goose chase again?"

Caught.

But I'd never admit it.

"I'm looking for someone."

"A man named Dan Franklin," Bitsy said.

"Another victim of your crazy imagination?"

I didn't want to get into it. So I'd been wrong. He didn't have to keep bringing it up.

"Listen, Dr. Bixby," I said, hoping that keeping things formal might convince him I hadn't meant to run into him. "We're supposed to meet with Mr. Franklin. He came into the shop for a tattoo, and there's a problem."

Immediately Colin Bixby's hand went to his chest. I knew what was under that lab coat. A small Celtic knot just over his left nipple. I'd tattooed it myself, when he was still speaking to me and I thought that maybe we were connecting in more ways than one.

"What sort of problem? Does he need medical care?"

"We're not sure," Bitsy said quickly. "That's why it's imperative that we find him as soon as possible."

"Why doesn't he go to the emergency room?"

He was asking valid questions, but we had to keep up the charade.

"Maybe if you could come with us," I suggested.

Bixby rolled his eyes. "All right, fine. But you know, we don't usually let the public into that department."

"Why not?"

"Let's just say the animal rights people don't like us doing research on animals. Even though we are complying with all guidelines for those animals' care, according to federal regulations." He sounded like a brochure for the Humane Society.

But who was I to say anything? He was leading us down the hall toward an elevator.

"So what are you doing here?" I asked. Last I knew, he was an emergency room doctor at the University Medical Center.

"I teach a class once a week," he said as he pushed the elevator button.

"It's lucky we ran into you," Bitsy said.

He pushed the button again, as if he couldn't wait for the elevator to get there. It was clear *he* didn't feel lucky.

Inside the elevator, he swiped his card and pushed a button for a floor that didn't have a number, only LL. As the elevator jerked downward, I asked, "How's your mother?"

He looked at me as if I had three heads. I knew, however, that his mother lived down the hall from him in his condominium building, and I was just making small talk, thank you very much.

He was having none of it. Until the doors slid open, his eyes watched the floors drop away on the little flashing sign.

We were in the basement. LL. Lower level, most likely.

Steel doors flanked the hallway.

"Don't the critters need sunlight?" Bitsy asked, indicating the concrete walls and fluorescent lighting that made our skin look jaundiced.

Colin Bixby snorted. Not a pleasant sound.

"Those animals are being tested on," I said in a stage whisper. "They don't exactly need sunshine and three meals a day."

"Those animals, as you call them, are treated humanely. They have a sleep schedule, an eating schedule. We make them as comfortable as possible." Bixby's tone was definitely frosty. And he was staring at my arm. The one with the koi that Jeff had tattooed.

"That's new," he said matter-of-factly.

I nodded.

He leaned over and studied it so closely I could feel his warm breath on my skin. But it seemed as though I was the only one getting all hot and bothered. I was only a specimen to him.

"Are you going to get another?" Bitsy asked him.

His head snapped up so fast I thought he'd give himself whiplash.

"Another what?"

"Tattoo," Bitsy said, exasperation lacing the word.

"No." Colin Bixby might as well have been playing *Who Wants to Be a Millionaire?* because I knew that was his final answer.

But I also knew people should never say never.

A sound like thunder echoed through the hall, and at the very end, where the hall came to a T, a large stainless steel cart came into view. A person dressed in blue scrubs and a yellow smock was pushing it. The person—and I couldn't tell whether it was a man or a woman because of the white cap that looked like a shower cap and a surgical mask—rolled the cart, which had several steel shelves lined with cages, toward us.

When he—or she—saw us, the cart jerked to a stop.

"Who are you?"

Bixby stood a little taller, held out his ID card, and said, "Dr. Colin Bixby. These women are looking for . . ." He looked back at me, the question in his eyes.

"Dan Franklin," I said.

"Dan Franklin," he repeated.

"Do you know where we can find him?"

The person gripped the cart, and I noticed now that he or she was wearing rubber gloves. They matched the rubber boots.

What the heck was on that cart?

I took a step closer and peered at it.

Tiny quick movements and a few whiskers indicated rodents. But why would he or she be wearing all that stuff? Were they contagious with something? Maybe we shouldn't have come down here. We had no idea what was going on behind those steel doors.

A glance at Bitsy told me she was thinking the same thing.

Dr. Bixby, however, looked more relaxed now that we had some company.

"Haven't seen Dan today," the person said. "You could check with Roz. She's in room seven." The person paused. "You know, they're not authorized to be here."

"I'll take responsibility," Bixby said, although from his tone, I could tell he was already regretting it.

We hadn't even gone out. Okay, so we'd shared one kiss. And it was one fantastic kiss. But that was all. There had been no promises made. I'd jumped to a conclusion that wasn't right, and he was making me pay for it.

He did live down the hall from his mother. Maybe it was better this way.

The cart rattled past us, and now we had a clear view of

those cages. They were most definitely rodents, rats or mice or both. I didn't much make a distinction. Rodents were rodents.

Bitsy started walking down the hall, and Bixby and I followed, noting all the numbers by the doors until we found number seven.

"Here it is," Bitsy said, then pointed to a small metal box next to the door where someone would have to swipe an ID card. She looked at Bixby. "Can you get us in here?"

Colin Bixby looked as though it was the last thing he wanted to do. His mouth was set in a stern line as he gripped his ID card.

"Let me do the talking, okay?" he asked, looking from me to Bitsy and back to me.

We nodded, and he swiped his card.

As we heard the latch click, Bixby pushed the door open, and we stepped inside.

I'd thought a stainless steel cart full of rats in cages was bad.

This room was a hundred times creepier. Rows of cages were lined up on stainless steel shelves, which stood in three rows to our right. A stainless steel sink on steroids was in the center of the room. A row of steel cabinets hung above a shelf with boxes of latex gloves and wipes and other implements that looked like something out of *Frankenstein*.

I wanted to set all those rats free. They could all live in my trunk if they wanted.

Bixby read my mind.

"Brett, have you ever had a family member or friend with cancer?"

Immediately I thought about my grandmother in hospice, covered with the patchwork quilt she'd made when first married to my grandfather way back during the Depression, her bony, transparent fingers clutching my hand as she told me she was going to be okay, that I could let her go.

I nodded, swallowing the lump in my throat.

"These animals—the testing that's done on them—they

can help. They can help us find cures, treatments for all sorts of illness and disease. You have to look at it that way."

I could see both sides.

"Excuse me?"

A woman had come around the corner of one of the banks of steel shelves. She wore the same scrubs and yellow smock as the guy in the hall, and as she pulled off her mask, I caught my breath.

Roz was Rosalie. Rosalie Applebaum Marino.

Chapter 22

"Brett," she said. "Do you have news about my father?" Her panic was evident in the tremble of her lips and the set of her jaw.

She thought I'd found her to tell her about Bernie and Sylvia. I shook my head.

"No. I'm sorry."

Puzzlement crossed her face. "Then why are you here?" Her eyes slid toward Bitsy and then to Colin Bixby. She touched her cap as if she were brushing a hair away from her face. I thought about how stylish she'd been when she showed up at Jeff's shop earlier.

"We're looking for Dan Franklin," I told Rosalie. "The wedding-chapel owner says he hasn't been there in a couple days, and his phone's no longer in service. Has he been here?"

Rosalie shook her head. "I haven't seen him, either, but he's not on the schedule until tomorrow. I didn't know about his phone. Do you think something happened to him, too?"

"What's going on?" Bixby interrupted, justifiably curious.

"My father and his new wife have disappeared, and we're all trying to find them," Rosalie said.

"And we're trying to find out if that dead guy in Brett's trunk had anything to do with it," Bitsy piped up, eager to dispense as much information as she could. She couldn't help herself.

"A dead body in your trunk?" Colin Bixby was legitimately confused.

"She found it yesterday," Bitsy explained. "Sylvia and Bernie borrowed her car for their wedding, and then they brought it back to her, and then Brett went for a hike and found the dead Dean Martin impersonator in the trunk. With a dead rat," she added.

Rosalie tensed up. "A dead rat?" Obviously, Jeff hadn't told her about that.

"A dead Dean Martin impersonator?" Colin Bixby was having a really hard time wrapping his head around this. Admittedly, it wasn't exactly something you heard every day, so I could cut him some slack.

"Because of the rat, you think Dan was involved?" Rosalie asked.

I nodded.

"How well do you know Dan Franklin?" Bitsy piped up.

Rosalie looked at her. "He's a nice guy. He loves his job here, and he loves singing at the chapel. Lou did tell me no one over at the chapel has seen him. He thinks whoever killed Ray got to Dan, too. Until now, I thought that was a little crazy, but now I don't know." She paused. "Do you know Lou got mugged?"

I nodded. "Will Parker told me."

"Will?" Rosalie asked. "When did you meet Will?"

"This morning," I said, and since I didn't want to explain how, I quickly added, "He said someone tried to run him down. Who would want to hurt those guys? What's the motive?"

She bit her lip, and her cheeks grew pink as she mulled the question. Then, "All you have to do is look across the street at that other chapel. Sanderson's been trying to put Tony out of business for years now."

Interesting theory, but a little weak.

"So there wasn't a beef between any of the Dean Mar-

tins?" I asked. "Will Parker said the trouble started when
Ray Lucci started working there."

For the first time, Rosalie's eyes skittered across the
room and landed on Bixby's face. "I don't know anything
about that," she said, but I could tell she was lying.

"How's your husband doing?" I asked.

Her hand went up to caress her other arm, over the spot
where I knew the tattoos were. The bruise around her eye
was fading, and I wondered whether another one would
soon replace it. I'd never met Lou Marino, but I didn't
think I wanted to.

"He's been talking to Sanderson about a job over there,"
she said.

So he'd allow himself to be coerced, if in fact Sanderson
was the one causing all the accidents.

Rosalie glanced around the room, saying, "I really have
to get back . . ."

"We'll get out of your way now," Bixby said, taking my
arm.

I resisted the urge to shrug him off, but I had to ask one
more question.

"What do you do here? Are you a technician, like
Dan?"

Rosalie seemed to relax now that I wasn't asking about
Lou. She nodded. "That's right."

"How long has Dan worked here?"

"About three years, I think."

"How did Dan Franklin end up working at the
chapel?"

Rosalie smiled. "He's always wanted to perform. I told
Lou about him, and Lou got him the job over there."

"So they're friends?"

The smile faded slightly, but she fought hard not to let it
go completely. "I suppose," she said softly.

That was enough for Bixby. He started steering me out,
his other hand on Bitsy's shoulder. "Thank you for your
help," he said, as if he was the one who wanted it in the
first place.

"I'll let you know if I hear anything about your dad," I tossed back as we left the room.

Bixby didn't say anything until we were behind closed doors.

"I can't believe you lied to me," he said.

"I didn't completely lie," I said. "I did talk to Dan Franklin, but he wasn't the one with the tattoo. The dead guy in my trunk? He came to my shop posing as Dan Franklin. And then we found out Franklin went missing and his phone's disconnected."

"I can't believe the things you get into."

Him and me both.

But if I admitted that, he wouldn't believe me.

The elevator door slid open, and we stepped out. Bixby crossed his arms over his chest.

"Do you have everything you need?" he asked.

Who ever has everything they need? I wanted to ask. And looking at him, I thought maybe I wanted a second chance, needed a second chance.

I took too long to answer.

He sighed and looked down at Bitsy. "Nice seeing you again," he said.

"Thanks, Doc." She grinned.

He started to walk away, then stopped and stared at me. "You know, I'd just about forgotten about you," he said softly before he turned his back on me and went down the hall.

I felt a slap on my wrist and looked down to see Bitsy making a face at me.

"You can daydream about him later," she admonished. "We've got to get out of here. All those rodents gave me the creeps."

We walked around the atrium and out the glass front doors. The sun beat down on the sidewalk, but it wasn't hot. There was a slight chill in the air, and I wished I had my jean jacket with me.

"Maybe it'll snow tonight," Bitsy teased.

"It's snowed here before."

"For like a nanosecond. One day, like three years ago."

It had been more recent than that, but I couldn't remember when. I didn't really want to argue it.

We maneuvered around the cars in the parking lot, and I spotted the Jeep up ahead.

But before I could point it out, a blue car swung around the bank of cars, skidding on the pavement as it careened toward us.

Chapter 23

I grabbed Bitsy's arm and yanked her out of the way as I dove onto the hood of a Dodge that had seen better days. The blue car screamed past, and I looked up too late. All I saw was a shadow of the back of a head in the rearview mirror as the car sped away.

I thought about how someone had used my car to try to run down Will Parker. But I wasn't a Dean Martin impersonator.

But then my memory flashed on something else. A blue car. The one in Dan Franklin's driveway. Had Franklin really been home after all, hiding out and watching me and Jeff? Had he followed me?

I slid off the hood and brushed dirt off my skirt as I asked Bitsy, "Are you okay?"

She had flattened herself against the Dodge's grill.

"It was close enough so I could feel it," she whispered. All color had drained from her face. "Did you see who it was?"

"No."

"Did you get the license plate?"

"It went by so fast it was a blur. I didn't notice the number."

As Bitsy brushed at her slacks, I could see her hands were shaking. "Why would someone do that?" she asked.

Why, indeed? Because we'd been questioning Rosalie about Dan Franklin? Because I'd been asking everyone about Dan Franklin? Because I'd almost broken into his house? Because Jeff Coleman and I had stolen his bank statement out of his mailbox?

"Who knew we were coming here?" Bitsy asked.

"Colin was the only one who knew, and we ran into him here," I said.

"Maybe he called someone after he left us," Bitsy suggested, and her eyes grew wider. "Maybe *he* was the one driving that car."

"Oh, give me a break. That's ridiculous."

"He's still really upset with you," she reminded me.

"But enough to try to run me down? No, this has to have something to do with Dan Franklin. Bixby was a coincidence."

"I don't believe in coincidences."

That's right. She doesn't. And I usually don't, either. But I didn't want to make the same mistake twice: think that Dr. Colin Bixby was out to kill me. In retrospect, it didn't make sense the first time, and it didn't make sense now.

And then I remembered another blue car. Will Parker's blue car. The one he wanted to whisk me away in.

Had that been Will Parker? Had he found out that it was my car someone used to try to run him down, so he was reciprocating?

"Will Parker drives a blue car," I said softly.

Bitsy whirled around on her toes. "Aha! Like I said, no coincidences. What did you do to him?"

"What do you mean, what did I do to him? Nothing. He's coming in for a tattoo touch-up. He seems like a nice guy."

A nice guy who just happened to have an appointment at the Venetian a couple hours after I met him at the wedding chapel. Who just happened to decide to come talk to me. Did he really have an appointment, or was he stalking me? Did he follow us here?

No, it was more likely Franklin. Although I couldn't seem to get Parker out of my head, either.

There were too many blue cars. And too many weird

things going on. I wished I'd gotten the license plate. Then we could narrow this down.

We began walking to the Jeep, our eyes skirting the parking lot, making sure that blue car didn't come back. When we got to the Jeep, we scrambled up inside, strapping the seat belts across us. I put the engine in first gear as we went toward the lot's exit.

Bitsy's feet weren't touching the floor, so she pulled her legs up and tucked them under her.

"What's the game plan?" she asked.

"I think we should talk to the cops."

She snorted. "About what? That a grown man hasn't been to either of his jobs in a couple days? That he hasn't been home? The cops won't take us seriously. They'll say, *Maybe he's holed up in a casino somewhere, losing all his money*. Not like that hasn't happened around here."

"You've proved my point. We don't have to go running around after Dan Franklin. Someone tried to run us over." The light turned green, and I lifted my foot off the clutch and gave the Jeep some gas. "I think that was a definite signal that we should stop snooping around."

"You like snooping."

"Not when someone tries to kill me."

She rolled her eyes at me. "That means we're close."

"Close to what?"

"Finding out who the murderer is."

"And you're suddenly Jessica Fletcher?"

She smoothed out the front of her shirt and grinned. "I love Angela Lansbury."

"That's not the point."

"Oh, I know. You're scared."

"Scared of what?"

"To find out what's going on. The police will say that Dan Franklin's a grown-up and they won't bother looking for him. But he did have a dead rat, which means that maybe there was something going on, something that does need to be investigated."

"But that's what the police are for." I pulled into the

parking garage at the Venetian. Our conversation was going in circles, as we were, heading up to the sixth level. I eased into a parking spot, and we both climbed out. I locked the doors, and we headed to the elevator.

We were both quiet, and I knew she was thinking about this crazy mess, too.

We walked along the canal, the gondolas passing, music emanating from the square. I wondered whether Will Parker had gotten the job.

"Earth to Brett." Bitsy snapped her fingers up near my chin somewhere. That was as far as she could stretch.

Ace was sitting at Breathe, the oxygen bar, a tube up his nose. It seemed a tad unsanitary, but who was I to bring that up?

I tapped him on the shoulder, and he opened his eyes, smiling. "Oh, hello."

"Hello yourself. Who's at the shop?"

He looked from me to Bitsy, then shrugged. "Joel."

"Is it time for you to go back?"

Ace sat up a little straighter and made a face at me. "You've been gone ages. I just finished a tattoo. I need a break." And he leaned back and closed his eyes again.

Bitsy and I started toward the shop. It wasn't worth getting into. He was right. I had been gone too long, and it was time for me to shoulder my responsibilities.

Joel was at the front desk, tapping his fingers on the sleek mahogany to the stylings of Lady Gaga, his new latest favorite singer. I wasn't so sure about his musical inclinations, but if I had my way, we'd have Springsteen all day, every day.

"Hey there," he said, looking up.

"Thanks for holding down the fort," I said, slinging my messenger bag on the floor.

Bitsy walked around and picked the bag up with one finger, handing it back to me. "Staff room."

"Right." Bitsy had rules about keeping order.

Joel put both hands on the desk and heaved himself up. Despite his Atkins loss, there was still a bit of weight to deal with.

Bitsy slid into the chair, her feet dangling. She looked up at Joel, a scowl on her face. "Didn't anyone answer the phones while we were gone?"

Joel sighed. "Ace and I both had clients. The phone rang once, but I couldn't run out, and I guess Ace couldn't either."

"What would've happened if someone came in?" she asked.

Joel shrugged. "The buzzer would've sounded and I would've gone out to see who it was. No one came in," he added defiantly.

The phone was blinking with one message. Bitsy hit the button.

The voice bounced off the wall behind us.

"This is Dan Franklin. You have to stop looking for me. I'm fine. Leave Rosalie out of it." And then the message ended.

Chapter 24

"Check the number," I told Bitsy, who was one step ahead of me.

She shook her head. "Restricted," she said, checking the readout. "What's the point in caller ID if you can't get the caller's ID?"

My question exactly.

"Maybe it was Dan Franklin in that blue car and not Will Parker," Bitsy said.

"But then why would he call us?"

"To make sure we got the message?"

Joel was scratching his head. "I have no idea what you two are talking about."

That was fine with me. The fewer people who knew what we'd been up to, the better. But Bitsy didn't seem to mind.

"Brett and I went over to the university to find out about this guy Dan Franklin and what his story is."

Joel chuckled. "I can see you now: Cagney and Lacey."

Bitsy ignored him. "And we met up with Colin Bixby and a lab tech who's got a husband who beats her and happens to be a Dean Martin impersonator."

"You know about Rosalie and the abuse?" I asked.

Bitsy rolled her eyes at me. "I remember her. Domestic-violence ribbons on her biceps. But I didn't remember her name."

As I hadn't when I saw her at Jeff's.

Joel was a few sentences behind. "Colin Bixby? As in *the* Colin Bixby?"

I sighed. "Yes, Joel, Colin Bixby."

"Is he still hot?"

Before I could answer, Bitsy said, "He looks better than I remember. What do you think, Brett?"

I thought again about Colin Bixby and his clear green eyes and almost-punk look. Give him some guyliner and an eyebrow piercing, and there's no telling what I'd do.

"He's still okay," I said, trying to sound casual.

Joel laughed. "What about this Dean Martin impersonator? Who rates better?"

"I don't think rating them is fair," I started, but Bitsy interrupted.

"The good doctor, hands down. I mean, at least he has a steady job, a good income. This Will Parker—Well, Brett, I'm sorry, but he's another actor, and you've already had one of those, and see how that turned out."

Bitsy didn't have to remind me about Paul Fogarty, my onetime fiancé, an actor on Broadway in Manhattan, whose whole life was consumed by his work. So much so that he felt compelled to belittle my career. There had been enough time between then and now for me to do some self-analysis, and I'd realized Paul's insecurities. But it wasn't enough for me to try to contact him after fleeing across the country to shed his abuse.

However, Bitsy's words brought out the contrarian in me.

"At least Will Parker doesn't live down the hall from his mother," I said haughtily.

"How do you know that? Have you Googled him? Have you been to his house? Maybe he lives *with* his mother."

Bitsy's words rang true. I had no clue about anything regarding Will Parker except his job and that he was sexy. And he had a blue car.

"Touché."

"Hungry, anyone?" Joel looked hopefully from me to Bitsy.

Bitsy shook her head. "Ace has a client coming in any moment, and you two"—she looked in the appointment book—"have clients in about half an hour."

Joel grinned at me. "Just enough time to pick up Johnny Rockets burgers."

I was getting really tired of burgers.

Walking past the pricey high-end shops away from the canal, I stopped in front of one window, admiring a floppy straw hat I could totally see myself wearing if I ever went back to the Jersey Shore for a vacation. I'd never be caught dead in it here.

"Not you," Joel said flatly, noticing the hat.

"Great beach hat," I said.

"Not you," he said again. "You're not a hat person."

"How do you know? Have you ever seen me in a hat?"

He studied my face and head for a second, then grinned. "Have you ever once worn a hat so I could find out?" he asked, grabbing my hand and pulling me into the store.

It was full of hats. Everywhere. And Joel started plopping them on my head one by one and announcing, "No, no, no," for each.

I personally liked a small black one that perched on the back of my head, with a netting over my forehead and eyes, like they wore in the forties and fifties. For a second, Joel was starting to agree but then pulled it off my head and said, "You look like a gangster's moll."

"And what's wrong with that?"

"We're trying to destroy the Mob stereotype here in Vegas."

"We?"

"Me and Steve Wynn."

"Oh, and you're best buddies, are you?"

He chuckled and put the black hat back on its mannequin head. "I've seen him."

"From a distance."

"In the men's room."

"No." I knew what he was saying.

"Close enough to touch him," he added.

We fell laughing out of the store's doorway, back into the mall. It was nice to think of something other than dead people and rats and blue cars for a little while.

"I worked up an appetite," Joel said.

"I can't have another burger. I'll start mooing," I said. "I'm sorry, Joel, but I need Chinese or even a hot dog."

The minute I said Chinese, he started salivating. "Noodles?" he said.

"Opposite direction," I said.

We turned and almost ran back toward the Shoppes at the Palazzo, which were announced overhead on a sign at the end of the Venetian Grand Canal Shoppes's canal.

We were circling around the walkway, about parallel with the magnificent yet incredibly wasteful waterfall, when I thought I saw someone familiar up ahead.

I grabbed Joel's arm and yanked him over to the edge of the walkway so I'd have a better view of the short elderly woman with a large cheetah-print tote bag hung over her shoulder. Her white hair was pulled up into something that looked like diamonds. A tiara, maybe. I was too far away to see exactly what it was.

But I wasn't too far away to see the tattoos.

"That looks like Sylvia Coleman," Joel said loudly.

The woman turned. And waved.

It *was* Sylvia Coleman.

Chapter 25

I was so stunned to see her that I couldn't speak for a few minutes. She scurried over to us, her smile wide.

"Fancy meeting you here!" she exclaimed.

"My shop is just down there," I said, pointing behind us.

"Oh, that's right, dear." She waved her hand through the air absently. "This place confuses me. All these stores and that silly river. What's a river doing in the middle of a mall anyway?"

I totally agreed with her. But I didn't have time to think about that. I wanted to know where she'd been and how she'd ended up here, now. I opened my mouth to ask, but she spoke first.

"I'm looking for a bathroom."

I knew there was a ladies' room downstairs and behind the escalator, near the Blue Man Group Theatre. It was tucked away in a corner that was fairly isolated when the Blue Man Group wasn't performing, and there I'd be able to question her without anyone listening in. "I can take you," I said, nodding at Joel. "Can you go get some take-out? I'll meet you back at the shop."

Joel didn't want to go. He wanted to stay and find out what was up with Sylvia, too, but he couldn't come to the ladies' room with us, so he nodded reluctantly. "Sure. What do you want?"

"Anything but beef," I said.

"He's a big one," Sylvia said as we watched Joel lumber away. "But it looks like he's losing some weight."

"He is," I said.

Sylvia tucked her hand into the crook of my arm. Her cheetah-print bag hung on her other shoulder. "Now, dear, I really do need that toilet."

Not wanting any sort of accident, I whisked her around and down the escalator, a little bit of the waterfall spray hitting our faces.

"That feels good," Sylvia said, "but rather unnatural in a desert, don't you think?"

Exactly.

"Cat got your tongue?" she asked.

"Where have you been? Jeff's been all over looking for you. Your car was found at the Grand Canyon. We've been worried sick." Once I started, I couldn't stop. I hadn't meant to say anything until we were alone.

Sylvia rolled her eyes, threw a hand up in the air and said, "Oh, that. That car finally broke down. I told Bernie we should've taken the Gremlin."

"But how—"

"We hitched a ride."

"Hitched?"

She stuck out her thumb. "You know. You're not that young, are you? Hitching was the only way to travel once upon a time."

And I could see her, too, throwing her thumb into the wind and seeing where it could get her.

"But how—"

"We got a ride on a bus. A bus full of old people. Can you imagine?" Sylvia chuckled. "They felt sorry for us. We took their tour to Sedona. We paid them," she added quickly, as if she would be accused of being a moocher.

"So you've been in Sedona this whole time?"

"That's right, dear."

"And what are you doing here?"

She looked puzzled for a second, as if she didn't quite know. Then, "We got here last night. This was the last stop on the tour. Since we paid, we got a room, like everyone else. Figured we might as well take advantage. Never stayed in one of these fancy-schmancy places before. Do you know how many pillows you get on the bed here? Unbelievable."

Yes, it was unbelievable. "You've been in town since last night?" I asked. "Why didn't you let Jeff know?"

Sylvia looked at me quizzically. "Am I supposed to check in with my son on my honeymoon?"

"No, I guess not," I said. "How long do you have your room here?"

"Two nights. I'm starting to get a little antsy to get home, though. There are just so many pillows I can take after a while."

She was dead serious. And she wasn't done yet.

"Bernie did go out earlier to pick up the Gremlin, but he said something was wrong with it, so he ended up renting a car instead. Until we get the Buick back."

I wasn't surprised something was "wrong" with the Gremlin. The almost-forty-year-old car shouldn't have even been on the road.

"Where's Bernie now?" I asked.

"Bernie likes to gamble. A little, not a lot. He's in the casino, trying his hand at the tables. But me— Well, I need that toilet."

I didn't want to point out that there were restrooms in the casino. How she ended up wandering around the Palazzo shops was a mystery. But then again, much about Sylvia didn't make sense.

We had walked around the waterfall, and I led Sylvia to the ladies' room. As I suspected, there was no one else there.

She unhooked herself from my arm and went into one of the stalls. I looked in the mirror and ran a hand through my short hair, tucking it back behind my ears and peering more closely at my face. I'd thought I was getting a zit this morning, but I still only saw a small red spot on my chin. I wondered whether Colin Bixby had noticed.

The toilet flushed, and Sylvia emerged, a big grin on her face.

"Now I feel better," she said as she washed her hands.

"So you haven't talked to Jeff yet? He doesn't know about the bus trip?" I asked.

Sylvia pushed the button on the air hand dryer, and the motor roared, and for a few minutes she rubbed her hands under it and didn't answer. When it finally stopped, she wiped her hands on her blue dress and cocked her head at me.

"I'm not sure why you're harping on this. I'll call Jeff when I get home."

"He's been looking for you. Worried about you," I said.

She chuckled. "He's always worrying. Too much. I thought I taught him better. I need to have a life, too, you know." She winked at me.

I thought a second and then said, "The police have been looking for you, too. They found your car."

"I told Bernie not to leave the car there, but he didn't want to call the Triple A. Was too angry at that car to do anything but abandon it, like a kitten or something."

I pictured them arguing about it by the side of the road, the big tour bus seeing them with their thumbs out. The image made me smile, but then I remembered where I was going with this.

"Well, Sylvia, it seems there was a problem after you left." I paused, and Sylvia waited. "Did you know there was a body in the trunk of my car when you brought it back to me?"

"Dear, I don't like to judge, but have you had a drug-related hallucination?" She was totally serious.

I sighed. "One of the Dean Martin impersonators was dead in my trunk. He was killed, I think, by being strangled with a clip cord around his neck."

"You think?"

"Well, the police haven't exactly told me the cause of death."

"Why don't you ask your brother, that cute detective?"

I'd have to tease Tim that an elderly woman thought he was cute.

"That's not the whole thing, either." I wasn't quite sure

how to broach the next sentence but figured I'd just jump in. "The dead man was Ray Lucci."

Sylvia had put her hand on the restroom door to go out, and it froze there as her face turned white.

"Ray?"

I nodded.

"And the police want to talk to me?" It was sinking in.

"I don't think they think you had anything to do with it," I said quickly, "but they think maybe you saw something that might put you in danger."

She took a deep breath and pushed the door open. I followed her out to a small bench a few feet away, where we sat.

I'd never seen Sylvia's face sag, and I put my hand over hers. She gave me a small, sad smile and patted my hand with her other one, the cheetah-print tote still hanging from her shoulder.

"You know, don't you, dear?"

"About Ray?"

She nodded.

"Yes. My brother told me."

"Does Jeff know?"

I shrugged. "I don't think so. Why didn't you tell him?"

"It was a long time ago. I met a man I thought I was in love with. When I told him about the baby, he left me." Her hand stopped patting mine, and she stared into my eyes. "Abortion was illegal, and I was afraid. I gave him up after he was born, but I never forgot him. I found him a few years ago. We've been corresponding."

I nodded. "I know."

"He was trying to turn his life around. I gave him some money; Bernie's son-in-law got him that job over there at the wedding chapel." Her voice faltered. "I don't remember anything that day, except he sang for us. A beautiful voice that boy has. Not like Jeff. Jeff sounds like a toad."

I couldn't say anything. I'm tone-deaf myself.

Sylvia bowed her head and turned her face away. I could see a tear slip down her cheek.

The tattoos crept out over the scoop neck of her dress.

Swirls of color: birds, flowers, butterflies. Most were faded from time, their edges leaking into her wrinkles, but a new one, one I hadn't seen before on the side of her neck, was bright and sharp.

"That's Amore," in script.

Chapter 26

"When did you get that?" I asked.

"What?" Sylvia looked up and wiped her eyes.

"The new ink. 'That's Amore.' "

Her eyes flickered a second, as though she was trying to think of what to say. Then, "I got it in Sedona. Bernie wasn't happy, but I said I wanted a souvenir of our wedding."

I thought a second before saying, "Ray got one, too. It said the same thing. Came to my shop for it. Joel did it. And then his clip cord went missing."

Sylvia didn't say anything right away, as if she was taking all this in and deciding what it meant. Finally, she said, "I didn't know Ray was getting a tattoo. And do you think he took the clip cord?"

"I don't know," I said honestly. "He told us his name was Dan Franklin. When he came to the shop. And we found out that Dan Franklin works with him at the chapel. Did you ever meet him?"

"My dear, I meet a lot of people, but at my age, I'm lucky if I remember one of them. So no, I don't know this Franklin fellow. And I don't know why Ray would impersonate him."

I opened my mouth to ask another question when my cell phone rang deep in my bag. I took my hand out from under Sylvia's and swung my bag around, digging until I found it.

I glanced at the number on the display, flipped the phone open, and said, "Hey, Jeff. Guess who I'm sitting with."

"I don't have time for games, Kavanaugh."

"You'll have time for this, Jeff. I'm with your mother."

Silence, then, "How?"

I told him how I'd seen her on my way to Noodles and we were hanging out near the Blue Man Group Theatre.

"Can I talk to her?"

I handed Sylvia the phone, and she got up and walked several feet away for more privacy. I studied the plants in the planter behind the benches. I thought about Sylvia and how she found her son after all those years and wondered how she'd tell Jeff. Because he was going to find out, and it would be best to tell him before the police did. While Tim was sensitive about the issue, I was willing to bet Flanigan wouldn't be.

My thoughts wandered back to Sylvia's new ink. It seemed too much of a coincidence that she and Ray Lucci got the exact same tattoo, albeit in different places, at the same time. She'd hesitated before telling me where she got hers. Was she lying?

I thought about how new the ink was. How it still had that pinkish hue. It had a sort of wet look, too, which meant she could be using Tattoo Goo, a product I gave my clients to keep the area lubricated right after giving them the tattoo.

Ray Lucci had gotten his tattoo the morning of Sylvia and Bernie's wedding. It was possible he'd told Sylvia about it. Maybe that was how she got the idea for it, and it would mean something even more special than just her wedding day. It was the same tattoo her long-lost son had.

Even though Sylvia was covered in body art, she'd once given me the grand tour and told me the stories of each tattoo. Each had meaning to her. It was a long, but very interesting, afternoon.

I felt a tap on my shoulder and looked down to see Sylvia handing me the phone. I stuck it in my bag. "Everything okay?" I asked.

"He's meeting us in the casino," she said. "He's going to take us to Rosalie's. I hope she's got supper."

My antennae went up. "Rosalie's?" I thought about how

I'd left her only a little while ago at the university lab. Jeff must've been mistaken. "You need to talk to the police, let them know you're all right. You might remember, too, if you saw anything that could help in the investigation."

She threw up her hands, the cheetah-print bag swinging violently back and forth. "If you want to argue with Jeff, be my guest."

I didn't really, but I didn't think I had a choice. He had to realize that going to the police would be the right thing.

Sylvia tucked her hand in the crook of my arm again, and we started walking back toward the casino.

"Are you sure you didn't see anything that day? Something unusual?" I pressed.

Sylvia gave me a sad smile. "I saw my son. And two other Dean Martins. They were pretty good, although sober as a preacher. It wasn't exactly realistic. I asked them if they wanted to go get a martini or something, on me."

I chuckled.

"Lou was one of them—you know, Bernie's son-in-law." She *tsk-tsk*ed. "I don't know what Rosalie is doing with that man. He treats her like dirt. No woman should let a man treat her that way."

"I heard someone mugged Lou," I said.

Sylvia made a face. "Serves him right. Flashing his money clip all the time, his big gold rings and chains around his neck. He's such a guido."

She didn't have any problems being politically incorrect.

"I guess the mugger cut him with a knife."

"I bet he cut himself just to tell that story," she said.

I frowned. "Why would he do that?"

"Because he always needs to be the center of attention."

"You don't like him."

"No."

We paused on the edge of the casino, the sounds echoing in my head: the slapping of the cards on the table, the clink of ice in glasses, the soft music that replaced the clatter of coins as they fell from the slot machines. Everything was automated now. Tickets took the place of quarters and nickels and dimes. I missed the little buckets whose weight indicated how lucky I'd been. Or how unlucky. It was too quiet in here.

But even with the changes, a casino is a casino: the black orbs in the ceiling, where the cameras watched our every move; the bright carpet patterns that made you look up at the tables, which enticed with their promise of luck; the dealers flipping the cards or turning the wheel or pushing chips across the tables.

Sylvia stood on tiptoe, and her head swiveled from side to side like a bird as she surveyed the room. I had a better view and said, "Over here."

Bernie sat at one of the blackjack tables. He had a pile of chips in front of him and wasn't ready to leave.

"In a minute, in a minute," he said without taking his eyes off the table.

Bernie Applebaum was bald, with wisps of white hair around his ears and on the back of his head. He was a little stocky, a little hunchbacked. But he had a quick, warm smile, and the wrinkles around his brown eyes accentuated his kindness. He'd owned a deli in northern New Jersey, not too far from where I grew up, but I didn't think I'd ever had one of what he called his "famous" pastrami-and-Swiss-on-rye sandwiches. Rosalie finally talked him into selling the business and moving out here with her after he'd had a heart attack a few years back. If I had to guess, I'd say Bernie was older than Sylvia, probably around eighty. He was in good shape now, swimming every day, which was how they met.

We watched Bernie play a few hands. I was still trying to figure out how to persuade them to talk to Flanigan about Ray Lucci, but when I started to make my case again, Bernie waved his hand in dismissal and Sylvia shushed me.

I felt a light touch on my shoulder and turned to see Jeff Coleman. His other hand was on his mother's shoulder.

"How are my girls doing?" he drawled, his grin wide as he leaned down to kiss his mother's cheek.

She turned her face up to meet his, but I slid out from

under his hand. I didn't want him to think I'd welcome a kiss, too. Our relationship had moved forward, but not that much.

He gave me a wink, and I told myself it wasn't because he was reading my mind but because he was happy to see his mother.

"Ready to go?" he asked.

Bernie shook his head. "In a minute."

I tugged on Jeff's sleeve and pulled him away from the table, out of earshot.

"Your mother says you're taking them to Rosalie's? What's up with that? They need to talk to Detective Flanigan. With a little prodding, maybe they'll remember something that could help solve Ray Lucci's murder. And I thought Rosalie was at work, anyway." I wasn't in the mood to tell him about my little visit to the university yet.

Jeff sighed and ran a hand across his salt-and-pepper buzz cut. "I get it, Kavanaugh. You want me to do the right thing. But I am doing the right thing. Trust me."

"I don't see how it's the right thing," I argued.

Jeff hesitated a second, looking toward his mother and then back to me.

"I'm taking them to Rosalie. Not her place. She's at the hospital. Her husband got clipped by a car. Not sure if he's going to pull through."

Chapter 27

I could barely concentrate on work. I felt the machine in my hand as I tattooed a young man's calf with the image of his pet dog, but I was on autopilot. The dog was one of those little ones, the ones that look like hairless rats, which didn't help my state of mind because I kept thinking about Dan Franklin and that dead rat in my car and Lou Marino getting hit by a car and being almost run over myself in the parking lot at the university.

I wondered whether he'd gotten hit while Bitsy and I were over there talking to Rosalie.

There had to be a connection with what was going on with the That's Amore Dean Martins, and as soon as I got home, I'd talk to Tim about it. For about a nanosecond I considered calling Flanigan, but then it would've been all official and everything, and I might've not been able to get that good night's sleep I was hoping for.

It had been a long day.

But before I went home, I wanted to stop by the hospital to check on Lou Marino and see how Rosalie was holding up.

Granted, considering her black eye, I supposed I shouldn't be concerned about her husband, but it was the right thing to do. Sister Mary Eucharista was urging me on.

And sure, I could've called Jeff Coleman instead, but when I tried, his phone just rang and rang.

Bitsy was wiping down Joel's room. Joel had left half an

hour ago; his last client hadn't taken as long as mine. Ace was long gone.

"Are you almost done?" I asked.

Bitsy looked up. She was standing on her stool, the one she dragged around with her to reach those places she couldn't, as she cleaned up Joel's ink pots.

"Just your room left," she said.

"I already did it," I said, and a grateful smile crossed her face. She'd had as long a day as I'd had, and I wanted to give her a break.

I surveyed how much she had left to do in here and silently joined her, putting the needle bar in the autoclave, wiping down Joel's client chair, collecting the trash and putting a new liner in the can. The room was, as Mary Poppins would say, *spit spot* in no time.

We got our stuff from the staff room and went out front, where I locked the glass front doors, then pulled the gate down and locked that, too. The rest of the mall shops were locking up, as well. Time to turn into a pumpkin.

I left Bitsy at her MINI Cooper, which she'd had outfitted to accommodate her size. I wished I could fit into one of those comfortably, but it was a lost cause.

We said our good-byes. I could see the weariness in the lines around her eyes. Mine probably looked the same, and I wondered whether I shouldn't head straight home, but once I got into the Jeep and pulled out onto the Strip, the lights flashing across the windshield, I got a second wind.

Jeff had said Lou Marino had been taken to University Medical Center, so I pointed the Jeep in that direction.

I told myself I wasn't going over there hoping for a glimpse of Colin Bixby.

He worked in the emergency room there, when he wasn't teaching classes at the university.

He probably wasn't working tonight anyway.

The parking garage was all lit up like a Christmas tree. I found a space and parked, heading down to the hospital entrance, where I pushed my way in through the heavy doors and stepped up to the information desk.

An older woman with bright white hair and too much makeup scowled at me. "May I help you?" She so obviously did not want to help me.

"I understand a friend"—okay, he wasn't my friend, but his wife was a client and his in-laws were friends—"was brought in here earlier. Lou Marino. He got hit by a car."

Her fingers were already moving on her computer keyboard. After a second, she looked up at me. "Are you family?"

I was too tired to lie. "A friend of the family. I really want to say hello to them. See how they're doing. See if they need anything."

"I can't let anyone up who's not family," she said curtly, turning back to her computer.

I stood there, shifting from one foot to the next. I didn't want to leave yet, and it didn't have anything to do with the fact that I would still have to pay five dollars for an hour of parking even if I was here only ten minutes.

Well, maybe that did have something to do with it.

"Is there any way I can get word to them?" I persisted.

The woman rolled her eyes at me. She didn't even pretend to hide it.

"You're not family," she said flatly.

I tried the only other thing I could think of. "Dr. Colin Bixby, is he on shift tonight?" I kicked myself for even asking, but he might be able to actually tell me something if he was here.

She rolled her eyes again. I pretended not to notice.

After a minute, she picked up the phone and spoke so softly I couldn't hear what she was saying. I didn't want to know what she was saying. Finally, she put her hand over the receiver and asked brusquely, "Name?"

"Brett Kavanaugh."

She went back to her phone, then hung it up and pointed behind me. "He'll meet you outside the emergency room."

Which was all the way around the building. I trudged along the sidewalk and finally saw the bright lights streaming out onto the pavement. Colin Bixby stepped out from behind a shadow.

"Twice in one day? And you're now harassing the staff?"

I couldn't tell whether he was teasing me.

"I could file a restraining order against you, you know." I saw the smile then, the one he tried not to show.

"Thanks for seeing me," I said. "I didn't know what else to do." I told him about trying to see how Lou Marino was doing and wanting to see Rosalie.

"They told me you were asking about a patient," he said. "But I don't know why you asked to see me."

"You're the only doctor I know over here. I didn't know if you'd be here."

"So you figured dropping my name would get you in?"

I shrugged. "I guess so."

He ran a hand through his dark, spiky hair. Even in the shadows he was hot. I felt I needed to say something.

"I'm sorry, you know, about before."

He gave a short laugh. "You mean when you thought I was going to kill you?"

"I was sort of a mess then," I said.

"No kidding." From his tone, I could tell he thought I was still a mess.

"A lot had gone on."

He nodded, his hands in the pockets of his white lab coat now. "So tell me what you were doing over there at the lab this afternoon. Really."

"It's like I said. A guy's body was found in my car along with a dead rat. I thought maybe it could be traced to Dan Franklin. I wanted to talk to the guy. But now he's missing, and someone tried to run me and Bitsy over when we were out in the parking lot, so maybe someone doesn't want me asking questions."

"What? Someone tried to run you over?" Concern laced his voice.

"It was a blue car; that's all I know."

"Maybe you should stop asking questions," he suggested.

No kidding.

Before I could stop it, I yawned.

"And maybe you need to go home," he added.

"I want to find out about Lou Marino," I said. "And see Rosalie. Then I'll go."

"Promise?"

I couldn't see through the shadows whether he was kidding me or really did want me to leave. Bitsy was right. I did screw it up with him. And I had no idea how to put it right.

"Scout's promise," I said, holding up my hand and forming a "V" with my fingers.

"That's the Vulcan sign," he chided.

"So sue me," I said.

He laughed. Really laughed. "Why is it I like you?"

He liked me? Could've fooled me.

But then he stopped laughing.

"I can't let you in to see Lou Marino's family," he said. "I'm sorry."

"Why not?"

"Because Lou Marino died half an hour ago."

Chapter 28

I wrote a note to Rosalie saying I was sorry and to please tell Jeff I'd call him in the morning. I gave it to Bixby, and he said he'd deliver it.

And then he kissed me good-bye.

Not like the fireworks kiss we'd shared a few months back, but his lips lingered on the corner of mine a tad longer than I thought they would. I felt a spark. It was small, but it was there. I swear.

He didn't say he'd call me.

Baby steps.

I pulled into my driveway at the same time Tim did.

We met in the kitchen, where I slung my messenger bag over a chair and shrugged off my jean jacket. He slipped off his sport jacket and tossed it on another chair.

"How was your day?" he asked.

I thought about the question and how I'd answer it. I finally said, "Well, interesting."

"Interesting how?" He took two beers out of the fridge, took the caps off them, and handed me one. I don't normally drink beer—I prefer wine—but it seemed like the thing to do right now.

"I'm not sure where to start."

He took a slug of his beer and set it down. "So start at the beginning."

With all that had happened, I'd lost track of the time line. When I rewound my memory, it landed at the wedding chapel with Jeff Coleman. I didn't want to tell Tim about that little adventure. And then there was the visit to the university lab. Another thing Tim didn't need to know about.

Although, leaving those two things out meant that a lot of other things had to be omitted, and suddenly there wasn't much to tell at all.

"I can't believe you're doing this again." Tim's voice shook me out of my thoughts.

"Doing what again?" I asked as innocently as I could.

"Sticking your nose into police business."

"I haven't even said anything."

"But I can tell. What have you been up to?"

"I don't know why you think I'm doing anything."

Tim snorted. "It's not all about you, Brett."

I knew that, but why did it feel like it sometimes?

"I think something might have happened to this guy Dan Franklin. Ray Lucci used his name when he came into my shop for a tattoo. He's another Dean Martin impersonator. He also works at the university. He's an animal-lab technician. He works with rats."

Tim sighed. "How did you find out he worked at the lab?"

I couldn't very well tell him I'd seen Dan Franklin's wallet and his university ID, so even though I'd dismissed trying to pull a fast one and telling Tim that I'd forgotten Franklin told me on the phone yesterday, I reconsidered and said, "He told me. When he called me back after we left a message because we didn't know Ray Lucci had used his name."

"Why have you made Franklin your own personal crusade?"

I shrugged. "Considering what's going on with all those Dean Martin impersonators, it seems like we need to find him soon. Someone might be gunning for him, too."

Tim closed his eyes and sighed, then opened them again. "We? *We* need to find him?"

So I felt as if I had a personal stake in this. But I didn't say anything because Tim was looking pretty angry at the moment, and the last time I'd seen him like that was the

time I told his girlfriend that he was out with another girl.
It wasn't malicious. I was just a kid and didn't realize it was
a no-no. But it hadn't mattered to him. I'd screwed up.

And it looked as though I did again.

But I couldn't let it go.

"You know Lou Marino died after getting hit by a car
tonight, right?" I asked.

"Who?"

"He's another Dean Martin. He's married to Rosalie,
Bernie Applebaum's daughter." I paused a second while
Tim absorbed this last bit of information, and then said,
"You know, I found Sylvia and Bernie."

Tim looked as though his head were going to explode.

I quickly told him about seeing Sylvia at the Palazzo
shops, her story about how they took a bus trip to Sedona
and ended up back at the Venetian. "Jeff came to take them
to the hospital to see Rosalie, because of Lou Marino's
accident."

Tim didn't say anything, but he pulled out his cell phone
and punched in a number. He walked out to the living
room, slid open the glass door to the outside patio, and
stepped outside. As I drank my beer, I tried to hear what
he was saying, but his voice was muffled. He was probably
calling Flanigan to find out whether he knew about Sylvia
and Bernie.

I'd left out the little bit about how Bitsy and I were
almost run over. I wasn't quite sure how to broach that,
since he was already pretty upset with me and my amateur
sleuthing and he didn't know about our little trip to the
university. But if I didn't tell him, he'd be even angrier. As I
rinsed out my empty beer bottle and put it in the recycling
bin under the sink, I tried to figure out what I should say
that would have the least impact.

Right.

Tim was closing his phone, coming back inside.

"Flanigan?" I asked, indicating the phone.

He nodded. "He saw them at the hospital."

"So he knew about Lou Marino?"

Tim took a deep breath and nodded again. "He's been

keeping tabs on those wedding chapel guys. Guess this isn't the first attempt on Lou Marino."

"He got mugged and cut up," I said without thinking.

"And how do you know that?" he asked, leaning toward me, his hands gripping the edge of the granite island countertop.

Uh-oh. But I couldn't back out now.

"I met one of the other impersonators. Guy named Will Parker. He stopped in the shop." I thought quickly and decided I had to lie. It was too bad I'd gotten rid of my rosary beads years ago. "He also told me someone tried to run him over. *With my car.*" I put a lot of emphasis on the last words. "Although he doesn't know it was my car. But it seems pretty likely it was."

Tim was nodding. I kept talking.

"This guy Parker said Ray Lucci had been a car thief and he was eyeing my car when Sylvia and Bernie drove up in it."

He didn't seem all that surprised for some reason with my revelations. He just kept nodding.

"This is why you can't get involved in any of this," he chided.

"But I did get involved," I said, deciding now to come clean. "And someone knows it." I was whispering now. "Someone tried to run me and Bitsy down in the parking lot at the university."

Tim's face grew red with anger. "And you didn't think to tell me that first? What's wrong with you? And what were you doing over at the university? No, let me guess. You were trying to find out about Dan Franklin. And then someone tries to run you down. Can't you see this is dangerous? You need to let the police do their job and stay out of it."

I sighed. He was right. Then something struck me. "Did you know about my car? That it almost ran over Parker? Did Flanigan tell you that?"

"I know you've got a personal stake in all this, Brett," Tim said. He was trying to pull himself together, stay in control. "But you really have to stay out of it. There's something I haven't told you."

All my muscles tensed. What more could there be?

"Ray Lucci's fingerprints were found in your car."

I blinked a couple of times. "Why wouldn't his finger-prints be there? I mean, he was in my trunk."

"No, Brett. His fingerprints were found on the gearshift, steering wheel, window controls, radio, and air-conditioning buttons. Flanigan thinks Lucci really did steal your car."

Chapter 29

"Do you think he was the one who tried to run down Will Parker?" I asked when it all sunk in.

"Possibly." He wanted to say something else, but stopped himself.

I didn't have that much self-control. "So how did he end up strangled with a clip cord and in the trunk?" I asked.

"That's what we're trying to figure out. Flanigan is, I mean."

"Anyone else's fingerprints in the car?"

"Only yours."

The words swirled around in my head. "Flanigan doesn't think I had anything to do with it, does he?"

"No."

"But?" I sensed that there was a "but" in there somewhere.

"I am not happy you're interfering with the investigation. Someone has already threatened you."

"I don't know anything, though. I didn't find out anything."

"Maybe you did and you don't realize it."

I pondered that a few seconds.

While I was pondering, Tim kept talking. "You're not to do anything else pertaining to this case," he said. "You are to go to work and come home, and that's it. Understand?"

"You're not my mother."

"If you insist on poking your nose where it doesn't belong, I'll call Mom and have her come out here for a visit."

There was no greater threat than that, and he knew it. He smiled smugly, because I knew he would do it. He totally would do it. And Mom would come out here and babysit me.

No, thank you.

Not that I didn't have a good relationship with my mother. Other than the fact that she couldn't deal with my choice of profession, we had a pretty decent relationship. Except when she was badgering me about how I should get married.

Okay, so we had some issues. Big issues. But she was my mom. It could be worse.

Tim was watching me.

"What?" I asked, irritated.

"Are you going to stay out of this and let Flanigan do his job?"

"Yeah, yeah, yeah," I said, sliding off my chair. "I'm going to bed."

"Hold on," he said, putting his hand up.

I sat back down. "What now?"

"What can you tell me about the car that almost hit you and Bitsy?" His tone had changed; it was his cop voice, one that I hadn't heard too many times.

As I told him about the blue car, what had happened, and how I didn't get a license plate number or even the make of the car, he took notes in a notebook he pulled from his back pocket.

"I'll give this to Flanigan," he said, getting up and starting for the living room. "You can get to bed. I'm going to watch a little tube." As I started to pass him, he reached out and held my arm for a second. "You know I'm only worried you're going to get into trouble, right?"

I gave him a peck on the cheek. "It's not your fault you're turning into Dad. It's in the genes."

I slipped out of his grasp as he rolled his eyes at me.

I was totally not responsible for what happened the next morning. I want to make that clear. I was minding my own business, reading the paper and having my coffee when the doorbell rang.

Sylvia stood on the doorstep, a small white car parked in the driveway behind her. Must have been that rental she told me about. She wore a long-sleeved T-shirt tucked into a cotton skirt. Tattoos crawled up out of the neck of the shirt and down her legs, but this was the most covered up I'd ever seen her.

"No one knows I'm here," she said as she came into the house and closed the door after her.

"Why are you here, then?" I asked. "Do you want coffee?"

Sylvia smiled, patted her white hair, which was pulled up into a neat bun in the back, sans rhinestone butterfly clips today, and said, "My dear, if I have coffee, I'll be in the bathroom all day, and I don't have time for that."

Way too much information.

"I'll have some prune juice," she said, plopping down into one of the kitchen chairs.

"Um, Sylvia—"

"Don't have any, huh? Jeff never used to, either, but now he keeps some just for me."

I wasn't quite sure whether Sylvia was telling me she'd be stopping by for breakfast often enough so I'd have to stock up on prune juice. I let it go.

"What's going on?" I asked, slathering a bagel with cream cheese.

Sylvia watched. "I could take one of those. Without the cream cheese, though."

As the bagel toasted, Sylvia took in her surroundings: the kitchen that opened up into a big family room with a sleek leather couch and big flat-screen TV plastered to the wall. Tim had gone a little crazy after Shawna moved out, taking all her Southwestern-motif furniture and decorations with her. Tim immediately painted over the blue and mauve walls with an eggshell color that contrasted sharply with the black leather. The long Scandinavian coffee table gave the room an elegance it hadn't had before.

But then again, Tim said once you get rid of cactus-themed wall quilts, anything would look elegant.

"Less is more, right?" Sylvia said as I put the bagel in front of her and sat down again.

"Yeah. Sylvia, what are you doing here? I don't think you came here just for breakfast."

Sylvia grinned and took a bite of bagel. "You're a smart girl. I tell Jeff all the time, that girl's smart."

It was hard sometimes to keep Sylvia on point.

"You're here, why?" I prodded.

"Well, I went for my morning swim over at the community pool. That detective kept us late at the hospital, asking all sorts of questions. He wanted us to come to the police station, but Jeff wouldn't have it. He said he'd bring us over today. But I snuck out so I could get my swim in. Clears the head, you know?" She tapped the side of her head and nodded.

I nodded, too, wondering where she was going with this.

"I need your help with something."

Uh-oh. I tried to keep an open mind. Maybe she only wanted me to take her to the store to get some prune juice.

She pushed her chair back a second and rummaged in the front pocket of her skirt. She pulled out a piece of paper and handed it to me.

It was all crumpled up, and I smoothed it out. It was a receipt printout from a company called Tattoo Inc.

Clever.

The receipt was for a clip cord. It had been shipped to Ray Lucci at the wedding chapel.

Chapter 30

"**W**hat do you think it means?" Sylvia asked as I stared at the receipt.

I had absolutely no clue, but ideas were starting to form.

"Why are you showing this to me?" I asked.

Sylvia sighed. "I haven't told Jeff yet. About Ray. I don't know how. And then Bernie hands this to me this morning. He said it was in the glove box in the Gremlin. I let Ray borrow the car last week. He must have left it there."

Little bits of Ray Lucci were ending up in the oddest places. Sylvia's car, my car.

I thought about what Tim would say.

"You should give this to Detective Flanigan," I said. "Not me. It's a clue." It proved that Joel's missing clip cord probably wasn't the one that strangled Lucci. And it would be great if that little bit were cleared up, so we could all get on with our lives.

I couldn't help but wonder, however, why Lucci would buy a clip cord. And if it was the one around his neck, how did his own cord get used against him? Just like how did he end up stealing my car and then end up in the trunk, with the car right back where Sylvia and Bernie had left it for me?

I tried not to think about Tim. How on earth could I possibly let this one go?

Sylvia tucked a stray hair in back of her ear. "I don't want to get Ray in trouble."

"But Ray is dead," I said softly, and not unkindly.

Sylvia reached over and patted my hand. "I know that, dear."

Sometimes I'm not sure what Sylvia knows or doesn't. So I have to make sure.

"You need to tell Jeff about Ray," I said.

"So you really think I should turn this over to that policeman?" Sylvia obviously wanted to change the subject. "He was dressed all fancy. Bernie says he doesn't trust a policeman who's got more money than he does. He thinks he's on the take."

On the take? What were we? In a Scorsese movie?

"I think you should give it to Detective Flanigan," I said again, knowing Tim would be happy I was doing the right thing.

She picked up the last piece of her bagel and chewed slowly.

I'd put the receipt on the table and now picked it up again.

"He had it delivered to the chapel, not his home," I said. "Where was he living?"

Sylvia touched the corners of her mouth with her finger, to brush away any leftover crumbs. "He had an apartment up in North Vegas."

"Why wouldn't he have the package delivered there, then?" As I asked the question, I realized the probable answer. He didn't want it in his apartment. Did he plan to use the clip cord against someone else, who then used it against him?

My thoughts were all mixed up like a milk shake in a blender.

"Why would Ray need a clip cord?" Sylvia's voice interrupted. "He could've asked to borrow one, if he needed one."

If Ray was planning something that he didn't want anyone to know about and he didn't want anyone to know he had a clip cord, why be so careless and leave the receipt in the car?

Maybe he forgot about it. It's not as if that doesn't happen.

I looked at the receipt again. It had a customer account number on it. I hadn't heard of Tattoo Inc., but there were a million Web sites that sold tattoo equipment. I could even contact the place where I get my equipment; maybe someone there had heard of it.

"Can I make a copy of this?" I asked Sylvia.

She nodded. "What are you going to do with it?"

I wasn't sure exactly. I went into the small den off the living room, where we kept our printer, which was also a copy machine and a scanner. Amazing what a hundred bucks can get you these days.

I made a copy of the receipt and gave the original to Sylvia. "Detective Flanigan," I said again.

"But I won't tell him you have a copy." Sylvia winked at me.

I smiled. "No, that might not be the best idea."

"You've got a plan, don't you, dear?"

"No—I don't know," I said. "We'll see." I looked at the wall clock. It was almost eleven. I needed to get into the shop. Sylvia saw me and got up, smoothing out her skirt as she stood.

I walked her to the door but stopped her before she went out.

"You need to tell Jeff about Ray," I said. "Does Bernie know?"

She nodded.

"You need to tell Jeff. Today. Before Flanigan does."

Sylvia squeezed my arm. "I know, dear. Thank you." She shoved the receipt back in her pocket and went out to the car. I watched as she got in, started the engine, and backed out of the driveway.

When the little white car had disappeared around the corner, I went back into the house and found my laptop. I put the URL for Tattoo Inc. into the address field, and the site popped up immediately.

Tattoo Inc. promised all your tattoo needs would be

met—at the lowest prices, of course. And as I perused the site, I wondered whether maybe I shouldn't be changing my purchasing policies. These prices were far lower than what I was paying.

Granted, I'd have to talk about it with Bitsy. She did all the purchasing for the shop, and maybe she'd already found Tattoo Inc. and decided for some reason that it wasn't worth saving a few pennies.

I went to "My Account," entered Ray Lucci's name and account number in the space allotted, and waited for the page to load.

When it finally opened, I couldn't believe it.

Ray Lucci hadn't ordered only a clip cord.

Three days ago, the day before he was killed, he'd ordered all the parts needed to build a tattoo machine. And he'd had them shipped to That's Amore.

Chapter 31

It was all right there in front of me on the laptop screen, but I couldn't figure it out.

Why would Ray Lucci want to build a tattoo machine? I scanned the items he bought: coils, armature bar, grip, binding posts, frame, tube clamp. It would be easier to buy a tattoo machine already assembled. And why order a clip cord but not the power supply or the foot pedal? A tattoo machine without the last two items was useless. A clip cord that couldn't clip to a power source made no sense, either—unless you were going to strangle someone with it. But Lucci didn't strangle himself.

I remembered, though, how I'd suggested to Tim that maybe he *had*. That autoerotic-asphyxiation thing that you hear about occasionally, usually in hushed tones.

I shook away the thought. Not because it was weird and kinky, but because the theory was probably stupid.

But then again, he'd stolen my car, and he owned a clip cord. No sign that anyone else was with him.

Except that the car was returned to my parking spot. And there was that rat.

I was going in circles.

I looked at the laptop screen again, at Ray Lucci's order. There was a tracking number for the shipment. I clicked on it, and the UPS page popped up. The parts had been shipped the day he ordered them, and he'd paid extra for faster mailing. According to this, the package had been delivered. Yesterday afternoon.

I closed my laptop and took a deep breath.

I hoped Sylvia would call Flanigan, but mostly for selfish reasons. So I could tell Tim that I talked her into it. Maybe then he wouldn't be mad at me for what I was going to do next.

The wedding chapel was still as tacky as I remembered it from the previous day. Today there was a large number of motorcycles, all Harleys, in the driveway, under the long awning. I heard the strains of "That's Amore" coming from the direction of the drive-through window and spotted two Dean Martins swaying as they sang. I squinted and saw the bride astride her bike, the black leather jacket with the Harley logo faintly visible through the long tulle veil that cascaded down her back. When the Dinos stopped singing, the guy on the bike next to the bride grabbed her and kissed her as she held her bouquet of white flowers high over her head. A cheer rose up from the crowd.

"Changed your mind, Kavanaugh?" I heard Jeff Coleman's voice behind me and turned to see him leaning against the side of the Jeep, a cigarette dangling from his lips.

"I thought you quit," I said, pointing to the cigarette.

"I only did it for you, and then you jilted me," he teased, but he took the cigarette out of his mouth and tossed it, grinding it out with his heel. "So what are you doing back here?"

I didn't quite know how to explain I was here looking for a package delivered to Ray Lucci, so I figured I'd turn it around on him. "What are *you* doing here?"

"I told Rosalie I'd come by and pick up Lou's last paycheck."

"He didn't have direct deposit?" I asked.

Jeff reached toward his breast pocket, but it was empty.

"Your doctor said not to smoke anymore," I reminded him.

He grinned. "I'll keep that in mind, Kavanaugh. And no, Lou did not have direct deposit. Rosalie needs the cash now, to help pay for the funeral."

"How's she doing?"

Jeff shrugged. "They were married for ten years. He beat the crap out of her for most of that time. How do you think she's doing?" He tried to keep his tone light, but the anger seeped out underneath his words.

"Did you know her before your mother met Bernie?"

"No. I didn't meet her until a few weeks ago. She and Lou brought Bernie over to the shop to meet up with my mother. I could tell from the get-go that Lou was bad news."

Interesting. "How?" I prodded.

"He dominated the conversation; she stood there with her head down, and only spoke when he looked directly at her. She laughed at his stupid jokes. Bernie hated him, the way he treated her."

"So he's not too broke up about his death, huh?"

Jeff cocked his head and looked at me sideways. "What are you getting at, Kavanaugh?"

"I don't know." And I really wasn't sure. "Seems pretty convenient for Rosalie that Lou's dead now."

"You think she had something to do with it?"

"No, guess not. Sounds like whoever did this did her a favor. It's probably the same guy who killed Ray Lucci and also tried to run down Will Parker."

"Who? Oh, yeah, the guy you were making eyes with yesterday."

Making eyes with? What century did he live in?

I chose to ignore him. "I'm just saying that I think somehow someone wants to kill off these Dean Martin impersonators." Something Will Parker had said to me yesterday poked my memory. "You know, Will said that the Elvis chapel across the street keeps stealing the Dean Martins."

We both instinctively looked over at the larger-than-life Elvis, dancing over the white wedding chapel. It was too much, but almost everything in Vegas was too much. You get used to it after a while.

Jeff laughed. "You think there's some sort of Elvis–Dean Martin war going on here?"

It did sound ridiculous, but then again . . .

"Maybe," I said.

Movement in the corner of my eye made me turn. Uh-oh. Anthony DellaRocco, owner of That's Amore, was scurrying toward us, a big smile on his face, his arms outstretched.

"You've come back!" he said. "Have you gotten over your cold feet?"

The latter was directed at me, because, of course, I walked away yesterday.

Before I could say anything, though, Jeff put his arm around my shoulders and said, "We decided a church is the way to go."

We did, did we?

"I'm afraid we're here for a sadder occasion, though," he added.

DellaRocco frowned, confused.

"Lou Marino's widow is my sister-in-law," Jeff continued. "She asked if I could pick up Lou's paycheck."

DellaRocco's face registered recognition. "Jeff Coleman? She called to tell me you were on your way. Come with me."

Jeff held on to my shoulder, steering me behind Della-Rocco. I was glad I now had the excuse to get back in that building, but I wished I didn't still have to pretend I was going to marry Jeff Coleman to do it.

DellaRocco led us inside and down the hall, turning into an office to our right. It was neat as the proverbial pin. A file cabinet stood against the far wall, a big metal desk sprawled catty-corner to it, an expensive big leather swivel chair behind the desk. The top of the desk held a wire basket with some paperwork and a pencil holder with three sharp pencils, and a stapler sat next to that. A framed photograph of a pretty brunette with laugh lines around her eyes faced the swivel chair.

A brown parcel perched on the far edge of the desk.

Anthony DellaRocco sat in the chair and swiveled so he could pull out his top drawer. He slid out a white envelope and handed it to Jeff, who was also looking at the package.

DellaRocco noticed.

"Came for Ray Lucci yesterday," he said. His eyes moved from Jeff to me and back again. "Some tattoo place."

Jeff and I exchanged a look.

"You two look like you know your way around a tattoo parlor," DellaRocco said with a wide grin, his big voice booming.

"What are you going to do with it?" I asked, ignoring him.

DellaRocco looked startled for a second, as if he didn't get that I was referring to the package. "Oh, you mean this," he said, tapping it.

"Did you make sure it's not ticking?" Jeff asked; his tone was ominous, as if it might really be ticking.

DellaRocco's eyes widened, and he pushed back in his chair, away from the desk. "Didn't even think to. You think it might have something to do with his murder?"

I was the only one who knew what was in the package, and I knew that it didn't, but I shrugged, as if it could be the bomb Jeff suggested.

Jeff was leaning down, his ear now close to the box. He shook his head. "Don't hear anything. You're lucky," he said to DellaRocco. "You know, you should tell the cops about this." He cocked his head at me. "Her brother's a detective. Why don't we take this and she can give it to him?"

DellaRocco's eyes narrowed. "A detective?"

"He's with the Las Vegas police department," I offered. "I'm sure he'd appreciate getting the package. It might be a clue to his murder. You might actually be responsible for solving it." The last bit was a bit much, but he was nodding as though I was telling the truth.

"I see what you mean." He paused. "They wouldn't be upset if I didn't call them myself?"

Jeff chuckled. "She's practically a detective herself."

He didn't see the dirty look I threw him.

"And even if it's not ticking," Jeff added, "remember the anthrax that went through the mail and killed that woman in Connecticut after 9/11?"

That did it. DellaRocco pushed the parcel over to Jeff. "Okay, fine. Get it out of here."

Jeff picked it up and swung it under his arm. He threw his other arm around my waist and started steering me out. "Thanks, Tony," he said.

"Thank *you*," DellaRocco said.

Jeff was pushing me so quickly out the door that I tripped over my feet. "What's the hurry?" I said. "Do you really think there's a bomb in that package?"

"Maybe I want to get my fiancée home," he said with a leer.

I squirmed to get out of his grasp, but he was too strong.

"A few more minutes, Kavanaugh, and you'll be a free woman again."

"I'm already a free woman."

Jeff chuckled. "Why is it so easy to get to you?" His words were light, but there was something underneath his tone that made me take pause.

"What's going on?" I asked.

He didn't answer. He pulled me over to the Pontiac.

"I've got the Jeep," I said.

"Just get in, okay?"

We'd barely gotten into the car before Jeff started opening the package.

"Why are you opening it?" I asked.

"Because I've done business with Tattoo Inc. And this isn't their logo, even though it's got their name on it." As he spoke, he ripped the cardboard box open.

I peered over the top to see what was inside.

It was the biggest gun I'd ever seen.

Chapter 32

"Smith and Wesson .45," Jeff said, picking it up out of its packing material and studying it.

"Put it back," I said, leaning far enough away so my back was plastered against the door behind me. "You don't know if it's loaded."

"It's not loaded."

I gave him a look, and he rolled his eyes at me. "I know a little bit about guns, and it's not loaded. Okay?"

That's right. Jeff had done a stint in the Marines.

I'd always had guns in the house, since my dad and brother both were cops. But I'd always kept my distance, not wanting to get too close to one. They made me uncomfortable. All those accidental shootings you read about in the paper. I didn't want to be a statistic.

"What would Ray Lucci want with a gun?" I said, more to myself than to Jeff.

But Jeff answered. "He was an ex-con," he said, as if that explained everything, and he put the gun back in the box and folded over the top flaps.

I studied the logo. It was the one on the Web site. But this certainly wasn't tattoo machine parts.

"You've ordered from Tattoo Inc.?" I asked.

Jeff nodded. "They've got great prices."

"But this isn't their logo?"

"Uh-uh."

I reached over my shoulder and pulled my messenger bag into my lap. Rummaging around, my fingers finally landed on the Tattoo Inc. receipt. I took it out and waved it at Jeff. "Something's going on," I said.

Jeff plucked the receipt out of my hand and studied it before looking up at me, his eyes quizzical. "How did you get this?"

I'd forgotten that Sylvia came to me privately this morning. I had to think fast. "I can't tell you." So lame.

A smile tugged at his mouth. "You can't tell me?"

I shook my head. "It doesn't matter how I got it. All that matters is, something's up with this order. It says tattoo-machine parts, but it's a gun. And they're using Tattoo Inc.'s name. That's fraud."

I had no idea what I was babbling about. I couldn't tell Jeff that Sylvia gave it to me. Because then he'd ask why and I'd be stuck. It wasn't my place to tell him about Ray Lucci.

Why hadn't Sylvia told him yet?

"Do you think this order has anything to do with Lucci's murder?" I asked, grasping at straws, trying to make sure Jeff was distracted enough to keep from asking me questions. "Do you think he thought he was in danger and needed the gun?"

"If so, it came too late," Jeff said, handing me back the receipt. "You didn't seem surprised to see the package on his desk."

"I wasn't. I used the account number off this receipt and tracked it. I knew it came in yesterday."

"So that's why you showed up here?" Jeff grinned.

"He also ordered a clip cord," I said, ignoring him. "He got that a couple weeks ago."

"But if the tattoo-machine parts weren't actually tattoo-machine parts, and they were really a gun, who's to say the clip cord was really a clip cord?"

He had a point.

We sat for a few minutes pondering that until Jeff broke the silence by saying, "Do you have time to follow me to my shop?"

I glanced at my watch. "Guess so. What are you going to do?"

He gently picked up the box and leaned over, putting it on the floor behind the passenger seat. "I'll meet you there," he said, indicating I should get out. So I did.

The whole way to Murder Ink, I wondered how that box of tattoo-machine parts became a gun. I also wondered how long it would take Sylvia to tell Jeff about Ray Lucci.

Jeff parked in the alley behind the strip mall where his shop was, but I preferred the Bright Lights Motel lot across the way. He met me at the front door, opening it for me and leading me back to his office.

He'd put the box with the gun in it on his desk, next to another one about the same size. That one had a logo for Tattoo Inc. that did look different, but not so much so that it was noticeable at first glance.

He pointed to it. "See?"

I nodded, not that he paid attention. He sat behind the desk and moved his laptop around in front of him. I came around the desk so I could look over his shoulder.

Jeff clicked on a bookmark named Tattoo Inc. A Web site popped up, and it looked like the one I'd seen. "That's it," I said.

"Give me the receipt."

I took it out of my bag and handed it to him. Jeff typed in the account number. We waited a couple of minutes, and finally, a box popped up saying it wasn't a valid account number.

Jeff picked up the receipt again and studied it. After a second, he leaned back and grinned at me. "Did you Google Tattoo Inc. or type in this URL on this receipt?" He waved the receipt at me.

"I typed in the URL," I said.

"That's what's wrong," he said, stabbing his finger at the screen where the URL for the real Tattoo Inc. was.

The URL on the receipt was a ".com" URL. I hadn't thought anything of it. But the real Tattoo Inc. was in England. With a ".co.uk" URL.

"But it looked like tattoo parts," I started. "Go to the site."

Jeff Coleman and I skimmed pages for the fake Tattoo

Inc. Nothing looked out of the ordinary. We found Ray Lucci's account again, and it was as I'd seen it earlier. But then I remembered something Jeff had said.

"I wonder what it was that he got instead of a clip cord," I said.

"Another gun, maybe."

So now we were back to Joel's clip cord as possibly the murder weapon. I didn't much like the idea of that.

Jeff was clicking all over the Tattoo Inc. site. "There's no place here where you can place an order online," he said, "but there's a phone number." He grabbed his cell and punched in the number.

"Yes, I understand I can place a special order," he said, then paused as he listened to the response. "Yes, I have an account." He rattled off Ray Lucci's account number. "Yes, I'll hold."

I went around the desk and sat in an old metal chair in the corner, tapping my fingers on the armrest as I watched Jeff Coleman. After a few seconds, he said, "Yes, I did receive my order. . . . Yes, it's just as you said. . . . Yes, I'm happy with it. . . ." He was absently clicking around the Tattoo Inc. Web site as he spoke.

But then he sat up straight and said, "Yes, yes, I know where it is. Thank you." And he flipped his phone shut.

Jeff's eyes were wide as he looked up at me. "Kavanaugh, there's more than murder going on. Check it out."

I got up and came around the desk. The tattoo equipment I'd seen had been replaced by guns. All different shapes and sizes.

"How'd you find that?" I asked.

"I clicked on the logo, and it popped up." He twisted around to look up at me. "Ray Lucci was buying illegal guns."

Chapter 33

"Do you think this had anything to do with his murder?" I asked.

Jeff rolled his eyes at me. "Is the pope Catholic?"

Smart aleck.

"But then what about Lou? And the attempt on Will Parker? And where's Dan Franklin? What about that rat?"

"So we've got a few loose ends."

"A few loose ends? The whole freaking thing is barely held together."

Jeff chuckled. "You know, you're cute when you get mad."

I felt my face flush. I *so* didn't need him making fun of me right now.

Jeff leaned back in his chair and pointed at the guns on the screen. "You probably should tell your brother about this."

I probably should, even though he'd get mad at me for "getting involved" again. I hadn't asked Sylvia to give me that receipt. It seemed innocent enough, I suppose, if you looked past the clip cord. But now we'd gone into unchartered waters. And this was best left for the police to look at.

I couldn't shake the feeling, though, that this might not have anything to with what had been going on.

"Where did you get the receipt?" Jeff asked, interrupting my thoughts, his voice soft, his eyes searching mine.

I stepped away from the desk. "I told you, I can't tell you."

"Okay, fine, be that way." He pointed at the Tattoo Inc. box. "You should take that to your brother."

I didn't want to be that close to the gun, much less driving around with it.

"I don't know about that," I said. "What if I get stopped or something? I could be arrested."

Jeff laughed out loud. "Stopped or something? Kavanaugh, you drive slower than my grandmother. You stop at every yellow light."

"So what if I'm a careful driver?"

Jeff slowly shook his head from side to side. "Okay, fine. I'll follow you to the police station, you can call your brother, and we'll hand this over. Is that a plan?"

Jeff's face was twitching with amusement. He knew if he came with me, then he'd find out how I got the receipt.

Sylvia had to tell him about Ray.

"Where's your mother?" I asked.

"Why?"

I shrugged, as if it were a casual question. "Just wondering. Usually she's here when you're not."

"She and Bernie are at Rosalie's."

"Can we stop there first? I really would like to give my condolences to Rosalie."

"She already got that note. The one that doctor delivered last night." The way he said "doctor" made me hesitate. "I thought you and he were all over. I mean, you did think he was going to kill you."

I wished people would stop rubbing that in. I'd said I was sorry, and I really needed to move on.

"Can we stop at Rosalie's first?"

"You know, Kavanaugh, you need to get over yourself."

A bell jingled from somewhere in the distance.

Jeff pushed away from the desk and stood up. I followed him out into the front of his shop.

A young man with a big grin and a mop of dark curls held out his hand. "Bobby Douglas. Am I on time?"

From the look on Jeff's face, I knew he'd forgotten about

his client. As he pointed Bobby to a workstation, he turned to me.

"You have to go on your own. Take the box. No one will stop you."

He saw me hesitate and chuckled. "It's not loaded," he said, reading my mind. "You'll be fine."

That's what he thought.

"I still want to stop at Rosalie's. Where does she live?" I asked.

Jeff took a deep breath, told Bobby to hang tight, and grabbed a piece of tracing paper and a pencil. He scribbled directions and handed them to me. "She's out in Summerlin. On the way to Red Rock."

I put the paper with the directions on top of the box. Granted, Rosalie's was in the total opposite direction than the police station, but I wasn't exactly relishing the idea of turning over this gun and explaining everything to Tim right away. The box would be safe in the Jeep. After all, if you looked at it, you'd think it had something to do with tattoos.

As I balanced the box in my arms, Jeff opened the door for me.

"You'll be fine, Kavanaugh," were the last words I heard before the door shut behind me.

I put the box on the floor under the passenger seat and found myself looking at it every few seconds. As if it were going to do magic tricks or something and I didn't want to miss it.

I drove up Charleston, the mountains coming closer and closer as I drove. Despite my trepidation about the parcel I was traveling with, I could feel the muscles in my shoulders and back relaxing instinctively as I gazed at the red-and-brown rocks that pierced the deep blue sky. I wanted to chuck it all—forget about Sylvia and Jeff and Ray Lucci and the other Dinos and that gun—and put my boots on and feel the hard desert under my feet.

The longer I thought about it, the more I wanted to play hooky.

The Red Rock Casino Resort Spa came up on my left. It

was out here off the beaten path, away from the Strip and its craziness, almost at the foot of its namesake.

The light was red, and it was a long one. I tapped the steering wheel impatiently. No one was behind or in front of me. On the other side of the four-lane road, a lone blue car sat like I did, just waiting.

That other blue car, the one that came too close for comfort at the university, flashed in my brain. The cars were similar, but I couldn't say for sure what model the sinister one was. It had gone past so quickly, and I was too busy trying to get out of the way to take notice. This one was a Ford Taurus. Fords and Chevies sometimes have the same sort of body. They're probably all made on the same chassis.

And then I remembered. Dan Franklin's blue Taurus. In his driveway.

I leaned forward a little, squinting to see the driver. A shadow was cast across the windshield, obscuring my view.

I knew I was being paranoid, but almost getting run down gave me a pass on that. I might always have a problem with blue cars now. Good thing my car was red. If I ever got it back. If I ever wanted to drive it again after it had been used as a coffin.

My phone rang in my bag, and I leaned over and pulled it out.

"You've got a client in an hour," Bitsy reminded me before I could even say hello.

"I know. I'm on my way," I lied, my eye on the blue car as my thoughts swirled around in a stream of consciousness.

"Why is Colin Bixby coming in later?"

I stopped paying attention to the blue car.

"Bixby?" I asked. "What do you mean?"

"He called and made an appointment for later. I made sure he and that Dean Martin guy weren't coming in at the same time."

I was barely comprehending. "Does he want another tattoo?" I asked. "And what's this about a Dean Martin guy?"

"Who? Oh, the doctor. I don't know. The Dean Martin guy's getting a touch-up."

"Which Dean Martin?" I asked, but then I remembered I'd offered to touch up Will Parker's tattoo. Bitsy confirmed that it was him.

The light turned green. As I put my foot to the accelerator, the blue car sped through the intersection.

And a police cruiser with its lights flashing came up behind me and indicated I should pull over.

Chapter 34

I hung up on Bitsy, tossed the phone onto the passenger seat, eased the Jeep over to the curb, and cut the engine. I leaned over and opened the glove box. A flashlight and a couple of CDs. I didn't see the registration. Where did Tim keep it?

A glance in the rearview mirror told me the cop was almost to the door. I sat up straighter, looking around for some other hiding place but not seeing anything.

Except the box on the floor. The one that had the big gun in it.

My heart started flip-flopping inside my chest, and I was having a hard time breathing. Especially when I saw who the cop was.

Willis. The fireplug cop who showed up at my house when I found Ray Lucci in my trunk.

So not my lucky day.

I flashed a smile at him, even though I was having a panic attack. Maybe he wouldn't notice.

"Do you know why I pulled you over?" he asked, as if he didn't know me from beans.

I shrugged, swallowing hard to push back the panic.

"You were not using a hands-free device for your cell phone."

This was totally why I adhered to the rules of the road. Although people talk on cell phones all the time while they're driving and there's absolutely no enforcement, it figured that I'd end up being the poster child for it.

"I was stopped at a light." Great. The moment my voice comes back it's belligerent. "I was not driving."

"You were going through the light, and you were on your phone," Willis said sternly. "I need to see your license and registration."

This was the sticky part.

"I've got my license," I said. "It's in my bag. I'm leaning over to get it." And I did as I said, sliding my hand in my bag and taking out my wallet. I slipped the license out and handed it to him.

He held it for a second, his eyes skipping around the inside of the car.

"Registration?"

I made a kind of twittering sound. "That's the problem," I said. "This is my brother's Jeep, and I thought the registration was in the glove box, but it's not, and I don't know where it is."

He studied my face a second, probably trying to see whether I was lying, then said, "Your brother's Jeep?"

I rolled my eyes before I could stop myself. "Tim Kavanaugh. Detective Kavanaugh," I said.

"I know who he is," Willis snapped at me. "Step out of the vehicle."

This wasn't going well. I did as asked and stood by the door as Willis looked around the inside of the car.

"What's in the box?" he asked.

My chest constricted, and I couldn't breathe. My mouth was as dry as the desert.

"The box? What's in it?" he asked again.

I tried to swallow. "Tattoo stuff," I croaked.

"I'd like to see it."

Now, I know how to talk to cops. And when a cop wants to see something in my car, I should just let him.

Why hadn't I gone straight to Tim rather than come out here?

I walked slowly around the Jeep and opened the passenger door. Willis was right behind me. I leaned in and picked up the box, handing it to him.

Willis's eyes widened when he saw the address on the front.

"This belongs to Ray Lucci?" he asked.

I nodded. "I can explain."

He flipped up the box flaps and looked inside.

Willis looked back up at me. He held the box with one hand, grabbed my arm with the other, and said, "Let's go."

"I was bringing it to Tim," I started.

"You're not exactly in the neighborhood," he reminded me.

"I needed to make a stop first," I tried.

He started leading me toward the cruiser.

"Can I at least get my bag?" I asked.

He let go of me, went to the Jeep, and got my bag for me, but he didn't hand it to me. He indicated I was to keep heading toward the cruiser.

"Can I lock it up?" I asked, indicating the Jeep.

Willis sighed, as if I was the biggest pain in his butt all day. I probably was. He allowed me to get the keys and lock up the Jeep before he stuffed me in the back of the cruiser and we headed back downtown.

Willis put me in one of those concrete interrogation rooms you see on TV. It's really like that, except possibly more uncomfortable. I waited there about twenty minutes before the door opened and Tim stepped in. He was not happy with me.

"Where did you get the gun?" he asked without saying hello.

I told him everything. About Sylvia giving me the receipt this morning and then going to see Jeff and finding the box at That's Amore and deciding to go see Rosalie first.

Tim took it all in, pacing back and forth in front of me as I spoke.

"I couldn't find your registration," I said. "I thought it was in the glove box. Why don't you keep it there?"

Tim stopped pacing and shook his head. "You've got an illegal gun in my Jeep, and you're worried about the registration?"

"You can call Jeff Coleman so he can corroborate my story," I said.

"Don't worry; we'll do that," Tim promised.

"So am I free to go now?" I asked.

"I'm not letting you go by yourself," he said.

"What do you mean?"

"First off, my Jeep is somewhere in Summerlin. You have no way to get anywhere. Second, you obviously can't be trusted on your own, so I'm going to have to take things into my own hands."

"Take things into your own hands? What does that mean?"

"That means you go to work and you go home, no stops in between."

"Like I'm under house arrest?" While I'd been having panic attacks with Willis, now my heart was pounding with anger.

"Exactly."

My eyes filled with tears, and I struggled to keep them at bay. "I didn't do anything wrong," I tried.

"You're putting yourself in danger. What if someone else had found that gun in the car with you?"

I shrugged. "No one did."

"Because Willis stopped you first."

A knock on the door interrupted us.

Detective Flanigan stepped in. Might as well make it a party. It would be the only one I'd be able to go to for a while, it seemed.

"So, Miss Kavanaugh, you seem to find yourself in interesting predicaments, don't you?" Flanigan asked before turning to Tim. "Have you told her?"

"Told me what?" I asked as Tim shook his head.

"I haven't had a chance yet."

Flanigan took a deep breath and leaned against the wall, his arms crossed over his chest. My throat tightened. Whatever it was he was going to tell me—well, I knew it wasn't going to be good.

"Your brother here is taking a couple of days off. To make sure you stay out of trouble."

Chapter 35

I stood up and faced Tim, ignoring Flanigan.

"You're going to be my babysitter?"

Tim nodded. "That's right."

"I'm not a child who needs watching."

"That's what you think."

With a huff, I plopped back down into the chair, my face in my hands. This was *so* not cool.

"It's for your safety," Tim said softly. "Someone already tried to run you down, too."

Logically, I could understand his concern. Maybe I was getting too involved with all this. But this gun thing, well, that wasn't my doing. I didn't go looking for it.

"That should be that," Flanigan said. "Hopefully, all this will be over soon."

It was the way he said it that made me take pause, and I lifted my head up.

"Do you have a suspect?" I asked.

Tim rolled his eyes, and Flanigan shook his head as he left the room.

"What?" I asked Tim.

"*What?*" he mimicked. "This is exactly why this is a good idea."

"But you're using vacation days, and you wanted to go hiking in Alaska."

"I'll still get there. I've got time."

Super.

"I have a client, you know. I have to get to the shop."

"I'll take you."

I was about to argue, then realized he was right: The Jeep was in Summerlin, and my car was somewhere being probed by the police. I did need a ride.

I felt like such a loser.

As we settled into Tim's department-issued Chevy Impala, which had all the personality of a dishrag, I asked, "Did Flanigan tell you that you had to watch me or did you volunteer?"

I saw it in his expression. This wasn't voluntary.

He knew I knew. "It's for your own good. I don't want to have to explain to Mom and Dad how you got killed because you were too nosy. They'd end up blaming me, and I'd have to live with it."

"So that's why you agreed to this? So you won't feel guilty?" Sister Mary Eucharista would be proud.

He turned down Las Vegas Boulevard. "You know, Brett, some nosy people are satisfied just poking into other people's medicine cabinets and bathroom drawers."

"So sue me. I'm not just some nosy person."

Tim wanted to laugh. His jaw muscles twitched, and the faint hint of a smile tugged at his lips. "Maybe you should've become a cop," he suggested.

"And maybe you could tell me how I could explain that to Mom."

"It wouldn't be any harder than explaining the tattoos."

Touché.

"So if you're hanging out babysitting me, maybe I should give you some ink," I said slyly. Tim didn't have a tattoo. He said he didn't know what he'd want marked permanently on his person, so he wouldn't get anything at all. "I've got books with ideas at the shop."

He ignored me.

Bitsy's eyes widened when Tim followed me into the shop.

"Hey, Bits," Tim said jovially, heading toward the staff room and disappearing inside.

"What is he doing here?" Bitsy asked in a stage whisper.

"He's my new babysitter," I said, quickly telling her what had gone on since I'd hung up on her.

"You had a gun in your car?"

Oh, right. Forgot to tell her how I came to possess a firearm. So I did.

As I spoke, the door swung open, and I looked up to see Will Parker coming in. I'd almost forgotten about him, but surveying the jeans and the button-down shirt and the way his blond hair flopped across his forehead, I figured I could have a lot worse ways to spend the next hour.

Tim, unfortunately, chose that moment to stick his head out of the staff-room door. Will Parker spotted him, and he did a double take.

"That's my brother, Tim," I said.

"The cop?" Will had a deer-in-headlights look about him.

I chuckled. "He's not going to arrest you until after I work on your tattoo. My room's this way." I led him down the hall and pointed to my room. "Wait a sec, okay?" I continued to the staff room, where Tim was riffling through a file folder with some stencils in it.

I grabbed the folder from him and put it back on the light table.

"You can't check out all the clients," I hissed. "You'll scare them away. I'm going to be about an hour, so you can go get a drink or lunch or something if you want. You can bring something back for all of us."

Tim was grinning. "Okay, fine, don't get all mad. I'll go get food."

He started out, and I remembered something. "Joel's on Atkins. He needs some sort of meat."

"Really? It looked like he'd lost some weight. But don't people on that diet gain it all back later anyway?"

"Don't tell him that." I shooed him out and went into my room, where Will Parker was seated, checking out my tattoo machine. He was caressing the clip cord far too intimately. I took the machine and cord and put them on the shelf behind the chair before I sat down next to him.

"Roll your sleeve up," I said.

"All business, huh?" he asked as he did what I said. "You're kidding about your brother arresting me, right?"

I made a face at him and didn't answer. The tattoo was on the top of his forearm. The skull was bleeding outside the lines, the black faded to a dull gray. It was really an outline, no color. The daggers through the eyes were also black, and while I'd initially thought with a quick glimpse the other day that it was good work, I was definitely re-thinking that now.

"How about a little color," I said. "I could do some red, some silver in the daggers, make the skull white, the sockets blacker, and it'll be really striking."

As I readied the inks and slid the needle into the machine, I felt myself go into autopilot. I pushed Tim from my head, and everything that had gone on the last couple of days faded like Will Parker's ink. When I finally put my foot to the pedal and the machine started its familiar whir-ring, I was focused on the tattoo and nothing else.

He didn't even flinch.

"You must have a high threshold for pain," I said as I wiped the excess ink with a soft cloth.

"Always did," he said.

"Can you twist your arm around a little to the right?" I asked, and he did, giving me a better angle so I could work on the outline of the skull.

It also gave me a better view of the bruises on his hand.

Chapter 36

The bruises looked as though they were a few days old, already turning purple and yellow.

"What happened here?" I asked, tapping one.

He flinched then.

I looked up and saw a glimpse of panic before he composed himself.

"It's nothing," he said. "I fell."

I wasn't an idiot, although I was wondering whether he was. Did he think I wouldn't see this when he came in?

He saw my expression and sighed.

"Okay, it was this girl. It got a little rough." To his credit, he blushed, as if embarrassed. "I'm not really seeing her."

But he'd seen enough of her. I got the picture. And I certainly wouldn't go out with someone who "got a little rough." Made me happy I hadn't gotten into his car the other day.

I pressed the needle to his skin.

"It's none of my business," I said softly, focusing on my work.

He didn't say anything.

I didn't know whether that was a good thing or bad.

Not that it mattered much right now. I went through the motions, the machine's gentle whirring echoing in my head and blocking out everything else. I was in my zone.

Finally, I sat up and took my foot off the pedal. I gently wiped the last of the ink off the tattoo. What had been a rather boring tattoo before stood out now. I'd added some embellishment to the dagger hilts, gold swirling through the silver, showing off the stark black and white of the skull.

Will Parker stared at it.

"Is it okay?" I asked. The worst thing is when a client hates what I've done. It doesn't happen much, but it's happened a couple of times. Although admittedly more in the early days of my career.

Will swallowed hard, then looked at me. "It's fantastic. I had no idea you were so good."

I swiveled my chair around so I could put the tattoo machine on the shelf. The inks would be thrown away, as would the needles I'd used. Everything was disposable. Much like Will Parker. Those bruises had told me more about him than any sexy smile, and I wasn't willing to go there.

When I turned back to him, he saw it in my face.

"It was a one-night stand," he tried.

I shrugged. "Like I said, none of my business. Let me get some stuff for you about how to take care of the tattoo, and I'll cover it up before you leave so it won't get all over your shirt."

He tried a grin on for size. "I never want to cover it up."

I smiled back, but it wasn't as enthusiastic. "Thanks for the endorsement. Tell your friends." I slapped a bandage over it anyway.

I went out to the front desk, where Bitsy and Tim were deep in conversation. When I approached, they both looked up, startled as if I'd interrupted something important.

"If I didn't know better, I'd think you two had something going on," I teased.

They exchanged a furtive look, and I frowned.

"Don't tell me . . ."

Tim put his hand up. "No, no, Brett, it's nothing."

But from the look on Bitsy's face, I knew it was definitely more than "nothing." She tried to cover it up by asking, "So how's it going in there?" and giving me a sly grin.

I shrugged. "The tattoo came out pretty good."

She frowned. "But what about *him*?"

I leaned toward her, and Tim leaned in, too, so he could hear.

"He's into some rough stuff with women," I whispered.

"He told you that?" Bitsy exclaimed.

"Shh!" I put my finger to my lips. "No, but he's got bruises on his hand, and he said he'd been with someone and it got rough."

"Maybe he's into bondage," Tim suggested, his eyes twinkling with amusement. "You sure you're not up for that?"

I slapped his arm. "Give me a break. Maybe *you* are."

I grabbed a sheet with tattoo-aftercare instructions out of the desk drawer. I waved it in front of Bitsy's face. "Need to make more copies," I said, going back to my room and Will Parker.

He didn't expect me back quite so quickly. When I stepped through the door, his back was to me. He was holding my tattoo machine and fiddling with the power source.

I cleared my throat loudly and went over to him, taking the machine.

"I'd thank you to leave my things alone," I said, my voice cold as I checked the power source. He'd changed the settings.

"I didn't know how it worked," he tried.

"If you'd asked me, I could've shown you." I thrust the paper at him. "Here. This tells you how to take care of it."

"Should I come back and have you check on it?" He tried that seductive smile on me, but it was a bad move. It put me in a worse mood.

"Do what the instructions tell you. And Bitsy will take your payment out front."

He stood there a second, as if I was messing with him. "Is your brother still here?" he asked.

"What? Oh, right, yeah." Maybe he thought I'd sic Tim on him over the bruises. I turned my back on him, and as I fiddled with the power source, putting all the settings back where they belonged, he went out to see Bitsy.

"Psst!"

I turned at the sound to see Joel frowning in my door. He kept glancing out toward the front desk.

"What's going on?" I asked.

"You didn't just ink that guy, did you?" Joel's voice was barely above a whisper. I could hear Bitsy and Will talking out front.

I nodded. "Sure. Only a touch-up, though. Nice tattoo. Skull with daggers."

"He's been here before."

"Sure he has. He came by yesterday. He was going on a job interview here at the Venetian."

"No, no, that's not it," Joel said, his voice getting higher with anxiety. He'd stepped inside my room now.

"What's up, Joel?"

Joel's eyes were wide.

"He was here with that guy you found dead in your trunk."

Chapter 37

"What do you mean? He was here with Ray Lucci?" I asked. "Bitsy never said anything about him, and she was here, too."

Joel was shaking his head so hard I thought it would bounce off.

"She wasn't here when they got here. She came in late. Dentist or something. I don't know. All I do know is, that guy came in here with Franklin, or Lucci, or whatever his name was. He didn't stay long, but long enough to poke around in my room while I was getting my inks together."

I remembered how Will Parker had been messing with my clip cord and then my power source. I had another thought.

"He wasn't in there alone, was he?" I asked.

Joel's hand shot to his mouth, covering it, and I knew. Parker had been alone.

"I had to go get some red ink from the storage room. I was out. I wasn't gone but a few minutes. He was gone when I got back."

Probably with Joel's clip cord.

"You didn't tell the cops about him."

Joel sighed, his hand dropping down to his side. "I forgot all about him until I saw him now. It was a crazy morning. The phone kept ringing, we actually had a couple of walk-ins, and I had to schedule appointments." He paused. "Which Bitsy had to reschedule. I never said I was good at that."

"I didn't say you were. It just seems like this was pretty important, and you forgot."

Joel snorted. "It's this diet. I'm forgetting all sorts of things. It's like my brain is hardwired for sugar, and without it, I'm a complete mess. I'm so sick of meat."

I reached over and rubbed his arm in support. "I'm sorry," I said softly but then jerked my hand away. Joel frowned.

"We need to stop Will Parker," I said. "Where's Tim?"

I didn't wait for an answer. I went down the hall to the staff room, where Tim was leaning back in a chair, his feet up on the table, leafing through a tattoo magazine. He grinned and waved the magazine when I came in.

"Interesting stuff," he said.

"I don't have time for that now," I said, launching into what Joel told me about Will Parker being here with Ray Lucci.

A few words in, Tim pulled himself up and looked like a cat about to pounce. "Where is he now?"

"He left," Joel said from the doorway.

"How long ago?"

Too long ago, but I didn't want to burst his bubble if he thought he could catch up with him. "I don't know, a few minutes," I said.

Tim grabbed my arm.

"Hey!"

"You have to come with me. I only saw him for a few seconds; I don't know if I'd be able to pick him out of a crowd," he said.

We passed Bitsy, whose expression was asking what the heck was going on. I said, "Joel will fill you in," just as Tim pulled me out of the shop.

Once on the walkway, we stopped abruptly, Tim's head swiveling from right to left and back again.

"Do you see him anywhere?"

It had really been too long. I doubted we'd track him down now, but it was worth a shot. However, all I saw was tourists. I shook my head. Something told me to go toward St. Mark's Square, toward where the Renaissance dancers perform, and I started to walk in that direction.

A gondola sailed past, the gondolier's even strokes moving it along the canal. With Tim following, I went up the small footbridge over the canal. From the top of the bridge, I could see farther, so I scanned the crowds on both sides of the water and then in the square. There was no music now; there were no dancers prancing about, only the sound of chatter and a line at the gelato place.

"I think it's a lost cause," I told Tim. "I should've immediately gone after him, after Joel told me. But I didn't quite understand at first what he was telling me."

Tim tugged my arm and led me over the bridge. "Come on," he said. "You never know if he stopped somewhere along the way."

"Right. He probably went to the garage and got his car." As I spoke, Tim and I stared at each other.

"Well, that was pretty stupid of us," I added. "Considering one of us is a police officer. A detective, no less."

Tim rolled his eyes as we went back over the bridge and weaved our way around one of the small walkways that led away from the canal. I didn't have a chance to ogle the shoes in Kenneth Cole, as I usually do, although I did see Ace at the oxygen bar again. There should be a twelve-step program for air addicts.

We rounded the corner, passed the newsstand and kiosk, and pushed the glass doors open, making our way down the ramp and then through another set of glass doors into the parking garage. We stared at the concrete and the lines of cars.

"Another brilliant idea, Watson," Tim said.

The parking garage was huge. He could've parked anywhere.

Tim's Impala sat nearby.

Tim crossed the pavement toward the car. I scurried to keep up.

As we reached the door, the roar of an engine echoed through the garage, and I gave a little jump. A blue car screamed around the corner and sped up as it came toward us. Tim grabbed my shoulders and pulled me farther into the parking spot, wedged between the Impala and an SUV. The blue car flew around the corner and out of sight.

My heart was pounding, and from the way Tim was clutching his chest, I could tell his was, too.

But my heart was pounding because it was a total déjà vu.

"It was a blue car that tried to run me and Bitsy down yesterday," I whispered.

Tim's head whipped around, and he stared at me.

"Was it the same car?"

"I don't know," I said honestly. "Both times the car was moving so fast, I didn't have time to even notice the make of the car."

"It was a Ford," Tim said. "I only caught half of the license plate."

I regretted the snide teasing about him being a detective and not thinking clearly. This was why he was the cop and I wasn't.

He was already walking back toward the Grand Canal Shoppes. I skipped along behind him.

"So what do we do now?" I asked.

"Now I try to find out the rest of that license plate and who was driving that car. As for you, well, I think you have work to do, don't you?" he said matter-of-factly, holding open the glass door for me. Our mother would have been pleased. But then again, she was always pleased with her only son.

"But I'm a witness, too," I tried. "And what if it was Will Parker? I know what he looks like." I paused. "Will Parker does drive a blue car."

He stopped short, outside Kenneth Cole. There was a new pair of red patent leather pumps in the window. For a second I was distracted.

"You're sure he drives a blue car?" Tim asked.

I nodded. "I saw it the day I met him at the wedding chapel."

"Well, that makes it easier," Tim mused.

"Because you can check out Will Parker's driver information now, right?" I asked, pretty pleased with myself.

Tim started walking again. "You think you're smart, don't you?" he teased.

"We *are* cut from the same cloth," I said. "So if Will Parker stole Joel's clip cord, do you think he's the one who killed Ray Lucci?"

We'd reached the shop, and Tim pulled the door open.

"You never know," he said.

Bitsy hopped up from her seat at the front desk.

"Did you find him?" she asked.

We shook our heads.

"Don't you have your clients fill out forms with all their information?" Tim asked.

Bitsy nodded, knowing what he was looking for. She reached for the file folder with Will Parker's information in it. She handed it to Tim.

He opened it, scanning the forms, then looked up at Bitsy. "Credit card?"

Bitsy shook her head. "He paid in cash."

"I need a little privacy. Can I use the computer in your office?" Tim asked.

"Sure," I said, following him down the hall and into the office next to the staff room. I indicated the laptop on the desk.

Tim gave me a look.

"What?" I asked.

He knew he wasn't going to get rid of me. He sat behind the desk and booted up the laptop. After a few seconds, he connected to the Internet and pulled up Google Maps. I looked over his shoulder as he put in Will Parker's address.

Tim zoomed in to the location, then leaned back in his chair and pointed at the screen. "What's wrong with this picture?" he asked.

I peered at the screen and did a double take. It wasn't a residential neighborhood.

The address was for an In-N-Out Burger.

On Dean Martin Drive.

Chapter 38

"The guy pays in cash and puts an In-N-Out as his address," Tim mused. "What's up with this?"

I was still hung up on Dean Martin Drive. Was that some sort of joke? He was a Dean Martin impersonator, so he just happens to pick that In-N-Out Burger? Couldn't have been a coincidence. I pointed that out to Tim.

Tim sat back up and reached for the keyboard. He started tapping. Yahoo! People Search. Will Parker. Las Vegas.

Five hits.

"What if he lives in Summerlin or Henderson or North Las Vegas?" I asked.

Tim scowled at me. Okay, so I threw a wrench into his brilliant plan.

"Why don't you call the wedding chapel and see if they'll give you his real address? They must have it. And you *are* the cops," I said.

"But I'm not on this case," he reminded me.

"So call Flanigan," I said.

He didn't like that idea, though. I could see it in the way his brow furrowed, his eyes narrowing. It was the same sort of look our father got when he was stumped by something. Tim wasn't supposed to be investigating because I, his sister, was directly involved. He was supposed to babysit me so I would stay out of the way. But that look, the one I knew all too well, meant that he was going to go a little rogue.

"Can I go with you?" I asked.

"Go with me where?"

"Wherever you're going to find Will Parker. The wedding chapel's probably a good place to start. And will you call the department about that partial license plate number?" I was talking so fast I hoped he wouldn't have time to say no.

"Don't you have a client coming in?" Tim reminded me about Colin Bixby's unexpected appointment. "You need to stay here."

"He's not getting a tattoo," I said, again wondering what it was Colin Bixby wanted to talk to me about. Why he'd need to make an actual appointment. Maybe he *was* getting another tattoo. But somehow I didn't think he'd want *me* to do it. It was far too intimate the last time, and despite the little peck last night outside the emergency room, I didn't think we'd moved too far beyond the fact that he was still hurt by my previous unfounded suspicions.

"Brett, you can't go with me." Tim's tone sounded as it did when he told me I couldn't go backpacking with him to Europe the summer after he graduated from college. But this was a totally different thing. And I said so.

"No, it's not," Tim said. "Flanigan would have my ass if he knew I was out checking up on things, and especially if you were with me."

"But you're going to do it anyway," I tried.

"You have a business to run."

I didn't want to tell him that Bitsy was doing a fine job running things while I was out playing detective. He didn't have to know that, and I didn't want to think about it too much myself. While it was a good thing I had such a trusted employee, I knew it was wrong to count on her as much as I did. Even though I'd recently given her a nice raise.

"If Will Parker took Joel's clip cord, then I have a vested interest in all this," I said. "Not to mention that Ray Lucci was found in my trunk with possibly that very same clip cord wrapped around his neck."

"Okay, I get it," Tim said, "but I can't let you go with me."

I had one more card to play.

"If you leave me alone, then how do you know I'm not going to go out on my own anyway?"

"You don't have a car," he said.

Oops. Forgot that small matter. But I did have friends who had cars, who'd lent me cars in the past when I needed a way around.

Tim knew what I was thinking. "You can't call Coleman."

"How will you know if I do or not?" I asked, jutting out my chin defiantly.

"You can promise me you won't."

"And I can cross my fingers so it won't count."

We sounded exactly as we did when we were kids, when Tim would want to go off and I tried to finagle my way into his plans. Nothing changes. Except now he didn't have our mom to intervene and tell me to let him alone.

Tim shoved his chair away from the desk and got up, combing his hands through his hair. Exasperated.

"You won't let up until I say you can go with me, will you?" he asked.

"No."

"If you go with me, you have to let me do all the talking. You need to stay out of my way."

I tried not to grin too widely as I followed him out of the office.

Bitsy said Colin Bixby wasn't coming in for another two hours. She didn't grill me about where we were going, because Tim was with me, and she didn't want him to think she was a nag. I knew she'd get me later. But by then maybe I'd have some answers.

Tim and I didn't talk as we went out to the Impala. We climbed in, and I wondered how long the silence would last. We wound around the garage until Tim pulled out of the parking lot onto Koval Lane, waiting at the light to turn up to the Strip. He turned on the CD player, and the Ramones sang "What a Wonderful World."

I tapped my foot in time with the music—as well as someone who's tone-deaf can—as the palm trees cast their shadows across the road, tourists traveled in packs at the crosswalks.

"So why didn't you call to find out about Will Parker?" I asked, breaking the silence.

"Better in person."

"So you can show your badge. Prove who you are."

He didn't agree or disagree, but I figured that's what it was.

It wasn't until we pulled into the driveway at That's Amore Wedding Chapel that I realized Tony DellaRocco might wonder why I was here with Tim when I was supposed to be marrying Jeff Coleman.

I told Tim about my concern.

He grinned as he pulled off his shades. "Then I guess you'd better wait in the car." And he opened the door and jumped out.

Great. Now he wouldn't tell me what he found out because he wouldn't have to.

Business was down today. There were no cars with brides and grooms waiting to be married. No Dean Martins serenading.

I glanced across the street at the Elvis wedding chapel.

A line stretched almost onto the Strip. Three cars and a stretch limo with a logo on its side that I couldn't read.

Maybe word about the dead Dean Martins had spread, scaring away the married-to-be. Being serenaded by a Dean Martin who might end up dead the next day probably wouldn't bode well. Although it could be a good story if the marriage lasted.

I thought about how Will Parker had said the Elvis chapel owner—Sanderson, I think his name was—had tried to steal away the Dean Martins and turn them into Elvises. But I couldn't exactly rely on Parker to tell the truth now that I knew he lived in an In-N-Out Burger and he'd possibly stolen Joel's clip cord.

I wondered how long Tim would be.

Would it be long enough so I could go check out the Elvises?

Tim had gone inside, and there was no sign of him. I

opened my door and stepped out, knowing he wouldn't exactly condone this—but what else was I going to do? He'd
taken the keys, and I couldn't listen to any music. I was
bored.

I made my way to a crosswalk and pressed the button
to wait for the walking-man sign, all the time glancing back
to see if Tim had emerged from the building. By the time
the little green man flashed, Tim was still inside, so I jogged
across the street.

The Elvis chapel was even more tacky than That's
Amore, with tall white Greek columns at its driveway entrance and a high trellis with some sort of fake white flowers and greenery. I skirted behind the limo, hearing the
Elvis now, singing about how he was in love and all shook
up.

Whatever floats your boat, I guess.

I preferred That's Amore. But I've never been an Elvis
fan.

"No walk-ups!" The booming voice from somewhere to
my left made me jump.

Chapter 39

He was a big guy, not just heavy but maybe about two hundred pounds overweight. His jowls sagged into his ample
neck, which pillowed above his broad chest. Because of his
size, he wasn't really walking. It was more like waddling.

He stopped next to me, his hands clutched together in
front of his big belly. He had a swath of jet-black hair in
a pompadour, like Elvis's, and wore a stretchy white satin
bodysuit that should not have been part of such a large
man's wardrobe. He totally needed *What Not to Wear*.

"No walk-ups," he repeated, staring at me as if I had
three heads.

"I'm just pricing," I tried, wishing for the first time that
Jeff Coleman was with me. He was much better at this than
I was. "My boyfriend—um—fiancé and I want a wedding
that will be memorable."

A wide smile that matched his girth spread across his
face. "You'll get that here, at the Love Shack."

I hadn't noticed the name of the chapel on the heart-
shaped sign because the Elvis cutout was so large. But
Love Shack? Really? I mean, didn't he realize that was the
B-52s and not Elvis? At least Tony DellaRocco kept the
Dean Martin theme in the name of his chapel.

He stuck out his hand. "Martin Sanderson."

I took his hand, and he gripped mine tightly, pumping it
up and down as if he were trying to get water from a well. I
tried gently to pull away, finally having to resort to force. I
yanked back so fast I almost fell over. Sanderson laughed.

"You're a skinny little thing," he commented. "So have you been across the street?"

He must have seen me at the crosswalk.

I nodded. "They've got a good special going."

"I can do better. I've also got one of their former singers. He's much better as Elvis than Dean Martin."

Until a couple of days ago I had no idea there were wedding-chapel-theme feuds going on.

"I—um—like Dino," I tried.

"Elvis was the King," Sanderson said flatly.

"True," I agreed, "but he died on the toilet."

"Adds to the man's mystique." He was totally serious.

"So what are your rates?" I asked.

"Bring your own car, ten bucks."

Really? "How can you keep your business going with that price?" I asked.

He grinned. "Most couples don't want the quickie. They want the limo"—he pointed over to a limo with an image of Elvis plastered on its side—"and the rest of the amenities."

"Which are what?"

"Flowers. Serenading."

"So if I got the ten-buck special, I don't get Elvis serenading me?"

"Sorry." But he certainly didn't seem sorry.

"I can get the Dean Martins with any package across the street."

He snorted. Not a pleasant sound.

"That chapel's on its way out. No one wants to get married in a place where people are getting murdered."

That was my in. "Murdered?"

Sanderson waved a hand in the air. "Oh, one of the Dinos was killed a couple of days ago. Another one got hit by a car and killed. One of them has disappeared. Fortunately one of them came over here and probably saved his life."

"He switched sides?"

Sanderson gave me a look and then bellowed with laughter. "You're a card."

Right.

I wondered how I could talk to Alan, the guy who shed his Dino persona for Elvis. There wasn't really a segue into that, it seemed. It would tip off Sanderson that I was here for something other than pricing weddings.

"Would you like to come in and see what we can offer?" Sanderson asked, indicating I should follow him into the building, which seemed to replicate That's Amore.

I glanced across the street to see whether Tim had emerged. So far, no. The Impala sat by itself in the lot. I wondered what was taking so long, what he was finding out about Will Parker.

I followed Sanderson.

Rather than the bland concrete of That's Amore, the decor of the Love Shack was much more elaborate, like a real church chapel dressed up for Halloween. The walls were draped with white satin; marble stands sported simple vases with sprays of flowers. As we passed them, I touched one and found that the flowers were fake. We walked along a long red-carpeted hallway down to an actual chapel, although Sister Mary Eucharista would no doubt beg to differ. The whole place was white, with more flowers attached to long white pews. An altar sat at the end of the runner, but there were no crosses or communion plates or baptismal fonts. Instead, large speakers dominated the corners, and the strains of "Blue Suede Shoes" were emanating softly from them.

This was Elvis's chapel. Not God's. Although I'm sure Elvis fans would think those were one and the same.

I much preferred the Rat Pack across the street.

"This," Sanderson said, sweeping his arm across the room for effect, "is our alternative for those couples who might want a real church rather than the front seats of their cars."

I did have to hand it to him. It made good business sense.

"Oh, I didn't realize—"

The female voice from behind us startled me, and I turned to see a rather homely older woman in an unflattering brown tweed skirt and a wrinkled button-down blouse.

She shifted slightly, tugging at the skirt as though it were tight. It wasn't.

The whole Love Shack staff needed Stacy and Clinton's fashion expertise.

"Miss Gardner, this is . . ." Sanderson turned to me, his eyebrows high, asking me without asking me what my name was.

"Bitsy," I said without thinking. "Bitsy Hendricks." She would kill me if she found out I was taking her name in vain, but I wasn't willing to give my real name here.

Miss Gardner's eyes traveled down the tattoo sleeves on my arms, and I could swear she was channeling Sister Mary Eucharista. Not good for me.

"Are you here with your beloved?" she asked.

I shook my head. "No. He's working. I told him I'd come over and check it out." I'm not a good liar, and I felt my face flush.

She was onto me. Her face hardened and her eyes narrowed for a second before she turned to Sanderson.

"You've got a phone call," she said. "It's urgent." Her tone left no doubt that if he didn't answer this call right now, something horrible would happen, like world peace would never be achieved.

Sanderson gave me a sheepish smile. "Excuse me a minute, Miss Hendricks," he said, and went out of the chapel and out of sight.

Miss Gardner and I stood awkwardly facing each other. I shifted from foot to foot, not quite sure what to say.

She broke the ice first.

"You're not here to get married, are you?"

I couldn't get this one past her. "No," I admitted.

"Why are you here?"

She reminded me too much of my childhood and how I'd been reminded every day I'd go to hell if I lied. So I came clean.

"It's the Dean Martins at That's Amore. They're being killed, and I heard that the owner over there and Sanderson have some sort of feud."

Her lips twitched, as if she wanted to smile, but she didn't say anything. So I continued.

"I was wondering if I could talk to Alan, the guy who came over here from there."

"I'm sorry," she said. "He's not here today." She paused. "I'm not really sure what you're looking for, Miss Hendricks. If that's your real name."

I sighed. "It's not."

"My advice to you, miss, is that you go home and forget about all of this."

She was trying to be kind, but a warning laced her voice.

"Forget about what?" I asked.

Miss Gardner reached out and clutched my forearm tight as a vise. She leaned toward me, her breath brushing my cheek. "That Ray Lucci was trouble. The world is better off without him."

Chapter 40

As quickly as she grabbed me, she let me go, turning on her heel and walking swiftly down the aisle, like a bride who'd been jilted and wanted to get out as soon as possible before the questions started.

I stood alone at the altar, wondering exactly what she was talking about. How did she know Ray Lucci?

My cell phone interrupted my thoughts, Springsteen singing "Born to Run" in my bag. I dug it out and glanced at the caller ID. Uh-oh. Tim.

I flipped the phone open and said, "Hey there."

"Forget that crap. Where are you?"

He was angry. Really angry, and I guess I shouldn't have been too surprised.

"I'm across the street."

"Across—" He stopped as he figured out where I was.

I waited.

"I'll be over there in a minute. Be outside."

The call ended, and I stuffed the phone back in my bag, striding down the aisle. As I turned the corner, I bumped into Sanderson, who stepped back slightly and grinned.

"Whoa, where you headed, little lady?"

"My ride is here," I said, trying to step around him.

He moved so I couldn't.

"Who's your ride? Your fiancé?"

"No, my brother," I said firmly, attempting again to sidle past.

He got in my way again. "Your brother?"

It was time to play my hand.

"Yes, Mr. Sanderson. My brother. A Las Vegas police detective. He knows I'm here, so if I'm not out there in a few minutes, he'll come in here and make sure I leave safely."

Sanderson feigned surprise.

"Why wouldn't you leave here safely?"

I shrugged, trying to appear nonchalant, but something about this guy was giving me the willies. "I don't know. I just know he's here, and I have to meet him outside." Again I tried to step around him.

This time he let me squeeze past, so close that I could feel the layers of his flesh against my breasts.

He grinned as he got his cheap thrill.

I scowled. "Thanks for the information," I said.

"You're welcome, Miss Kavanaugh."

I stopped. "Excuse me?"

"Oh, I know who you are. I know you're here because you think I threatened DellaRocco. It's not that way. Believe me. It's the other way around."

"What's the other way around?" Tim would be even more furious with me if he had to wait too long, but I couldn't help myself. "Are you saying he threatened you?"

"He sent his thug over here."

"Thug?" What? Were we in a *Sopranos* episode?

"That ex-con."

"Lucci?"

Sanderson nodded. "That's the one. Says he can make life difficult for me. Well, I turned the tables on him, didn't I?"

He didn't seem to realize what he was saying, but its meaning was not lost on me.

"Did you have something to do with Ray Lucci's murder?" I asked. Sometimes the direct question is the best one.

Or not.

He grabbed my shoulder and shoved me against the wall. I landed with a thud, the wind momentarily knocked out of me.

"Hey!"

We both looked up to see Tim bounding toward us. He pushed Sanderson away from me, and before Sanderson knew it, Tim had his arm twisted up behind him so hard I could see tears forming in Sanderson's eyes.

Tim looked at me. "Are you okay?"

I nodded, standing up straight, trying to catch my breath.

Tim turned to Sanderson. "I could take you in right now for assault."

I rarely saw my brother at work. I was used to him lounging around the living room in a pair of jeans and a T-shirt, a beer in one hand, his other hand in a bag of chips, while he watched whatever game was on the big-screen TV. Sometimes there was a woman, usually not the same one from week to week. After Shawna and their three-year relationship, he was playing the field. I didn't blame him.

But now, his eyes were dark, his face tight, his voice deep with his threat. His muscles bulged in his arm as he strengthened his hold on Sanderson. He was all cop, and it scared me a little, like it was scaring Sanderson. Because, despite the hefty girth on the man and Tim's definitely thinner frame, Sanderson looked as if he was about to pee his pants at any second. If Tim pulled his gun, it would be all over.

"I didn't mean anything," Sanderson finally stammered.

Tim swung him around as if he weren't any heavier than a bag of potatoes. He let go of Sanderson's arm and put his hands on his hips, his feet planted on the ground like a cop in one of those TV reality shows.

"You did mean something, and if I ever find out that you did anything like that again, to my sister or to any woman, I'll come after you. And believe me, you don't want that to happen."

Scared the crap out of me, and I wasn't even on the receiving end.

Sanderson nodded like a bobblehead doll. "Yessir," he said, even though he must have had at least twenty years on Tim. But cops have that effect on people.

Tim turned his stare to me. "Are you ready?"

I nodded and shifted my bag a little farther up my shoulder.

Tim put his hand at the small of my back and steered me toward the door and outside. The glare hit my eyes, and I squinted, rummaging in my bag for my sunglasses. I slipped them on.

Tim opened the car door for me, and I climbed inside, settling into the seat, pulling my seat belt around me, and clicking it in. He got into the driver's seat and started the engine.

But then he turned to me. "You're not off the hook, you know, just because that guy was tossing you around in there."

I glared at him. "So you're going to finish what he started?" I challenged.

"Don't tempt me."

"He said Lucci came over and threatened him."

Tim's hands tightened on the steering wheel. "Did he say that?"

"I heard that Sanderson was trying to steal the Dean Martins. He got one of them. Alan something or other. I thought maybe Sanderson had something to do with what was going on, but he says it was the other way around. That DellaRocco was threatening him. Using Lucci as muscle."

Tim snorted. "Someone's lying."

It was the way he said it that made me take notice.

"What did DellaRocco say?"

Tim braked at the red light, and we sat idling. He stared straight at the light, as if willing it to change. I opened my mouth to ask my question again, but before I could, he spoke.

"DellaRocco said he found ten thousand dollars in a duffel bag in Lucci's locker the day Lucci was killed."

Chapter 41

My mouth hung open, and I couldn't find any words at first. Finally, I sputtered, "In cash?" My brain was working overtime, and it got hung up on something, but I needed to think about it a little first. See whether I was off base.

Tim nodded. The light turned green, and we continued down the Strip, Circus Circus to our left, the big top beckoning.

"He told the cops?" I asked.

Tim nodded again. "Flanigan."

"But Flanigan didn't tell you?"

"I'm not on the case, remember? The guy's body was in your car. I'm not supposed to be doing anything."

"So how did DellaRocco manage to mention this to you?" I asked.

"He thought I knew. He said something about the ten grand—had we figured out where it came from yet?—and I played along and, after a little more conversation, managed to put it together."

"Do you think DellaRocco will tell Flanigan you were here?" I worried a little about his job, but only a little. Tim had a way about him, something that let him get away with stuff that normal people couldn't. He could talk his way out of anything, like when he brought his girlfriend home way after curfew in high school and her father started to get on his case. He smooth talked his way out of it, and the father ended up taking him to a basketball game the next week.

"DellaRocco didn't exactly like Flanigan," Tim said. "They got off on the wrong foot."

That was good.

"So DellaRocco didn't know where the money came from?"

We stopped at another light. I could see the Eiffel Tower several blocks down, hovering over the Strip rather than the Seine.

"He assumes it has something to do with his death."

"Duh."

Tim chuckled. "You have a way with words. You know that, little sis?"

I punched him on the arm.

"So I don't get it," I said as the car started to move again after a minute. "Ray Lucci steals my car but leaves ten thousand bucks in his locker? Why didn't he take the money with him?"

"I have no idea. None of this makes any sense."

I had another thought. "Maybe he did bring the money, and then whoever knocked him off and stuffed him in the trunk took the bag back to the chapel and put it in his locker."

"Major hole in that story, Brett. Why would someone put the money back in the guy's locker? It was cash. It was a load of money. He'd just take it."

Okay, so I wasn't a real detective. I just played around with being one every now and then.

"But it was a thought," Tim said.

"What about Lucci threatening Sanderson?" I asked.

"I don't know about that. DellaRocco said Sanderson was stealing his performers. That's all. Anyway, if he was really threatening Sanderson, he probably wouldn't tell me."

"Probably not," I conceded. "I think we need to find out where that money's from." Although I had an idea.

"Follow the money," Tim said softly, almost as if to himself.

I was torn. If I mentioned the ten thousand dollars that Dan Franklin had withdrawn from his bank account two weeks ago, then he'd ask me how I knew about that. I wasn't sure whether I wanted to admit that Jeff and I stole his bank statement. This would have to be approached delicately, so no one would throw us in jail.

Tim turned into the driveway for the Venetian and steered the Impala into the self-parking lane. We passed under the brick facade of the fake Doge's Palace. Impressive. Looked almost real. If you took away the palm trees, the Mirage, and Treasure Island across the street.

Nah. It would never look even almost real. Because if you took those things away, you'd have only acres of desert. Venice was drowning. You couldn't do that here.

We went around and around in the concrete garage, parking in a spot near the elevator that would take us to the Grand Canal Shoppes. As we got out of the car, Tim looked furtively around him, as if that blue car would appear out of nowhere again and try to run us down.

Nothing this time, though. We got into the elevator and rode in silence to the third level, getting out and going through the walkway and into the mall.

Ace was not at the oxygen bar.

That was a change. Maybe he had a client.

"I need to make a few calls," Tim said.

"You can use the office," I said, wondering when my next client was scheduled.

When we got to my shop, though, my question was answered for me.

Colin Bixby was leaning against the mahogany desk, talking to Bitsy.

They looked up when I pushed the door open. Tim nodded at them and, without a word, went past them to the office in the back. That was odd. He didn't give Colin even a glance. They'd met a few months back, but maybe he didn't recognize him.

Bitsy raised her eyebrows at me, but I gave my head a quick shake, indicating she shouldn't ask now. I forced a smile for Bixby, still unclear why he was here.

"Hi there," I said.

It wasn't quite a smile, just a little hint at the corner of his lips. It seemed he was as unclear about his visit as I was. But I was willing to give him the benefit of the doubt. For once.

"Want to come back?" I asked, giving my head another little shake at Bitsy, whose eyebrows were now almost to her hairline.

Colin followed me to my room, and I indicated he should go in. I closed the door after us.

"Have a seat," I said, waving my hand toward the client chair.

Bixby stood awkwardly, his hands in his pockets, looking at the chair as if it were a wild animal that might bite him.

I laughed. "It's okay," I said. "I don't have my machine on."

The joke didn't do much to change his mood, but he sat tentatively on the edge of the chair. I swung my wheeled chair around and sat next to him.

"I guess you're not here for more ink," I said after a few seconds of loud silence.

The smile peeked out then, and his green eyes flashed. His gaze was intense, and I found myself feeling all hot and bothered, but in a really good way. There was definitely something still between us.

"You seeing anyone?" he asked.

I shook my head, not sure where he was going with this. He could've asked me that the other day or called me to find out. A personal visit wasn't necessary.

"I've been seeing someone." His words were like a gut punch, and I found myself struggling for a breath.

Okay, I was really in the dark now.

"Maybe you should tell me why you're here," I said after a second. My voice sounded oddly disconnected from my body.

"But it's not serious," he continued as if I hadn't said anything at all.

Something inside me switched, and I felt anger rising. He couldn't mess around with me like this. What sort of game was he playing? Sure, I'd screwed things up before, but we'd been perfectly happy not seeing each other. Hadn't we?

"Maybe you should spit it out," I said, the edge in my voice sharp as a knife.

It didn't go unnoticed.

He nodded. "I'm sorry, Brett, but seeing you again has sort of thrown me for a loop. It's brought back some feelings I'd forgotten about. Or tried to forget about."

I remembered what he'd told me when we met at the university the other day. How he'd just about forgotten me. I nodded.

"But I'll tell you why I'm here. I know you're curious."

I wished he'd get on with it.

"It's about Rosalie. Marino."

My confusion about Colin Bixby melted away with the abrupt change of subject.

"What about her?"

"You know about the abuse."

I nodded. "Yeah. I did her tattoos," I admitted. "The purple and white ribbons on her arm. The ones that symbolize survival."

Bixby leaned forward and I could smell his scent: a little citrus and honey with a slight hint of hospital.

"I treated her for the broken bones. The bruises." He paused a second. "And when she lost the baby."

Chapter 42

Now I really felt as though someone had punched me in the gut. Baby?

He saw what I was thinking.

"You didn't know about the baby?"

"No."

"But you're her friend," he said.

I wasn't. I barely knew her. She'd spent a couple of hours right here in this chair, but other than that, my contact with Rosalie Marino had been limited to the last couple of days. Because of our encounter at the university lab, it may have seemed to Bixby as though we were closer than tattooist and client. I shook my head. "No. Not really."

Confusion crossed his face. "But you came to the hospital to see her last night," he said. "I thought—"

"No. We're not friends. But I am friends with her father's new wife and her son. What's this about a baby?"

Colin hung his head in his hands. "I should have known."

He didn't answer my question. "Should have known what?"

"That things with you aren't always as they seem."

Okay, so he was right on that. But he didn't have to act as if it were the end of the world.

"I'm sorry," I said. "But you did come to me about something. Is Rosalie in trouble? I really am friends with the rest of her family."

"Her *new* family," he emphasized. "And I can't say any more than that now."

He shut down, his doctor-client confidentiality held close to the vest now that he knew I wasn't who he thought I was. His eyes skipped around the room, resting finally on the ink pots lined up on the shelf, the tattoo machine on its side.

"Do you want another one?" I asked softly. I'd warned him when I'd given him his Celtic knot on his breast that tattoos are addictive. It's rare to find someone who's content with only one. Maybe he'd never get more than one, but I was willing to bet he thought about it. I had quite a few repeat clients.

When Colin didn't answer, I tried a joke. "How about a stethoscope on your arm?" I could see it, too, how I would design it, and suddenly it wasn't a joke anymore. It could be really cool. The stethoscope could start on his bicep and swirl down to the crook of his arm, where I'd place the chest piece, which he'd use to check someone's blood pressure. I described my idea to him.

Colin Bixby's eyes flickered, and the temptation had been planted. He liked the idea. Liked it a lot.

"You could do that?" he asked tentatively.

"I could draw up something, see if you like it," I said, reaching for my pad and pencil. Quickly I sketched it out, shading here and there, and when I was done, turned it around so he could see it.

"Wow," he whispered, staring at it.

"You could think about it, make an appointment if you think it's something you want to do," I said. The last time he didn't think he would go through with it if I didn't do it right then, so I had. He'd flinched only at the first touch of the needle, didn't even seem as if he'd pass out at all—a problem more common than you'd think— which was why I thought perhaps he might not mind getting more ink. Despite his admission that he didn't like needles.

The thing with the tattoo machine is, the needles only go down into the second layer of skin, where they release the ink. I don't like needles, either, when they go farther than that. Granted, getting a tattoo still hurts, and knowing that the needles pierce the skin only so far is cold comfort.

I put the pad and pencil on the shelf. Colin got up and brushed imaginary lint off his jeans.

"It's possible that since her husband is dead now, Rosalie's going to be okay," I said, wondering whether I could somehow trick him into telling me what he came here to say. I was sure he was here to tell me something so I could either watch out for Rosalie or warn her about something. I didn't think he came just to spread information. That would violate his doctor ethics.

His head snapped up, and he stared at me for a moment. It wasn't one of those sexy stares, but I could see him thinking about something, wondering what he should say next.

Finally, "Did you ever find Dan Franklin?"

The name jolted me out of my thoughts. I thought about the ten thousand dollars again. "No," I admitted. "As far as I know, no one knows where he is."

"You should tell that detective brother of yours to try harder," he said, his hand on the doorknob.

Exasperated, I sighed. "Why can't you tell me why you're here," I said.

He shook his head and then smiled. "I might be back for that tattoo."

I grinned. "It could give you some cred with those guys who come into the ER."

He pushed the door open and went out into the hall and down to the front desk, where Bitsy sat facing us as if she'd been waiting the whole time for us to emerge.

"Care to make an appointment, Doctor?" she asked politely, but I could hear the curiosity in her voice.

Colin Bixby gave me a look that curled my toes, his green eyes all smoky and sexy, before saying, "Maybe. I'll call."

And he went out the door without looking back.

Bitsy and I stared after him.

"What did he want?" she asked.

"I have no clue," I admitted. "He wanted to tell me something about Rosalie Marino. He thought we were friends. But all he ended up saying was that we need to find Dan Franklin."

"What about Franklin?"

Tim's voice from behind made us both jump.

I related what Bixby told me.

"Pretty cryptic," Tim said, running a hand through his hair.

"It's pretty clear she lost a baby because of the abuse," I said. "But I'm not sure what Dan Franklin would have to do with that."

"He works with her," Bitsy piped up. "Maybe he's got the hots for her. Maybe he killed her husband."

Tim and I exchanged a look.

"Has Flanigan actually looked for Franklin?" I asked him, thinking that if Flanigan focused on Franklin, it was likely he'd find out about the ten grand and I'd be off the hook.

"I have no idea. *You're* my assignment," he said with a shrug.

I thought about what Bitsy said, about Franklin possibly killing Rosalie's husband. Maybe Franklin was one of those guys who decided to go after men who abused women. I voiced my thoughts.

Tim sighed. "That's possible, I suppose."

It was the only idea I had at the moment. But what about Ray Lucci? There *was* that rat.

The phone rang, interrupting us.

Bitsy picked it up. "The Painted Lady," she said.

After a few seconds, she looked up at me and handed me the receiver. "Jeff Coleman."

I took the phone. "Hi, Jeff." I hadn't talked to him since the previous day, when he came to take Sylvia and Bernie to Rosalie at the hospital. "How's Rosalie holding up?"

"Listen, Kavanaugh, you and I both know that Rosalie

is better off without that scumbag. I don't even care if the cops never find the guy who did this."

The words hung between us for a second before he spoke again.

"But I think I know who did it."

Chapter 43

"Who do you think killed Lou?" I asked.

"Dan Franklin."

Everything seemed to come back to him.

"Why him?" I had my own suspicions, but I wanted to know his.

"That car's gone."

"What car?"

"That Ford Taurus we saw in his driveway."

I gave a quick glance at Tim, who was watching me intently. He raised his eyebrows, wordlessly asking me what was going on, but I shook him off.

"So that could mean anything," I said.

"Maybe. Except that Detective Flanigan said they think it was a blue car that hit Lou."

"They think? Don't they know the color?" In books and on TV, the cops always know the color of the cars in hit-and-runs. They can even track down the kind of paint to determine what make of car it was. I had no reason to think they couldn't do that in real life, too.

"He didn't want to say for sure. Maybe they've still got tests to do or something. But Franklin's car is blue."

So was Will Parker's, but I wasn't sure what Parker's motive would be. Dan Franklin seemed a better suspect at the moment.

"So what are you up to, Kavanaugh?"

It was the way he said it that made me wonder what was up with him.

"I'm working."

"What did your brother say about the gun?"

"Oh, that. Well, it sort of got all messed up. I was on my way over to see Rosalie—"

"She said you never showed."

"No, I didn't. I was talking on my cell phone, and a cop pulled me over."

He chuckled. "You can't tell me that they gave you a ticket."

"Worse than that." I gave Tim another sidelong glance. "He found the gun in the box addressed to Ray Lucci and took me down to see Tim and Flanigan." I didn't want to tell him about Tim's new assignment as my babysitter.

"So what did they say about it? Did they know about this illegal-gun stuff?"

Now that was a question I hadn't asked. "I'm not sure," I said. "They sent me back to work." I paused. "Hey, how do you know Franklin's car is gone?"

"I happened to take a ride over there. The mail in the box is gone, too, along with the newspapers on the stoop. Looks like the man came home after all."

"So he's not dead."

Tim's eyebrows were just about popping off the top of his head, and Bitsy was hanging on my every word.

"Probably not."

It was killing me that I couldn't hop in my car and drive over to see for myself. Maybe after Tim and I got home and after he went to sleep, I could take a little midnight stroll over to Franklin's house.

Maybe I *was* too nosy, as Tim said. Because even to me that sounded a little crazy.

"Listen, Kavanaugh, gotta run. I'll give you a call tomorrow." And then he was gone.

I hung up the phone, putting up my hand before Tim could speak.

"Flanigan says they think it was a blue car that hit Lou Marino."

Tim pondered that a second, but as he opened his

mouth, Bitsy said, "Like that blue car that came after us at the university?"

And like that blue car that almost hit me and Tim in the parking garage. Was it the same car? Who knew? Franklin and Will Parker both had blue cars.

I shrugged.

"Why does he think it's Franklin?" Tim finally got to ask a question.

"He says Franklin drives a blue Taurus. It was in his driveway, and now it's not." Oops. Might have been a little more information than I wanted to give.

Tim caught on. "How does he know it was in his driveway and now it's not?"

I sighed. "Okay, Jeff and I went over to Dan Franklin's house. We saw the car in the driveway. There was also a pile of mail in his box and newspapers on the stoop, and Jeff says those are gone now, too. So Franklin came home after being gone for what looks like a couple of days."

Tim's face was so red I thought he was going to have a coronary.

"You have to stop this, Brett."

Bitsy took that as her cue to skedaddle off to the staff room. She saw what was coming.

I was tired of it, though. "Okay, fine, I've been doing a little snooping. But it's only to help."

"Do I need to lock you up in the house until all this is resolved?"

Now that was going a little too far, and even he knew it. Tim threw up his hands, said, "I give up," and went to join Bitsy back in the staff room.

I sat at the front desk, watching the people milling around outside. Suddenly I needed to feel not so much like a prisoner anymore. I also needed chocolate. Godiva was across the canal.

"Anyone want chocolate?" I asked loudly.

Joel's head stuck out from his room. "I do," he said gleefully.

"Can you have that on your diet?" I asked sternly.

He took a deep breath and said, "I don't really care."

Joel was back.

I grinned. Call me an enabler.

Tim was standing in the staff room doorway.

"I'm going across to Godiva," I said, getting up and going around to the front door. "Want anything?"

He must have been as tired of me as I was of him because he shook his head and disappeared again. I could hear his and Bitsy's voices murmuring, but I ignored them as I pushed the door open and stepped outside.

I could just keep walking, I thought as I strolled along the canal to the end, where a line of tourists awaited their turn in a gondola. A glance back at the shop told me Tim wasn't waiting in the doorway, watching me. I saw the top of Bitsy's head, but no one else.

I stepped up my pace and didn't round the end of the canal as I should've if I was going to Godiva. Instead, I moved into the Shoppes at the Palazzo, passing Michael Kors's store, not even pausing briefly to admire the shimmering cobalt strapless gown in the window—although I promised myself I'd be back later to check it out—and going around the maze of walkways until I faced Double Helix, the bar.

I really wanted a drink. But more than that, I wanted to feel a little invisible.

The problem was, I was all too visible.

The hand gripped my shoulder, and I felt his hot breath on the back of my neck as he said, "Just the person I was looking for."

I tried to turn around, but I couldn't.

"Who are you?" I asked. "I'll scream."

"Don't scream." Anxiety laced his voice, and he loosened his grip, moving around so he was facing me.

I recognized him then. From his ID picture.

Dan Franklin.

Chapter 44

All I could think about was how Jeff Coleman said he thought Dan Franklin killed Lou Marino. It wasn't the most calming of thoughts. I felt my heartbeat ratchet up, thumping in my chest as if it were trying to break free. Sort of like I'd been when I left the shop just moments ago.

Bad move.

I found my voice. "Where have you been?" I was surprised it came out so normally, as if I were just meeting an old friend for drinks at the bar. "And why are you looking for *me*?"

"I heard you were at my house."

"How did you hear that?"

"With neighbors like mine, who needs a security system?"

"They must have pretty good vision," I said.

"You sort of stand out. You're so tall, and you've got that red hair." He cocked his head toward my arm with the koi swimming on it. "Not to mention the tats."

That's right. I wasn't wearing my jacket when Jeff and I were poking around Franklin's house.

"You made a positive ID on me from that?" I clicked my tongue. "I find that hard to believe. It could've been anyone. How did you know to look for me?"

"You did call me. We spoke. I looked you up online."

He'd found the Web site, as I suspected.

"So what do you want?" I asked, knowing now that I

couldn't weasel my way out of this. "Why are you grabbing me?"

Granted, this might not be the way to talk to a possible killer, but despite what Jeff Coleman had said to me, I wasn't getting that vibe off Franklin. Not anymore, anyway, after that first moment. As I assessed his appearance, too, I saw that he couldn't be less threatening. He did look remarkably like Dean Martin, much more so than Will Parker, who needed the wig and the tux to complete the transformation. Franklin was tall, his dark hair a little wavy, his eyes small, his face long and jowly. He wore a pair of beige slacks and a button-down shirt under a Windbreaker.

Dan Franklin looked as if he was heading out for a game of golf.

He indicated Double Helix. "Can I buy you a drink?"

I'd come over here for that, so why not? Maybe I'd get some questions answered, so I could stop snooping around and Tim could stop babysitting me.

We went around to the entrance of the bar. It felt like an amusement-park ride, with a low wall circling the bar and the rest of the place open-air. We slid onto two barstools, and the bartender came over.

"What can I get you?"

Franklin looked at me, waiting for me to order first. He really didn't seem like a killer right now.

"Margarita," I said, "rocks, salt."

"Gin and tonic," Dan Franklin said.

"No martini?" I asked.

He looked confused a second, then smiled shyly. "Because of the Dean Martin thing, right?"

The bartender busied himself making our drinks, and Franklin tapped his fingers on the bar top.

"Where have you been the last few days?" I asked. What I'd initially thought of as a hostile meeting was turning into something rather civilized.

Franklin stiffened slightly, and if I hadn't been looking for it, I would've missed it.

The bartender put our glasses in front of us, and Franklin took a quick sip, as if he was buying time. I swished the straw around in my margarita before taking it out and sipping from the brim, making sure I got some salt, savoring the tang and the kick of the tequila.

Dan Franklin could take his time if it meant we could sit here and enjoy our drinks.

He seemed to notice that I wasn't exactly pressing him for an answer, and the muscles in his neck relaxed a little. He sipped his own drink before finally saying, "I had to lie low. When you called about Lucci, I knew they'd come after me."

"Who?"

"The cops."

"Why?"

"Why what?"

"Why would they come after you?" I tightened my grip around my glass.

He shifted a little on his stool. "Lucci and I didn't get along."

"Didn't sound like he got along with anyone," I said. "Why do you think the cops would focus on you?"

"Rosalie," he said softly.

"Did you have a relationship with Rosalie?" I asked softly.

His eyes widened, getting that deer-in-headlights look. "No, no, not that way. She's a beautiful woman, but she's married. I respected that."

And I believed him. His reaction seemed sincere, and because of that I also knew he loved her. Was in love with her and had been for a long time.

"How does Lucci figure in all this?" I asked, taking another sip of my drink.

Dan Franklin fidgeted a little more, his foot tapping the rung on the barstool, his fingers drumming his knee. Little beads of sweat started to form on his forehead, and he swallowed hard.

"He found out how I felt about Rosalie. He threatened to tell her husband. And then he killed Snowball."

"Snowball?"

"She was my pet rat. She was so innocent." He wiped his

forehead with the back of his hand, his eyes cast down as he got caught up in the memory.

"Why did he kill her?" I nudged.

"He said she had no business at the chapel. I'd wanted to keep her there for one shift. She wasn't feeling good. I told him that, and then when I came back from my serenade, she was dead in her cage."

"Are you sure he killed her?"

Dan Franklin gave a little high-pitched sob. "Of course he said he had nothing to do with it. But her neck was broken."

Much like Dan Franklin's heart, it seemed. But none of this really explained why he'd gone missing. So he had a dead rat, and he suspected the murder victim to be the killer.

I opened my mouth to ask another question, but he was shrugging out of his jacket. It fell against the stool back, and as he reached over to pick up his glass, I saw it.

The tattoo.

It said "That's Amore" on his arm.

Chapter 45

He caught me staring.

"It's not what you think," he said, a little panicky.

What? That he really was the guy who came to The Painted Lady after all, and not Ray Lucci? Because that was exactly what I was thinking right that second.

Every muscle in my body was taut. I was ready to run. But I did want some answers, especially now. His gaze had wandered over to the entrance to the bar. I could see him figuring how long it would take him to get over there.

I clamped my hand down on his knee.

"So you've never been in a tattoo shop before, Dan?" I asked, my voice low and possibly a bit threatening.

He started shaking his head so fast I thought it would spin right off his neck.

"No, no, no, I'd never been in *your* shop before," he insisted, moving his leg to try to release my grip, but my hand was holding on pretty tight.

"I don't think I believe you," I said. "This is exactly what my tattooist tattooed on you. Isn't it?"

"It wasn't me."

"What else are you lying about? Is that why you've been hiding? Because you're guilty?"

"I didn't kill him," he hissed.

I took a shot in the dark. "So why did you give him ten thousand dollars?"

"I don't need to answer any of your questions." Dan Franklin pushed himself off the barstool. A piece of paper fluttered to the floor from his pocket as he ran toward the entrance. I started after him, but the bartender stood in my way.

"That's twenty bucks for the drinks," he said, then pointed to the ground. "And can you pick up your garbage?"

I totally did not have time for this right then. I tried to keep an eye on Franklin as I reached in my bag for my wallet, pulled out a twenty, and threw it on the bar before stooping down and picking up the hard piece of paper, which didn't belong to me, thank you very much. The bartender obviously wanted a tip, but I didn't have time. I almost slapped the paper in his hand but instead shoved it in my pocket as I sidled around him, stumbling out of the bar. I couldn't see Franklin any longer. There were three walkways he could've gone down, and I skipped from one to the other, but I didn't spot him.

"What are you doing, Brett? You were supposed to come right back to the shop."

I whirled around to see Tim walking toward me. I said the only thing I knew he'd respond to. "I ran into Dan Franklin. He's got a 'That's Amore' tattoo, like Ray Lucci, and he said Ray Lucci killed his rat, Snowball, and he withdrew ten thousand dollars from his bank account, and I think that's where Lucci got his money. And now he's getting away."

I could see the little wheels of Tim's brain working, and he was coming to the same conclusions I did.

After a couple seconds that felt like hours, Tim pointed down one walkway. "You go down there, and I'll go down this one. They do meet up eventually, right?"

They do, but this place was a maze of walkways and stairs and escalators and elevators. Dan Franklin could be across the street at the Mirage by now.

I jogged along my route and ended up at an ornate railing. As I was looking down at the rather spectacular crystal sculpture in the Palazzo hotel lobby, I saw Dan Franklin power walking past.

"Hey!" I shouted.

He glanced up and gave me a little finger waggle.

"How do we get down there?" Tim had come up next to me.

We had to go back to the escalators by the waterfall and then down to the first floor.

Dan Franklin disappeared.

Tim tugged my arm and said, "Come on." We made our way back around the maze of shops until we got to the escalators. We took the escalator two stairs at a time—at one point I thought I'd somersault forward all the way down—and landed at the bottom with a thud, running straight ahead, through the Palazzo casino and then coming to the statue. We rounded it to the front entrance.

We pushed our way through heavy doors and stood outside, breathing heavily from our workout. Remarkably, I saw Dan Franklin in the distance, on the sidewalk, heading south. But I was tired. I leaned over, my hands on my knees, trying to catch my breath, and the little piece of paper that bartender made me pick up fell out of my pocket and onto the ground.

Something about it caught my eye. I reached down, picked it up, and uncrumpled it.

It was a Las Vegas Monorail ticket.

I shoved it at Tim. "This fell out of Franklin's pocket. He might be going there," I said.

Tim nodded as he studied it.

"Where on earth do we find this Monorail?" I asked. "I know it exists. I see it every now and then, but I've never actually been on it."

"You and most of the city," Tim said. "I think we can get to it at Harrah's."

"You think? You don't know? You're one of Las Vegas' finest. You're supposed to know where everything is."

Las Vegas' finest had started toward the Strip. Harrah's was a little ways down from here. In the direction Dan Franklin had been headed. Sounded like a plan.

"So tell me about this ten grand," Tim said.

Uh-oh. I knew that was coming, but I hadn't quite figured out yet how to skip around it. It did, however, get Tim to help me chase Dan Franklin, so I had to think fast.

"Jeff found out about it." That wasn't a lie. Exactly.

"Coleman?"

I nodded.

"How did he find out?"

"How does Jeff find out about anything?" I asked.

Tim mulled that a second, then asked, "So Jeff found out Dan Franklin withdrew ten grand from his bank account?"

"That's right." And because I needed to get off the subject, as we passed the façade of the Venetian, I added that I thought Dan Franklin might have actually been in my shop, that it might not have been Ray Lucci after all.

"We have Dan Franklin's information, not Ray Lucci's. Why would Lucci pose as Franklin? That never made sense," I said. There was something about the tattoo that tickled my memory, something that was a little off, but I couldn't remember what it was.

We circled around a gaggle of Japanese tourists holding cameras up to get a shot of the Eiffel Tower in the distance. There was a lot of pedestrian congestion here: heavyset guys holding beer bottles—open container laws don't exist in Vegas—as they jostled each other, laughing; twentysomething women showing off bellies and tattoos; middle-aged couples wearing fanny packs and trying to sidestep all of the above. Three Hispanic men were slapping small cardboard cards against the palms of their hands before holding them out to passersby. Rejected cards sporting pictures of women with large bare breasts and phone numbers where they could be contacted lay scattered on the sidewalk.

I ignored them and craned my neck to see Franklin up ahead. He hadn't moved as quickly as I'd feared. Maybe he'd stopped for one of those cards.

"So Lucci had the same tattoo Franklin has," Tim mused. He was trying to figure out if that meant anything.

"So does Sylvia," I said, although the instant I said it, I regretted it because of the way Tim looked at me.

"What do you mean, *so does Sylvia*?"

"She's got a 'That's Amore,' too," I said. "She told me she got it in Sedona to commemorate her wedding. It looked new, so I'm sure she wasn't lying."

"What about Dan Franklin's?"

"What about it?"

"Did that look new, too?"

I saw where he was going with this. If Franklin was the one who got the tattoo at my shop last week, then it would still be healing with that bubblegum pink hue. I thought about the tattoo, but I wasn't sure.

"It was so quick," I said. "He took off his jacket, I saw the tattoo, and then, when I pointed it out, he swung around so I didn't have a chance to really look at it."

"But this is your job," Tim protested as we went through the doors at Harrah's.

"Okay, so I had an off day," I said bitterly.

The lights were flashing like a strobe; bells were ringing; music was playing. People were crowded around the slot machines, methodically hitting those little PLAY AGAIN buttons and hoping for the best. I refrained from shouting, "You'll never win," and stuck close to Tim as we maneuvered our way across the casino floor toward the back, where Dan Franklin's head bobbed up and down in the crowd. He didn't seem to know we were behind him, and he didn't look back. Maybe he figured he'd lost us back at the Palazzo.

It felt as if we were walking forever. Around slot machines, gaming tables, people, cocktail waitresses balancing trays of glasses. Like those rats in a maze.

Finally we left the casino and stepped into a small area with a couple of kiosks. A sign pointed us in the direction of the Monorail. We went outside along a concrete path between Harrah's and the Imperial Palace.

It dawned on me right about then that Tim was helping me track down Dan Franklin. Exactly the kind of thing he was supposed to prevent. But I certainly wasn't going to say anything. He was on autopilot; being a cop and chasing the bad guys was ingrained in his DNA. Although it could be argued we didn't quite know which side of the law Dan Franklin was on. The tattoo made him suspect, as did the facts that he'd been hiding out for days now, eluding any sort of questioning, and had withdrawn ten thousand dollars from his bank account.

As we approached the Monorail station, after walking what felt like miles, I realized there was one more thing that cast doubt on the man's innocence.

He had a blue Ford Taurus. So what would cause him to get around town on the Monorail instead of driving? An accident, perhaps?

Chapter 46

Sure, I was casting a wide net. It wasn't exactly that I wanted Dan Franklin to be guilty, but all the signs were there. Because I still wanted to distract Tim from Dan Franklin's banking activity, I filled him in on the blue Taurus as we went up the steps to the Monorail station.

"You're wondering why he'd take the Monorail," Tim said when I was done. No one could ever accuse him of not being with the program.

As he spoke, the sleek bullet-shaped Monorail slid along its track and came to a smooth stop at the station, which we were approaching. I didn't see Dan Franklin anywhere up there, but we didn't have the greatest view.

We had to buy tickets from a machine. Tim stuffed a ten-dollar bill into its slot, and it spit out a couple of tickets. He handed me one.

"Too bad there wasn't a person here," I said. "You could've just showed your badge."

He ignored me, and we slipped the tickets into the turnstile. The doors flipped open, and we took the stairs two at a time.

At the top, the Monorail's doors were closing, and as it started to move past us, going north toward the Sahara, I spotted Dan Franklin inside one of the cars, smiling and waving at us as the train picked up speed.

"We just wasted ten bucks," I said. "Because even if we get on the next train, we don't know where he's getting off."

Tim still hadn't said anything. He stood with his hands on his hips, surveying the tracks.

"This only goes to the Convention Center, the Hilton, and the Sahara from here," he mused. "The Convention Center doesn't make any sense; it leaves you off in the middle of nowhere, not close to the Convention Center or to the Strip. And the Hilton—it's too far off the main drag. No real reason to go there, either. The Sahara is the logical destination."

"For what?" I asked.

Tim turned and stared at me. "What do you mean, *for what*?"

"Why would he go to the Sahara?"

He sighed. "Think about it, Brett. If you want to be some sort of Nancy Drew, I think you'll have to do better than that."

And then the lightbulb over my head went on.

The wedding chapel wasn't far from the Sahara.

"You think he's going to That's Amore, don't you?" I asked.

Tim grinned. "So you're a little slow."

I started for the escalator but heard Tim say, "Where are you going?"

I turned back to see him staring at the track, as if willing a train to come by.

"What? We're going to take this?" I asked, walking back over to him.

"By the time we get the car, he could be long gone."

"And by the time a train comes, he'll be halfway to Mexico."

"But not if he doesn't have a car, like you suspect."

Okay, so he had a point. "But won't we need a car once we get there?"

"Maybe you can ask your friend Jeff Coleman to meet us."

Had aliens come and taken my brother away? Was he one of those pod people from *Invasion of the Body Snatchers*?

And then I knew. He wanted to ask Jeff how he knew

about the ten thousand dollars. I'd painted myself into a corner on that one.

"Call him, okay?" Tim said.

I had to try to turn it around a little. "Why don't you call Flanigan instead?"

"Because if I tell him I've got a gut instinct based on your gut instinct, he'll tell me to stay out of it."

I grinned. "And that doesn't appeal to you, does it?"

"Just call Coleman, okay?"

I didn't see any way out of it. As I reached into my bag, I saw another Monorail approaching. That didn't take too long.

I flipped my phone open and punched in Jeff's number.

"Kavanaugh?"

"Hey there, what are you doing right now?"

"Wouldn't you like to know?"

"I'm not kidding. Are you free now?"

"For what? Phone sex?"

I snorted. "No. Not phone sex."

Tim shot me a look, and I waved him off as the Monorail came to a stop in front of us. The doors slid open, and we stepped inside. It was like the monorail in Disney World. Clean and bright. Except that no one else was in this car, and as I remembered, the monorail at Disney was usually full of screaming kids and at least one balloon.

Jeff was talking. "Okay, so no phone sex. Maybe next time."

I ignored him. "Can you meet Tim and me over at That's Amore? We need a ride."

"Where's your car?"

"It's in the parking garage at the Venetian."

"So how are you getting to the wedding chapel? Are you taking a cab?"

"We're on the Monorail."

"The what? Kavanaugh, you do know that no one but tourists use that thing."

He was right. Although, looking around me, I didn't think even the tourists were taking advantage of it.

"So can you meet us?"

"What do I get if I do?"

I closed my eyes and counted to ten before I spoke again. "You get the satisfaction of possibly catching a killer."

"I told you I didn't care if the cops ever caught the guy who killed Rosalie's husband."

"But what about Ray Lucci?"

He was quiet a second, then said, "That's a little complicated right now." His voice was unusually soft.

"Sylvia told you, didn't she?" I asked.

I heard a short inhale, then, "Yeah. She told me you knew, too. Why didn't you tell me?"

"Not my place. Are you okay?"

"It's not the kind of news I was expecting."

I wanted to talk to him more about it, how he was handling knowing he had a half brother whom he'd never get to know, but sitting here on the Monorail with Tim watching me didn't seem like the right time. Jeff was the first to change the subject, though.

"So why are you heading to the wedding chapel?"

"I think you were right when you said you thought Dan Franklin was the killer. I ran into him a little while ago, and he ended up taking off. We're following him. We think he's heading to the chapel."

"You think?"

While the Monorail glided along its track, I managed to put the story in a nutshell by the time we reached the Convention Center station.

I was so immersed in my conversation that when Tim yanked me by the arm and pulled me up, I shrugged him off at first. But then I saw the look on his face and where he was looking. Outside the Monorail window.

Dan Franklin was striding across the parking lot at the Convention Center.

Chapter 47

"Change of plans," I said quickly to Jeff as Tim and I got off the Monorail. "He got off at the Convention Center. We're following him now."

We went through the automatic glass doors and spotted the escalators that would take us down to the first level and the parking lot.

"I'm just about there," Jeff said.

"What?"

"While we've been talking, I've been driving. I wasn't too far away. I was heading to my mother's; she's staying over at Rosalie's, and she needs a change of clothes."

I didn't much care about Sylvia's wardrobe at the moment.

"I'll see you in a minute." And Jeff ended the call.

Tim and I were running now. Dan Franklin was over near the Courtyard by Marriott, on East Desert Inn Road. So far I didn't think he'd seen us. I shoved my phone in my bag, which was slapping against my hip as I ran.

A blue car swung around into the Marriott lot near Franklin, parking sideways. Something was wrong with the car on the side facing away from us, but I saw it only a split second, and it hadn't totally registered.

Franklin waved at the driver, who climbed out.

As Tim and I drew closer, I could see who it was.

Will Parker.

And I remembered that Joel said Will Parker had been in the shop with Ray or Dan that day. So that song and dance Will told me about him and Dan having a tiff over Snowball the Rat might have been fabricated. Otherwise, why would Parker be here now?

Will Parker spotted us, and he must have said something because Dan Franklin turned around. We were gaining on them. But then Parker got back in the car, and it shot off, leaving Franklin in the wake of its exhaust. So maybe they weren't best friends after all.

Franklin didn't even try to run this time. In seconds, Tim had Franklin's arms pinned behind him.

"Call Flanigan," Tim said to me in his best cop voice, reciting the number so I could punch it in my cell. He held his free hand out and took the phone. "Kevin? I've got Dan Franklin." Silence, then, "We're at the entrance to the Courtyard by Marriott parking lot." He handed me back the phone.

"You can't hold me," Franklin said. "Who do you think you are?"

"You're wanted for questioning in Ray Lucci's murder," Tim said.

"What are you charging me with? I want to call my lawyer."

"We're not charging you," Tim said calmly. "We want to find out what you know about Ray Lucci. Ask you some questions."

Franklin sighed and hung his head. "I should've known he'd get at me, even after he was dead."

"Get at you how?" I asked.

Franklin's head snapped up. "You have no authority to ask me anything."

Ouch.

"Where did Parker go?" Tim asked, taking over.

"Parker?"

"Don't play stupid. That won't help you."

"He was here to take me to work."

"To the chapel?" I asked.

Franklin nodded. "I've got a shift in about half an hour. I called Will, and he said he could pick me up here and take me over."

"Where's your car?" I asked.

"It's in the shop."

"Why?"

"What do you mean, *why*?"

"Just answer," Tim ordered.

"Timing belt," he said. "Supposed to pick it up tomorrow."

"We'll need to know which garage," Tim said.

As he spoke, Jeff's familiar gold Pontiac swung in next to us and he climbed out. He assessed the situation and asked Tim, "Need any help?"

As if on cue, a police cruiser turned in. And just my luck, Willis was the cop on call. He glared at me, as if he was expecting to find another big gun on my person.

"Take Brett back to her shop," Tim instructed Jeff. "And I'll need to talk to you later."

Jeff's expression didn't change, but his eyelids flickered slightly.

I jumped in. "Won't Flanigan need to talk to me about my conversation with Dan?"

Tim nodded. "Later. But for now, he'll have other questions for him. And if you're right about that one issue"—I knew he meant the money—"we can verify that pretty quickly."

Sure they could. They were the cops.

"But aren't you supposed to keep watch over me?" I asked, unwilling to leave because I didn't want to miss anything.

"Take her," Tim told Jeff, "back to her shop."

"Come on, Brett," Jeff said, taking my elbow and indicating I should follow him.

"Tell Rosalie I'm sorry," Franklin said then.

We all stared at him.

"About Lou," he added quickly. "Tell her I'm sorry about Lou."

He certainly wasn't doing himself any favors saying anything like that.

Jeff held the door to the Pontiac open for me, and I settled into the seat, watching Tim and Willis and Franklin. As

Jeff got into the car and started the engine, I asked, "Do you really think he did it?"

He didn't answer as the car moved out of the lot, passing a Chevy Impala that looked remarkably like Tim's, Detective Kevin Flanigan at the wheel. Flanigan caught my eye, and I could see that he might not have been too happy about Tim taking over this whole Dan Franklin thing. Maybe we should've called Flanigan from the get-go, when we were following Franklin on the Monorail.

"You're really under lock and key, aren't you?" Jeff asked.

"I don't want to talk about it," I said, looking out the window. We were across the street from the Stardust, and I could see the Circus Circus big top a block or so up to the right.

Jeff was about to turn left onto the Strip, but I put my hand on the steering wheel.

"What?" he asked.

"Let's make a stop," I said.

His lips twitched as if he wanted to smile. "I told your brother I'd take you to your shop. He won't trust me ever again if I don't do that. And what is it he wants to talk to me about?"

I sighed. "I had to tell him about the ten-thousand-dollar withdrawal."

"You told him we stole his mail?"

I shook my head. "No, no, I sort of glossed over the details."

He narrowed his eyes at me and said, "Glossed over them how?"

"He knows you were involved."

He chewed on his lip for a second, then said, "But you left out most of the details, didn't you?"

"Does it matter? They'll check his account, and then they won't need us," I said, trying to convince myself. "But for now, I think we should go to the wedding chapel."

He grinned.

"Kavanaugh, I didn't think you cared."

I slugged him on the shoulder. "I don't mean we should get married or anything."

"I'm crushed."

I rolled my eyes. "Give me a break. There's something there I want to check out." I was thinking about Will Parker coming by to pick up Dan Franklin—in a blue car. Something about that car still tugged at my brain. Plus, Will Parker giving us an address for an In-N-Out burger joint stuck in my craw.

"Something or someone?" Jeff asked. "I'm not the kind of guy who drops a girl off to see another guy."

I leaned back in my seat and sighed. "Okay, fine, take me back to my shop."

But he'd already turned right. In the direction of the wedding chapel. I didn't say anything, just let him drive.

But when we approached the intersection—That's Amore on our right and the Love Shack on our left—Jeff took an unexpected turn to the left.

"What's going on?" I asked.

And then I saw it. A blue car sat in the front lot at the Love Shack. A blue car with the right headlight smashed in and the bumper a little bit askew.

Chapter 48

Jeff Coleman blew a long, low whistle.

"Looks like a bad one," he said.

"That's the car," I said. "Will Parker came to pick up Dan Franklin in that car. I thought something looked a little off, but the way he parked, I couldn't really tell until now."

"Do you think this was the car that hit Lou?"

I shrugged. "Could be."

"But you said it's Parker's car, not Franklin's. So what's up with him? And why is it over here and not across the street?"

I had no freaking idea. My head was a jumbled-up mess of thoughts all knocking into one another like kids in one of those Moonwalks.

"Maybe they're in on it together," I suggested. "There were some hints that Sanderson, the guy who owns this wedding chapel, might have been involved, too."

"I didn't take you as a conspiracy theorist, Kavanaugh."

"I'm grabbing at straws here," I admitted.

"Playing devil's advocate for a moment," Jeff said. "Why would Will Parker leave his smashed-up blue car so everyone can see it? If he used this car to run down Lou, then you'd think he'd hide it."

"But maybe he thinks no one will notice if it's parked over here. Then again, Dan Franklin's car is allegedly being serviced," I said.

Jeff fished a cigarette out of his front breast pocket. He put it in his mouth but didn't light it. He saw me watching him. "What? I'm not going to smoke it. I just think better with it."

Now there were so many ways to respond to that that I couldn't figure out which one to throw out at him. He noticed and grinned, the cigarette bobbing between his lips.

"No cracks, Kavanaugh."

I held up my hands in surrender. But before I could say anything, the door to the Love Shack swung open and Will Parker sauntered out.

Jeff and I ducked down in our seats, and I could only hope that Parker hadn't seen the Pontiac when Jeff and I were at That's Amore the other day. He didn't seem to pay any attention, though, as he got into his car, started the engine, and pulled out of the lot.

After a few seconds, Jeff eased the Pontiac out after it.

"What are you doing?" I asked.

"Following him," Jeff said, now taking the cigarette out of his mouth and balancing it on the empty ashtray in the center console. "I figured that's what you wanted, right?"

I hadn't really thought about it, but it seemed like a good idea, so I let him think that. I nodded. "Maybe now we'll find out where he really lives."

"If he goes home," Jeff said.

We were about two cars behind Parker, heading north on Las Vegas Boulevard. The Stratosphere tower was hovering over us; I twisted my neck to try to see the rides up at the top. There's something called the Big Shot, in which you get strapped in and shot a hundred sixty feet up at forty miles an hour, and then it drops you. Fast. And craziest of all was Insanity, which is totally insane because it's a huge claw extending sixty-four feet from the Stratosphere Tower, dangling you more than nine hundred feet above the Strip. And then it spins. Not that I'd ever want to ride it, but it sort of fascinated me: a ride spinning around that high in the air. Vegas was also big on roller coasters. Circus Circus had one in its Adventuredome, New York–New York sported a coaster that spun around its skyline, and the Sahara had one, too. MGM used to have a roller coaster, back in the day when it was trying to compete with Disney and Universal as a family attraction, but it failed miserably, and now the coaster was just a memory. In its place was the Monorail track. Not exactly an exciting thrill ride, as I could attest.

"Be careful he doesn't spot us," I warned. "This car sticks out like a sore thumb."

"Don't worry about that," Jeff said, and the way he said it made me take pause.

Jeff's stint in the Marines intrigued me. He knew how to pick locks, break into houses without breaking into them, covertly follow cars in traffic. I also had learned a few months back that he "knew" people who could give him information. While I was curious, I hadn't pried into his business. I was afraid if I did, he might think I was far more interested in him than I wanted him to think. Although the more I got to know him, the more intrigued I was.

"I wasn't a spy, Kavanaugh," he said, reading my mind. "I served my country like a lot of these kids these days. But it's worse now, over there."

"You were in the Gulf War."

"I never shot my gun in combat. It was a very short war."

"But you were in the Marines for how long?"

"Four years."

"So what did you do the rest of the time?"

Jeff grinned as he maneuvered the car so we were now three cars behind Parker.

"If I told you, I'd have to kill you," he said.

It wasn't worth trying to have a serious conversation with the man. I focused on Parker's car, which suddenly swerved and turned right down a side road, before the Little White Chapel. You could get married almost anywhere in Vegas.

Jeff immediately slowed down, but he didn't turn. As we passed the road, we could see there were no other cars behind Parker. We kept going straight.

"We're going to lose him," I warned.

"Too risky. He'd notice us."

"Do you think he already spotted us and did that to shake us off his trail?"

Jeff laughed out loud. "Shake us off his trail? I think you need to stick to tattooing, Kavanaugh. You're not very good at spy stuff."

No kidding.

"You need to call your brother, though."

"Why?"

"To give him the license plate of that car."

I hadn't even thought about doing that. Jeff was right. I'd make a lousy spy.

I punched Tim's number into my phone.

"What?" he barked.

"I've got a license plate number," I said. "Will Parker's blue car. Do you want it?"

He didn't even ask how I got it after I rattled it off; he just hung up.

I noticed that we were also going down a side street now, and Jeff made a quick turn to the right. Will Parker's car was two cars up. A white Bronco was between us.

I stared at Jeff. "How did you do that?"

He grinned and tapped the side of his head. "Leave it to me, Kavanaugh."

I didn't want to give him the satisfaction of a high five or anything, so I rolled my eyes.

"You're just jealous that you can't do this," he teased.

Parker turned left, and we were on Charleston. He turned right onto Las Vegas Boulevard. We were heading toward Fremont Street, close to where Jeff's shop was.

Parker's brake lights went on as we approached Murder Ink, and I caught my breath. Did Parker know we were following him? Was he baiting us?

He slid the blue car into a spot in front of Goodfellas Bail Bonds. Jeff eased the Pontiac into one two spaces away.

Parker climbed out of the car. But instead of going into Goodfellas, as I expected, he sauntered down the sidewalk and stopped in front of Jeff's shop.

Jeff sat up a little straighter, his hands tight on the steering wheel as he leaned forward. I held my breath. The shop was closed. I assumed the door was locked. Was Parker going to break in?

Turns out he didn't need to.

The door to Murder Ink swung open, and Parker went inside.

Chapter 49

We hardly had time to register what had happened when my phone rang. Tim. I flipped it open. "Hey," I said.

"That license plate. On the blue car. I got it."

"It's Will Parker's, isn't it?" I asked.

"Parker? No. It's that Love Shack guy. Martin Sanderson."

Sanderson?

Jeff had opened his door, and I put my hand on his arm to stop him from getting out right away as I said to Tim, "I'll give you a call back, okay?" and flipped my phone closed. "Where are you going?" I asked Jeff. My phone started to ring again, and I saw it was Tim. I turned off the ringer and stuck the phone back in my bag.

"Someone let him into my shop," he said, his eyes dark with anger. "My mother's at Rosalie's. I'm with you. No one else has a key. The shop was locked. I was here earlier and made sure everything was shut down."

Okay, so he had a legitimate reason to be concerned. If it were my shop, I'd be the same way. I pulled my arm away and nodded. "Okay," I said, opening my door.

That caused him to pause.

"You are not coming in with me."

"I am so."

"I told your brother I'd take you home, and I can't have you getting hurt or anything on my watch."

I glared at him. "I'm a big girl, Jeff. I can take care of myself."

I expected him to come back with some nasty retort, but instead he chuckled. "You're right about that. Just stay behind me, okay?"

We got out of the car and walked slowly up to the corner of Goodfellas. An alley between Goodfellas and Murder Ink stretched back to another alley where Jeff usually parked his car and smoked with the Mexicans who cooked at the Chinese take-out place on the other side of his business.

"I'm going down here," he whispered, "in the back way. Hopefully, I can catch them by surprise. But you stay here, in case someone comes out this way. Can you whistle?"

I cocked my head at him and rolled my eyes. "I pucker up and blow, right?" I asked, making my voice all husky and Lauren Bacall–like.

He caught himself before he chuckled. "Nice to know you're a Bogie fan," he said, then went down the alley, around to the right, and out of sight.

I leaned against the side of the stucco building that was Goodfellas Bail Bonds. I'd never seen anyone go in or out in all the time I'd known Jeff, but then again, their clientele might keep odd hours. Much like a tattoo shop.

I was concentrating so hard on watching the shop that when my cell phone rang again, I nearly jumped. I leaned down and felt around in my bag for my phone, finally finding it and flipping it open.

"Where's my Godiva?" Bitsy asked without saying hello, her tone definitely frosty. "Where did you get off to?"

I kept my eye on Murder Ink's door as I gave it all to her in a nutshell. I wondered what was taking Jeff Coleman so long. Was he inside with Parker and whoever had let Parker in or was he waiting for the right moment to go in the back way?

"You could've called earlier," Bitsy chided, interrupting my thoughts.

"I'm sorry," I said, and I truly was. I didn't need Sister Mary Eucharista on my shoulder to remind me that I was shirking my duties.

"When will you be back?"

Still nothing at Murder Ink.

"I'm not—" I started to say when the tattoo shop's door suddenly flew open and Will Parker came scrambling out with Jeff Coleman on his heels. "Gotta go—call you right back," I said, uncertain whether I could keep that promise.

Will Parker was coming toward me, and I stuck my foot out in the sidewalk.

He tumbled over it, did a somersault, and somehow landed back on his feet, like some sort of Cirque du Soleil acrobat. Come to think of it, maybe he *had* been with Cirque at one point. He was a performer, after all, and you couldn't throw a cat in Vegas without hitting one of those Cirque shows.

The image of him wearing tights for that Renaissance show had bothered me; a leotard would've been much worse.

I didn't have much time to ruminate, though, because Parker was halfway down the block with Jeff behind him. He wasn't even huffing and puffing. Maybe it was his Marines training. He certainly hadn't been off the cigarettes long enough to make a difference.

I hesitated to go after them. I wouldn't be able to keep up, most likely, and as I glanced back at the shop, I couldn't help but wonder where the person who'd let Parker into the shop in the first place was. Had Jeff managed to tie him to a chair or something before chasing Parker?

I tentatively went toward Murder Ink and peered in the window below the neon sign advertising tattoos. The sign was off, which made it easier to focus.

Jeff's tattoo stations looked as they normally did: chairs, shelves, flash lining the walls. I didn't see anyone else in there.

I pulled the door open and stepped inside.

Yup, everything looked normal in here. I touched the top of a box of baby wipes as I stood in one of the stations, checking everything out.

It all seemed so normal that I felt myself relax a little. So when I heard someone clear his throat, my heart started pounding.

Chapter 50

The light from the window caught the wisps of his white hair, illuminating them.

"Bernie?" I asked, my heart racing.

Bernie Applebaum was holding some sort of quilted thing. He held it up, and I could see now that it was a bag.

"Sylvia wanted me to pick this up for her," he said.

For a second, I wondered why. Jeff had been on his way to Sylvia's for a change of clothes, and he could've stopped here and picked this up on the way. But then I remembered it was Sylvia, whose requests usually didn't make much sense to anyone but her.

"So you let Will Parker in," I said.

Bernie was staring out the window at the street, and the sound of my voice seemed to startle him. He ran a hand over the top of his head, smoothing out the sparse white hairs.

"Oh, oh, yes," he said, looking at me again. "Is that his name? He said he was here for a tattoo."

Really? Will Parker had just had his tattoo touched up—by yours truly. I doubted that's why he was here, but couldn't figure out another reason.

Of course it could've been my own vanity, wanting to think that Parker wouldn't come to Jeff Coleman for another tattoo if he'd been happy with the one I gave him.

Okay, so I'd conveniently forgotten that Will Parker said he lived at an In-N-Out Burger and was driving a blue car that was all smashed up as though it had been in an accident and that Lou Marino was hit by maybe a blue car.

I hoped Jeff had caught him, but since he wasn't back yet, they were probably halfway down the Strip by now.

"So you don't know him?" I asked.

Bernie shook his head and indicated the quilted bag. "She said it was yellow. Is this yellow?"

It was a mishmash of fabrics, and some did have yellow in them. "I suppose," I said and had another thought. "Why did you let him in? The shop is closed. You couldn't help with a tattoo."

Bernie sighed. "I don't know. It was reflex, I think. He knocked on the door, and I saw him and let him in. I told him no one was here, no one could help him."

But he had been in here longer than a couple of minutes, which was how long it should've taken Parker to get the message and get out of here. Unless he knew we were waiting for him outside. It's possible he'd seen us pull up behind him.

"I didn't do anything wrong, did I?" Bernie asked tentatively. He didn't wait for my answer, though; he started back toward the office, where he undoubtedly had found Sylvia's quilted bag.

I took a step after him, but the bell on the front door made me jump, and I turned to see Jeff coming in. He was huffing and puffing now.

"Did you get him?" I asked.

He scowled at me. "Does it look like I got him?" he asked, his tone definitely testy.

"Bernie's here," I said to change the subject.

"Yeah, I know," he said, still taking deep breaths.

"It's a good thing you're quitting smoking," I said before I could stop myself.

"I think you need to shut up right now," he said between breaths.

Okay, got the picture. I made like I was zipping my lips and then locking them.

In a flash, his face lightened and he laughed out loud. "You are way too sensitive, Kavanaugh."

"So what happened with Parker? Where did he go?"

"I want to know what it is with these Dean Martins and public transportation. Guy hopped a bus. I think he paid the driver to close the doors before I could get on."

"So what happened? In here, I mean. You were in here a little while with him."

"He said he wanted a tattoo. I played along, but then I think he recognized me. You know, as the guy you were supposed to marry?"

"Don't remind me."

"It wouldn't be that bad, would it, Kavanaugh?" He was teasing me again, that little glimmer of amusement in his eyes.

I ignored him.

"That's when he took off?"

"Said he made a mistake. Apologized, then ran out the door. You know the rest."

I knew what happened, but I didn't know why. This didn't set right with me. I couldn't get past him having me touch up his tattoo only hours ago, and now he was visiting Murder Ink. Something wasn't right. But then again, there wasn't a whole lot right with the whole day.

A crash in the back of the shop made us both jump, and we went through the sixties-style beads into the office where Bernie stood over a metal ashtray that had apparently toppled to the ground. His eyes were wide.

"Sorry about that, buddy," he said to Jeff, who picked up the ashtray and put it on top of the file cabinet. Bernie was no longer holding the quilted bag. In fact, I couldn't see it anywhere.

"Where's Sylvia's bag?" I asked.

Bernie's face turned red and he wrung his hands. "I put it out in the car. I parked in the back, like Sylvia said."

Jeff put his arm around the elderly man's shoulders.

"That's all right. Do you need a ride? It's getting dark out. I can take you back to Rosalie's."

Relief washed over Bernie's face. "That would be great. But what about the car?"

Jeff looked at me. "Kavanaugh can follow us in your car, and then I'll take her home." He raised his eyebrows at me with the question.

I nodded. "That's fine. It works out perfectly. I just need to call my shop. Tell them I'm not coming back."

I stepped back into the front of the shop. It *was* getting dark out. The neon from the Bright Lights Motel sign across the street slipped through the window and cast a red glow on the floor.

Bitsy seemed resigned to the fact that I had skipped out and wasn't going to return.

"Joel's done at ten. Ace is already gone. Can I leave with Joel?"

"Absolutely," I said, eager to meet any demands she might have. The guilt was inching through me, and I could feel it settle between my shoulders. "And you can come in late tomorrow. I'll open."

"Thanks," she said, although it wasn't as heartfelt as I'd hoped. She was holding a grudge, and it was well deserved. I should wear a hair shirt to bed tonight.

Jeff stuck his head through the beads.

"Ready? We need to get Bernie back."

"Sure," I said, sticking my phone in my bag.

We all went out the back, and Bernie gave me the keys to the white rental, which I saw now was one of those little Chevy Aveos that are no bigger than my kitchen table.

"Drive safe," Bernie said nervously.

Jeff chuckled. "She's the safest driver I know. No worries." He began to steer Bernie toward the alley so they could go out front where the Pontiac was parked. "I'll wait out front for you," he tossed back at me before they disappeared.

The car was small, and my head almost hit the ceiling. It was almost as bad as Bitsy's Mini Cooper. But not quite.

Sylvia's yellow quilted bag sat on the passenger seat next to me. I picked it up and fingered the fabric, which was frayed around the edges. Why would she want this old thing? I opened it up and peered inside. Nothing, except a small piece of paper at the bottom.

I couldn't help myself. I plucked it out and turned on the overhead light to read it.

It was a bank withdrawal receipt. Sylvia had withdrawn ten thousand dollars from her account.

Chapter 51

I let out a long breath and sat back in my seat, holding the receipt. Between the ten grand in Lucci's locker, Dan Franklin's ten grand, and now this, we were looking at thirty thousand dollars floating around. Unless, of course, Lucci's money was from either Franklin or Sylvia.

I checked the date on the receipt.

The day before the wedding.

Had Sylvia given Lucci the money? Had she remembered about this receipt and asked Bernie to get it so no one would find out?

I tried to tell myself that Sylvia could've taken the money out for anything. It could've been to pay for their honeymoon. Although the Grand Canyon wouldn't cost that much, and they were driving themselves. And I knew how little it cost to get married at one of those wedding chapels, so that wouldn't cost much, either.

I stuffed the receipt back in the bag and resolved to ask her about it directly when I got to Rosalie's.

I wasn't sure I wanted to mention it to Jeff, in case I was way off base. He wouldn't like it if I was interrogating Sylvia. At least without telling him why ahead of time.

I pulled out of the alley and turned the corner to see Jeff and Bernie sitting in the Pontiac, waiting for me. Jeff made a sort of gesture with his hands that made me realize I'd taken way too long ruminating about that bank receipt.

In a few minutes we were on Charleston Boulevard, heading toward Summerlin—and Red Rock Canyon.

I'd never been out there at night, and I wasn't sure I wanted to. Because it was definitely night now, and the mountains blended in with the sky, so it looked like a black hole in the distance. It had gotten chillier, and I wished I'd thought to bring my jacket with me, but when I started out for Godiva, I had no idea where the journey would take me.

I shivered as I watched Jeff's turn signal flash red.

We pulled into a condo complex that didn't even attempt to look any different than any of the other condo complexes out here. In the dark I couldn't tell whether the buildings were brown or beige, but I was willing to bet they were one or the other. The plantings were nicely done, adding to the desert theme of the complex. No fountains that I could see, which made me happy. At least they weren't wasting water.

Jeff eased the Pontiac in front of one of the town houses. All the lights were on inside. Every room. Okay, so there was no water waste, but what about electricity? I parked the Chevy behind Jeff.

"Where were you?" he asked as I approached, my bag and Sylvia's bag in hand.

Bernie grabbed Sylvia's bag. "I'll take that," he said. As if he wanted to be the one to hand her the bag, since it had been his mission to go get it. I had no problem with that, even though I doubted it would make any difference to Sylvia.

Bernie led the way into the foyer, which was painted gray with a mauve trim. A wreath of dried flowers hung on the wall over a white table with three fat candles of varying heights that smelled like vanilla. A little precious for my taste.

"Where have you been?" Sylvia stepped out of the kitchen on our left, a dish towel wrapped around her waist, doubling as an apron. She wielded a wooden spoon.

I smelled it then, the distinct scent of tomato sauce. Homemade tomato sauce, not that stuff you get in a jar. My stomach growled. Loudly.

Jeff laughed. Sylvia merely patted my arm, then pulled me into the kitchen with her, the spoon leading the way.

"I've got a nice pot of sauce going. You make a salad."

It was an order. But I wasn't going to argue. I opened the refrigerator and started taking out lettuce, cucumbers, and carrots.

Sylvia had already put a bowl on the granite-top island for me. I dumped the salad makings next to it and began washing the lettuce while she stirred the sauce. I glanced around at the country kitchen, with its white French cabinets and sleek stainless steel appliances. Lou Marino must have done pretty well as an impersonator, or else Rosalie was making more money than I thought over at the university.

"So where did you find Bernie?" Sylvia asked as she produced a can of chickpeas and handed it to me.

I glanced around but didn't see Bernie or Jeff. Or Rosalie, either.

"He was at Murder Ink," I said.

"Why on earth was he over there?"

She had her back to me, so I couldn't see her face.

"He went to pick up your bag for you."

Sylvia didn't say anything for a second, then, "Oh, oh, that's right."

Something was off. Either she really didn't know why Bernie was at Murder Ink or she was having one of her all-too-frequent senior moments. I couldn't tell.

Sylvia came over next to me, wiping her hands on a towel, and peered into the bowl, where I'd already assembled a pretty decent looking salad.

"You'll find, dear, that men sometimes do the damndest things." And then she was back to the stove, emptying a box of spaghetti into a pot of boiling water.

I rinsed the chickpeas in the sink before putting them in the salad. Sylvia was nodding, watching me.

I couldn't help myself. No one else was in here with us, so it seemed as good a time as any.

"Do you know that Ray left a duffel bag with ten thousand dollars in his locker at That's Amore?" I asked as casually as I could.

"Where did he get that kind of money?" she asked.

I studied her face for any sign of recognition that she knew about the money, but nothing. I took a stab in the dark.

"You didn't give it to him, did you?"

Sylvia chuckled. "Do you think I did?"

"You withdrew ten grand from your bank account the day before your wedding," I said. "I saw the receipt."

No flicker in her eyes, no twitch of her cheek. She continued to smile at me.

"I think that's my business, don't you, dear?" And Sylvia went out into the living room to tell everyone dinner was on.

I nearly bumped into Bernie as I brought plates to the dining room.

"Don't harass her," he said softly.

"I'm not," I assured him, although I really wanted to press the issue. I'd have to find another way around it.

Rosalie came to the table, her black eye now faded to yellow. Soon it would be gone, like the man who'd given it to her. She was laughing at something Jeff said, her mannerisms less stiff and awkward than they'd been the other couple of times I'd seen her. Jeff was right: She was better off without Lou.

I started to say something about Dan Franklin, but Jeff kicked me under the table. I glared at him, but he was shaking his head and frowning. This wasn't the time.

I caught Rosalie looking at me thoughtfully a couple of times, and then she'd quickly look over at Jeff. I didn't want to know what she was thinking.

Bernie patted his daughter's hand all through dinner. Jeff caught my eye a couple of times and winked as his mother told stories about the old people on the bus to Sedona. It was a family dinner that seemed perfectly normal. Except for the fact that two people were dead.

I didn't want coffee. It would keep me up. It had been a

long day, and after we'd cleaned up I asked Jeff whether he could take me home.

Sylvia offered her cheek, and I gave her a kiss.

"Don't worry about anything," she whispered as she kissed me back.

I wasn't quite sure what she meant, but she'd already moved on to Jeff and was saying good-bye to him now.

Bernie had already taken Rosalie back into the living room, and Jeff and I stepped out into the night. It had grown cold, and I shivered in my T-shirt.

"You okay?" he asked as he opened the car door for me.

"Just turn the heat on," I said, settling back and closing my eyes.

He didn't say anything else as he climbed in his seat and turned over the engine. I felt the car moving, and it lulled me into one of those half-awake, half-asleep states.

I was so out of it that I thought the sound was in a dream. I opened my eyes and saw the bright lights straight ahead. They blinded me, and suddenly my body was jerked back against the seat as Jeff spun the wheel, the car skidding sideways across the pavement.

But he hadn't been fast enough. The impact of the crash caused the air bag to explode, and it slammed into my face so hard I thought my nose was broken.

Chapter 52

Suddenly it was quiet. Too quiet.

A streetlight a few feet away cast a dim yellow beam across the road, but everything around it was black. Like being inside with the lights on and not being able to see anything but your own reflection in the windows.

Then I heard something—couldn't put my finger on it—but the air bag began to slowly deflate.

"You okay, Kavanaugh?" Jeff's voice pierced the silence.

I turned my head slowly—everything hurt—and saw a glint of something in Jeff's hand. A pocket knife.

"What happened?" I asked, surprised that my voice sounded normal, even though it was too loud in my ears.

"Car was coming straight at us. I swerved right into a pole or something. That's why the air bags inflated."

But that wasn't what I'd meant.

A rustling outside the car caused me to tense up, pain tearing through my muscles. My eyes had begun to adjust to the darkness, but I still couldn't see anything outside the car.

"What is it?" I whispered.

Jeff put a finger to his lips, the streetlight illuminating his silhouette. He shifted down in his seat and indicated I should do the same. Pain shot through my back and up to my neck, but I moved past it as I heard more rustling. It sounded as if someone or something was walking through the shrubs along the side of the road, just beyond the car.

We were facing the desert. I glanced in the side-view mirror. Behind us, on the other side of the street, town houses stood in line like toy soldiers, but it was a development that was only half finished. No lights in any windows.

No cars on the road, either.

Nothing except that blasted streetlight, which was more of a hindrance than a help. I saw now that the pole we crashed into was another streetlight, but it wasn't working.

Jeff put his fingers to his ear, pantomiming a phone. I wondered where his was as I stretched my arm to reach my bag on the floor. As my fingers touched the fabric, an explosion rocked the air.

I yanked my hand back, my whole body shaking.

It wasn't an explosion. It was a gunshot.

Who was out there?

Jeff's hand encircled mine, and he squeezed tight, as if to say it would be okay.

But I wasn't convinced. Someone was out there. Someone who'd tried to run us down and was now shooting at us.

Well, one shot.

Made me wish Willis hadn't found that gun I'd had. Not that I knew how to use it, but it was big. Big enough to make a statement, even if I just waved it around.

After a few minutes of silence, I reached down again for my bag.

Another shot rocked the air.

Whoever was out there could see me.

"What's going on?" I whispered.

Jeff was holding on to my hand so tightly that when he squeezed it again, I barely noticed. I moved my head slightly, and he was looking out the front window. I didn't think he could see any more than I could. Unless his time in the Marines had given him some sort of natural night-vision goggles.

The air bags hung, deflated, in front of us like empty sacks. I was acutely aware that my face felt as though it were on fire. I had turned my face slightly when the bag inflated, and I sensed that my cheek had a huge rug burn.

I was afraid to touch my nose, as if any movement would cause whomever was out there to shoot again.

"We can't just sit here like this," I whispered.

"Got any ideas?" he whispered back.

"You're the Marine. What did you do when you got shot at in the desert?"

"I never got shot at in the desert. Except for now."

His other hand inched toward the door. Great. He was going to try to open it, and we'd both get blown away. But as I contemplated how to stop him, he fingered the knob that maneuvered the side mirror.

It moved a fraction of an inch.

And another gunshot pierced the air and shattered the mirror.

Jeff seemed to have been expecting that because he didn't move his finger.

"He's behind us," he whispered. "I saw the car."

"Could you see *him*?"

"I saw a shadow. He's standing right at the trunk, watching us."

A shiver shimmied across my shoulders and down through my legs. "What does he want?"

"Want to ask him?"

I tried to pull my hand away, but he held it tightly.

"I've got a plan," he said.

"Will it get us killed?"

"Hopefully not. But you have to scooch down further. He can't have a good visual."

That didn't make me feel very confident. But we couldn't just sit here, held hostage by some unknown guy with a gun.

"I'm going to start the car and back up into him," Jeff whispered.

"You're nuts. Can the car even start?"

"We'll find out, won't we? Get down."

I tried to slide down farther, but the seat belt pinned me to the back of the seat. I managed to maneuver under the chest belt so it was behind my head. The lap belt was tight across my abdomen, but I could live with it. The deflated air bag covered my legs, but I pulled them up as far as possible. I didn't want him to shoot my leg. Because I was certain he would start shooting.

Jeff let go of my hand, and I felt even more exposed. He shimmied down farther, too, but not as far. His seat belt was close to his neck, but still across his shoulder. He didn't move his legs. His foot was hovering over the accelerator.

"Hold on," he whispered as his hand moved to the ignition and he turned the key.

The engine roared to life, and he slammed his foot on the accelerator. The car shot backward, and I felt as if I was on a roller coaster, my body slamming back against the seat. I had shifted even lower, the seat belt strap across my neck, but I could still see out the front windshield. One of the headlights was out, but the other one illuminated the desert. It was ugly out here, brown with a few tumbleweeds and scattered yuccas.

The gunshots were steady now.

The car swerved around, and we were facing the road again.

"Down, Brett!" Jeff shouted as he put the car into first and we rocketed forward, shots ringing in my ears, barely discernible above the engine's roar, so much so that I thought the shots might have been my imagination. But then I saw the hole in the windshield. It had just registered when a body came up over the hood, smashed against the windshield, and then rolled off.

I couldn't discern the hole anymore, because the entire windshield had shattered into a mosaic with the impact of the body.

The car kept going.

I moved up in my seat and stared out my window, looking back to see who it was.

"Do you think he's okay?" I asked. My voice sounded too loud.

"Call 911," Jeff barked, the car still rocketing down the road.

I leaned down and grabbed my bag. We were getting

close to a traffic light, but Jeff wasn't slowing down. There were a couple cars waiting at the light.

"Aren't you going to stop?" I asked.

Jeff didn't answer, spun the Pontiac around the cars.

It was brighter here, too, the streetlights doing a better job than the one up the road. I turned to confront Jeff about the speed of the car when I saw it.

The gun had blown a hole through more than the windshield.

Blood was pouring out of Jeff's shoulder.

Chapter 53

I felt myself start to hyperventilate, but I took a couple of deep breaths. I still held my phone, but I hadn't opened it yet.

"You have to stop, Jeff," I shouted. "You're bleeding."

"We're going to the hospital. Call the cops. Tell them what happened."

My hand was shaking as I flipped up the cover on the phone. Instinct made me call Tim.

"What, Brett?" He sounded annoyed.

"Tim," I said breathlessly, still looking at Jeff's shoulder. All that blood was making me woozy.

"Talk to him, Brett," Jeff said sternly, although his voice wasn't nearly as strong as it should've been. "Don't look at me."

I closed my eyes.

"What's going on, Brett?" Tim's voice echoed through my head.

"It's Jeff. He's been shot." It was all I could concentrate on at the moment.

"Shot? Where?"

"In the desert."

"Where are you?"

I opened my eyes and looked through the windshield. The shattered glass gave it a sort of magnifying glass appearance. The lights from the strip malls and the gas stations and the apartment complexes glimmered against the broken windshield and bounced back off it in a halo effect. How on earth could Jeff see to drive?

"We're on the way to the hospital," I heard myself say, the question about Jeff's driving still bouncing around in my head like a pinball. "He's been shot." I didn't say he was at the wheel.

"Which hospital?"

There was only one on this road, so I figured that's where we were heading. "University Medical Center."

"I'll meet you there."

"Um, Tim? We hit the guy who shot at us. He's back there—I don't know—somewhere on the side of West Charleston Boulevard in Summerlin. Near a streetlight that's out. He forced us off the road. Then he shot at us. Jeff ran him over. We left him there." I couldn't stop talking; I didn't want to stop. I felt as though if I stopped, something even more awful would happen. My hand was still shaking as the phone vibrated against my ear.

"Brett, stay calm." Tim's voice was soothing. "Did you recognize the guy who shot at you, the guy you hit?"

"No, I never saw him. Even when he hit the car"—the words got stuck in my throat for a second—"I just saw a body. Not his face. Nothing to recognize."

"That's okay; don't worry about it. I'll meet you at the hospital. I'll send someone out to Summerlin. How's Jeff?"

I looked over at him. He was focused on the road; his hands were holding the steering wheel tight. The blood was spreading, and his breaths were short and shallow.

"He's okay," I lied to Tim, then closed the phone.

We were almost at the hospital. We'd run every red light, but, remarkably, we didn't see any cops. The emergency entrance was up on the next block. I sighed with relief.

Too soon.

As we approached the driveway to the hospital, the car suddenly swerved as Jeff's arms fell from the wheel.

I braced myself as we slammed into an ambulance. My neck snapped back and hit the headrest.

Security guards, paramedics, and doctors surrounded

the car in seconds. Faces peered through the windows. The door opened, letting in a cold gust of air that made me shiver. Jeff was white as a ghost; he looked as though he'd passed out. My heart leaped into my throat as someone tried to pull me from my seat.

"Help him," I begged, although they were already doing that. Jeff was out of the car; they had him on a gurney; they were rolling him away.

It was only then that I let myself be brought out of the car, unlatching my seat belt, reaching for my bag at my feet. My legs got caught for a second in the air bag before I wrenched them free and stepped out of the car. I felt as though I'd been at sea for days; my knees buckled, and I almost went down. Hands were under my arms, pulling me back up.

A familiar voice asked, "Are you okay?"

I turned my head to see Colin Bixby in his white lab coat, holding me.

I tried for a small smile, but I couldn't carry it off. "Yes. But Jeff . . ."

"We're taking care of him. Don't worry about him."

I wanted to worry. "He lost a lot of blood." I saw it then, on my arm, on my shirt. It had splattered all over me. Bixby was looking at me, wondering whether I'd been shot, too. "I'm okay," I said, lying again. Sister Mary Eucharista was giving me a pass, though. I asked her to look after Jeff.

"You weren't shot?" Concern laced Bixby's words.

"No."

He helped me around the ambulance, and I glanced back at the Pontiac. There was blood on the hood.

My knees buckled again, and I started to fall. Bixby leaned down and swept me up in his arms, carrying me like a child through the sliding doors into the emergency room waiting room. People who'd probably been waiting here for hours watched as we went through another set of sliding doors into the emergency room. I'd been here once before.

Bixby set me down on a bed and pulled the curtain around.

He peered into my face and gently touched it. I winced when his fingers probed my nose.

"Air bag?" he asked.

I nodded.

"It's not broken."

I sighed. "I feel like a truck ran over me." And then I thought about Jeff, helpless and bleeding on a gurney. Never having shot his gun during a war. But getting shot by a crazy person in the Vegas desert. The tears started then, and Bixby let me cry. His fingers probed my arms, my legs, my torso without a word. I barely felt them.

Finally he stepped back and said, "You'll be okay."

I sniffled. "Thanks."

The curtain snapped back then, and my brother came in. He didn't say anything. He came over and put his arms around me, pulling me into a tight hug.

It made me start crying all over again.

Bixby stepped back. "I'll check on Coleman," and then he disappeared, making sure the curtain was giving us as much privacy as possible.

"He's in surgery," Tim said. "He lost a lot of blood."

I nodded against his chest.

"What were you doing out there?"

That's when I saw him. Detective Kevin Flanigan was standing behind him. Tim saw where my gaze had settled.

"Tell us what happened," Tim said softly.

I knew it was procedure, but it still felt like an imposition. I didn't have a choice. I reared my head back and frowned. "We were coming back from Rosalie's. We had dinner with her and Sylvia and Bernie. Jeff was taking me home." It all sounded so benign, considering everything else that had gone on in the past couple of days. In the last hour. Who would try to kill us? Granted, I had been poking around a little too much maybe, but I didn't know diddly about anything. Although perhaps the guy shooting thought I did. I shivered at the thought.

"Can you tell us what happened?" Flanigan asked, a little notebook in his hand. His voice was kind, as if he had some empathy after all.

In fits and starts, I told them what happened on the road out there in the desert.

"I don't know why . . ." I said when I finished. "Who would do that?"

"You didn't recognize him?" Flanigan asked, the same question Tim had asked on the phone earlier.

I shook my head. "I just saw a shadow. He rolled onto the hood of the car, but I didn't see his face. The windshield shattered. I couldn't see much of anything too clearly."

Tim and Flanigan exchanged a look, and I could see they knew something.

"What?" I asked.

"The timing is convenient," Tim said to Flanigan, ignoring me.

Flanigan put his notebook and pen into the breast pocket of his pin-striped suit. He looked dapper, even when interrogating accident witnesses.

"What timing?" I asked.

"Let me see if we can locate him," Flanigan said, nodding a good-bye to me and disappearing around the curtain.

I turned my gaze on Tim. "You have to tell me. What timing is right?"

"Dan Franklin. We let him go about two hours ago."

Chapter 54

Tim's words sunk in slowly.

"You let him go?" I finally asked.

"We didn't have anything to hold him on. His car really had been at the garage, getting a timing belt like he said. Nothing about it indicated it had been in a crash lately. He told us about that rat, but there's no evidence that he put it in your trunk or killed Ray Lucci. He confessed to being in love with Rosalie Marino but swears she doesn't know."

Tim ran a hand through his hair and sighed.

The back of my bed was up, so I leaned against it, closing my eyes for a few seconds. I could see that body tossed up against the hood of the Pontiac like a rag doll. I opened my eyes again to get rid of the sight.

"Can we find out about Jeff?" I asked.

"He's in surgery," Tim said again. "We won't know anything for a little while." He paused. "We'll need to talk to him when he wakes up." He meant Flanigan. Of course Flanigan would have to talk to Jeff. Probably to make sure Jeff and I had the same story.

"He's tough," I said, mostly to myself. "He'll be okay. He was in the Marines. He was in a war. And he came home okay."

"Flanigan will probably need to ask you more questions, too."

I nodded and sighed. I knew that, but I wasn't in the mood to be interrogated again. Tim noticed and rubbed my shoulder. I winced as pain shot through my back. He jerked his hand back. "Maybe you're not okay," he said.

"We got into a crash. I might be sore for a couple days."

He cocked his head at my face. "You might want to wear a veil or something."

"It looks that bad?"

"It'll look worse tomorrow."

Great.

I wanted to close my eyes again, but I was afraid of what I'd see. The curtain moved, and Bixby stepped in. He looked at Tim.

"How is she?"

"*She* is fine," I replied, before Tim could. "*She* would love to take a shower." I didn't add that I wanted to wash off Jeff's blood, but I didn't think I had to.

Tim's phone started to ring, and Bixby frowned.

"I'll be back," Tim said, putting his phone to his ear and walking out.

"You really are fine?" Bixby asked.

"How is Jeff?"

"He's in surgery."

Same answer as Tim. Totally wasn't what I wanted to hear.

"You're the doctor here. Can't you find out how it's going?" I asked.

"You care a great deal for him, don't you?" Bixby asked, his eyes probing my face.

I knew what he was looking for. "He's my friend," I said softly. "Nothing else." Although as I said it, I remembered how Jeff had held my hand, how he'd called me by my first name, not Kavanaugh. "He's a very good friend," I added.

"Oh." Bixby turned his face slightly, and I could see disappointment.

"We're not a couple," I said. "It's not like that. It's different." I struggled with how to describe my relationship with Jeff Coleman. He was a royal pain in my butt, but he had helped me out on more than one occasion, and he created the koi tattoo on my arm, something that was permanent, that would never go away.

As I sat there and thought about him, I knew. I knew that if something happened to him, my life would be a little bit emptier.

I'd never admit that to him, though. He'd get some sort of stupid idea that it meant more than it did. Just as Bixby was having that stupid idea now. I could see it.

I crooked my finger at him and said, "Come here."

He did, and I sat up so our faces were mere inches apart. And then I kissed him. Gently, because my face hurt more than getting a hundred tattoos at the same time.

It seemed to pacify him, because when he pulled away, Dr. Colin Bixby wore a lopsided grin.

"I'll go check on Coleman's status," he said and went through the curtain, leaving me alone with my thoughts.

Sister Mary Eucharista wouldn't have been happy with me. I'd kissed the man to make him stop asking me whether I had feelings for Jeff. Don't get me wrong—I found the guy incredibly sexy. But kissing him to get him to stop asking questions wasn't exactly right.

I looked at my shirt and the bloodstains and decided I couldn't stay here like that. I swung my legs over the side of the bed, ignoring the shooting pain that moved through my body. My neck felt as though there were a vise on it. I moved toward the curtain, slowly, because now my muscles had decided to revolt. They'd been resting, they'd been happy, and now I was making them work after way too much trauma.

The curtain swung open just as I reached it. Tim frowned.

"What are you doing out of bed?" he demanded.

"I need a shower. Please tell Bixby to find me a shower." Tears sprung into my eyes, and Tim put his arm around me.

"Okay, okay. We'll find you a shower." He twisted his head and called over to one of the nurses. "Can my sister get a shower somewhere?" To me, he said, "I can call Bitsy, see if she can bring a change of clothes."

I'd forgotten about Bitsy. I'd told her she could go home

early, and I'd said I'd open up tomorrow. How was I going to manage that now?

A nurse in baby blue scrubs and green Crocs came over to me and smiled kindly. "Do you want to come with me?"

I nodded and followed her down the hall and out a door. She led me to another door and pushed it open. It was a full bath, hospital style, with plain fixtures and handicap rails. The shower had no tub, but a small plastic seat and more rails, in case I couldn't hold myself up. I might end up making use of them.

The nurse pointed to a soap dispenser.

"We don't have shampoo," she apologized.

"I'll use the soap," I said.

She shut the door behind her as she left. I locked it and stripped off my clothes. The blood had soaked through my shirt, and the skin around the dragon tattoo was pink. My heart began to pound, and I sat, naked, on the plastic chair, my head in my hands, and I began to sob softly. Somewhere in this building, Jeff was fighting for his life. I vowed to be nicer to him when he got better. I wouldn't get as annoyed with him.

After a few minutes, I pulled myself together and turned on the faucet, the hot water crashing down around me, beating into my skin and washing away the blood.

The nurse had left me some scrubs, and when I was done, I put them on and found Tim waiting for me.

"Better?" he asked casually, although I could see from his expression that something else was going on.

"What is it?" I asked.

"Cops found the scene. Couldn't really miss it. Pieces of car all over the place, lots of skid marks. A dent in that light pole you must have hit."

He was holding something back, though.

"What?" I asked again. "What's wrong?"

"There's nothing else there. No car, no injured person. No one at all."

Chapter 55

"So you think we ran ourselves off the road? That Jeff shot himself?" I asked indignantly. "Or maybe you think *I* shot him."

"Don't be ridiculous, Brett."

"Am I being ridiculous? You say that there was no body, no car, like I was lying or something. Like maybe it was all a figment of my imagination."

"I know you're not lying," he argued. "But obviously you didn't hurt the guy as bad as you thought."

"There was blood on the hood of the car," I said, shivering with the memory and looking around. "Where's Flanigan? Doesn't he want to take me in or something?"

"You're being unreasonable," Tim said, his voice full of exasperation. "Can you remember anything else that could help us?"

I didn't want to remember anything. I wished I didn't remember anything.

"Jeff said he saw the car in the side-view mirror. But he didn't tell me what kind of car it was."

It had been a little while from the time Jeff and I left to the time I called Tim. If the guy wasn't hurt too bad, he probably drove away. It had felt as if we'd slammed into the other car pretty hard, but maybe it wasn't as bad as it felt.

"Do you really think it could've been Dan Franklin?" I asked.

"He came after you this afternoon. He ran from us.

He seemed a little squirrelly when we questioned him, although he had answers for everything."

"Did he pick up his car from the shop after getting his timing belt?" I asked, emphasizing the words "timing belt" as though that was just a cover. Because it might have been.

I remembered something else. "What about Will Parker? He met Franklin at the Convention Center, right?"

"Franklin says he called him to pick him up and take him to work."

I vaguely remembered him telling us that.

I thought about Parker and how Jeff and I had followed him from the Convention Center.

"Sanderson. Martin Sanderson. The owner of the Love Shack, that wedding chapel across from That's Amore," I said.

"What about him?"

"Parker went there from the Convention Center."

Tim frowned. Oops. He didn't know Jeff and I had followed Parker. But considering where Jeff was now, I wasn't going to worry about it.

"Remember I asked you about that license plate number? Will Parker was driving the car registered to Martin Sanderson."

I filled him in on how Jeff had followed Parker, adding that Parker ended up at Murder Ink, where we found him with Bernie.

Tim scratched his chin. "He said he was there for a tattoo?"

"That's what Bernie said." As I spoke, I realized how stupid that sounded. Parker had been to my shop earlier for a tattoo touch-up. He hinted he might want more ink, but it seemed too soon to head to another shop for another tattoo. But what other reason would he have to go to Murder Ink?

"Maybe I need to talk to Bernie," Tim said. "See exactly what Parker wanted."

"Maybe you do. But keep in mind he's over eighty."

"Which means his memory might not be as good."

"Right."

"He's at his daughter's house?"

"That's where we left them." And then I realized I hadn't called Sylvia to tell her about Jeff. She had no idea her son was in surgery at the moment, shot in the shoulder by a crazy person. Considering that she'd lost one son, this would be terrible news. "I need to call Sylvia," I said softly. "She doesn't know yet, about Jeff."

But then I had another thought. I debated with myself for a second, then said, "Sylvia withdrew ten thousand dollars from her account the day before her wedding."

"How do you know that?" Tim's eyes were as wide as dinner plates.

I told him about the quilted bag and how I'd come to be in possession of it. "It was all pretty innocent," I added, "until I looked inside the bag and saw the bank receipt."

"So you think she's the one who gave the money to Lucci?"

"She says she didn't. When I asked her about it later, she said to mind my own business." I paused. "I guess it could've been for anything."

"Except that her son left a duffel bag with exactly that amount in his locker."

"But what about Dan Franklin's money? The money he withdrew?"

"I see where you might connect the dots, but that one's a dead end. Franklin did take the money out, but what you didn't see was that he put it right back into a CD. His bank was offering a pretty good rate. We verified it all with the bank."

Back to square one.

"So what about Sanderson? His assistant told me that Ray Lucci had been around threatening them," I said. "Maybe Sanderson wanted to get rid of Lucci. Parker was with Lucci at my shop—" I stopped. What about that tattoo that Dan Franklin had?

Tim read my mind. "It really was Lucci. We verified the shop where Franklin got his tattoo."

And then it came back to me in a flash. What had bothered me about Franklin's tattoo. Joel told me he'd tattooed "That's Amore" around Lucci's bicep. Franklin's tattoo was on his forearm. So much for that theory. But it didn't mean Franklin was off the hook completely. He *had* run from us for some reason.

"Going back to Parker—he was with Lucci at my shop. He was messing around with Joel's clip cord. He could've taken it and then killed Lucci with it later. Since Parker was driving Sanderson's car and he went over to the Love Shack today, maybe he and Sanderson were in on it together."

"And you think Sanderson hired him to do it?"

I shrugged. "You got any better ideas?"

He agreed. "It would make sense."

"Parker did say someone tried to run him down in my car. Maybe Lucci tried to kill him first."

"Or maybe he made that up."

Definite possibility.

"Why would he kill Marino?" Tim asked.

There were still too many questions. And Parker was in the wind, so we couldn't ask him.

"I'm going to take you home," Tim said.

"What about Flanigan?"

"He agreed that you could go home, as long as I was with you." He paused. "Of course he's not completely trusting me right now, either, because of the Monorail thing, but I managed to convince him we'd go straight to the house."

"I'm staying. I need to stay until Jeff's out of surgery." I heard a tinge of hysteria in my voice.

"There's nothing you can do." Tim sighed, then tried another tack. "You don't have any proper clothes."

"I thought you said you'd call Bitsy."

"I couldn't reach her."

I nodded, remembering. "I told her she could leave early. She's probably on a date or something. You know, you could go get me some clothes."

"Or you could come home, change, get a couple hours of sleep, and then I can bring you back when Jeff's in recovery." He stared me down. This was not unlike some of our childhood power plays, and fortunately for him, I was worn down enough by the night's events to give in.

I got off the bed and felt it in every muscle. Tim noticed. He took my arm as he pulled back the curtain with his other hand. Bixby was on the other side.

"Can you call me the minute Jeff is out of surgery?" I asked him.

"Sure," he said, and while I'd done my best to assure him that Jeff was no more than a friend, he still looked a little uncertain.

I was too exhausted, worried, and in pain to care now.

"Thanks."

Bixby leaned over and gave me a peck on the cheek.

Tim put his arm around me as we walked out the sliding doors and into the night. I shivered; the cotton scrubs weren't exactly warm, and it had gotten pretty chilly out. Tim shrugged out of his tweed sport jacket and handed it to me. I put it on, and between the warmth from Tim's body and the tweed, I felt a lot better.

When we were settled into the Impala, I turned to him and said, "I forgot to call Sylvia." I took my phone out of my bag, and as I flipped it open, I realized I didn't have Rosalie's number. I called information and was put through.

No one answered. The phone rang and rang.

"That's weird," I said as I closed my phone. "Sylvia was staying over with her."

"Maybe they're very sound sleepers," Tim suggested.

Maybe. But it felt as though something wasn't right. It was possible they wouldn't have heard the first ring, but I let it ring at least ten times.

"Unless they had the ringer turned off," Tim said when I expressed my concern.

Okay, so maybe I was seeing trouble where there wasn't any. But I hadn't expected the boogeyman to jump out in the desert, either.

Tim's phone rang. He scooted up in the seat and took it off his belt. "Kavanaugh," he said.

I could hear the other person talking but couldn't make

out the words. Finally, Tim said, "Okay. Thanks." And he hung up. He turned to me, his mouth set in a grim line.

"It was definitely someone from that wedding chapel who ran you off the road and shot at you."

Before I could ask how he knew that, he spoke again.

"They found a torn piece of a jacket at side of the road. It had the words 'That's Amore' on it."

Chapter 56

I didn't think I could ever hear that song title again without having a panic attack. I closed my eyes and let the movie play in my head: the car ramming into the light pole, the gunshots, the body slamming into the windshield.

I looked at Tim. "Do you think it was Dan Franklin?"

"Could have been."

"Why would he have changed into his Dean Martin tux, though?" I asked.

We sat for a few minutes pondering that. It didn't make any sense.

"Will Parker?" I asked.

"Maybe."

Or maybe it was someone totally unrelated to anything that had been going on tonight. Some guy with road rage who came after us.

No. It had to have something to do with everything that had been going on the last few days. Someone who felt threatened enough to try to kill Jeff and me.

Which reminded me, "We need to tell Sylvia about Jeff."

"So what do you propose to do? Go over and wake them up?"

I nodded. "Exactly."

"Why don't I get a uniform out there?" Tim said. "Then you don't have to worry. He'll tell Sylvia about Jeff and take her to the hospital to be with him."

The guilt I felt about leaving the hospital came rushing

back. "I should be with her," I argued. "I should tell her, and I should sit with her, waiting for Jeff."

We were stopped at a light. Tim shifted a little so he was looking at me.

"Is there something more than friendship between you and Jeff Coleman?" he asked.

He was totally serious. While I understood why I had to explain things to Bixby, I shouldn't have had to explain them to my brother.

"No," I said. "But I was in that car with him. It could've been me." And as I faced that thought, my whole body began to shake, but I kept going. "He would've stayed for me. I know that. He wouldn't have left."

Tim took a deep breath. The light changed, and he settled back into his seat and turned on the turn signal. In seconds, he'd spun the Impala around.

"Thanks, Tim," I said, as I found myself headed back out to Summerlin.

We had to stop at the scene. The road was filled with flashing blue and red lights, white spotlights illuminating the desert as detectives and crime scene investigators combed the ground for any clues.

"They're trying to re-create what happened out here," Tim explained. I already knew that; I watch TV.

Tim flashed his badge for the cop who stopped us.

"We're just heading up the road," he said. "Guy who got shot—his mother's in one of those town houses. We can't reach her by phone, so we're going to pick her up and take her to the hospital."

The cop shone his flashlight in my face, and I blinked. "Okay," he said, although I could tell he wanted to say more. He waved us through.

"He probably wanted me to stick around and re-create the crime," I said bitterly, spots in front of my eyes because of the flashlight.

"Hate to tell you, Brett, but you're not off the block yet. Flanigan will go over everything with you again."

"After he talks to Jeff? To make sure our stories match, right?" I couldn't keep the anger out of my tone.

"That's right. It's his job to get the story straight." His tone was measured, as if he knew he shouldn't rile me up even more.

I settled back in my seat and stared at the black sky ahead of us. I always counted on Red Rock for peace of mind, but I wasn't sure I'd want to drive out this way again anytime soon. Maybe I'd have to check out Lake Mead, over in the total opposite direction. There were some good trails out there, too, although it was farther to go, less convenient if I had to get to work at a reasonable hour.

Maybe I wouldn't find a body in my trunk when I came home from Lake Mead.

Ray Lucci was the impetus for all of this. What had he done that caused someone to kill him and stuff him in my trunk? That dead rat—Snowball—still nagged at me. I realized we were close now to Rosalie's complex. I pointed it out, and Tim turned right. Fewer lights than before. I had a hard time distinguishing one area from another and got us lost a couple of times, Tim circling the parking lot.

"Someone's going to call the cops thinking we're casing the place," Tim muttered.

Casing the place? I ignored him, not wanting to banter. I wasn't in the mood.

Finally, I spotted Rosalie's place. I recognized Bernie's white rental car out front.

"How did you not see that the first two times we passed it?" Tim asked.

"We passed it two times?" I honestly hadn't noticed.

He pulled up behind the white car and cut the engine. I peered out the windshield at the town house. No lights in any windows. Not even a glimmer or a glow.

"It's not that late," Tim mused.

I'd lost all track of time, and I could totally do with going to bed right now, so I wasn't one to speculate on when Sylvia and Rosalie decided to retire.

We got out of the Jeep and went up the steps to the front door. I pushed the doorbell, and we could hear it echoing inside.

We waited.

And waited.

Finally, Tim pushed the doorbell again, and again we could hear it inside.

This time, however, we also heard footsteps. The curtain in the kitchen window next to the door fluttered, then the outside light went on over our heads. We heard the dead bolt unlatch, and the door opened. Rosalie's head appeared around it.

"Brett?" she asked, her face scrunched up in a frown. "What are you doing here?" Her eyes moved from me to Tim, lingering on him for a second; then she added, "This must be your brother."

No kidding. But I gave her the benefit of the doubt because she'd been asleep. Her hair was all mussed up, and she had little creases in the side of her face from the pillow.

"We're looking for Sylvia," I explained. "There's been an accident. Jeff . . ." The words caught in my throat.

The door swung wide now, and Rosalie clutched her white bathrobe around her torso. "An accident?"

I nodded. "Jeff's in the hospital."

Her eyes grew wide. "Is he okay?"

"I don't know," I said honestly.

"We need to see Sylvia," Tim butted in. "She should be at the hospital when Jeff comes out of surgery. We're going to take her there."

Rosalie shook her head. "Sylvia's not here. She and my dad had a big fight. I don't know what it was all about, they wouldn't tell me, but they left."

Chapter 57

"Where did they go?" I asked.

Rosalie shrugged. "I figured they'd go back to Dad's house. Or Sylvia's, maybe."

"Can we call your father?" Tim asked.

Rosalie stepped aside and let us come in. She led the way into the kitchen and to a phone on the counter. She picked up the receiver.

"Why is their rental car still here?" I asked while Rosalie dialed.

"They took my car," she said. "Dad's going to take it to the shop tomorrow morning for me. I need an oil change." She put the phone back in its cradle. "No answer."

"What about Sylvia?" I asked.

"You don't have her number?" Rosalie asked.

I was embarrassed to admit that I didn't. I'd never needed to reach her anywhere but at Murder Ink. Neither Sylvia nor Bernie had cell phones, which was why we couldn't reach them right after I found Ray Lucci in my trunk.

Rosalie was already dialing. Tim and I waited. Finally, she hung up, frowning. "That's funny. No answer there, either."

I had a bad feeling about this. Where could they be? On a whim, I took the phone and dialed Murder Ink but got only the recording saying the shop was closed.

"Where could they be?" I asked no one in particular.

I thought about how they'd disappeared after their wedding. It wasn't unusual for Sylvia to do things spur of the moment, but considering Rosalie, I wouldn't think Sylvia would run off again and not tell anyone where she was going.

Maybe she and Bernie had stopped off for a late drink somewhere.

I said as much to Tim, who shrugged, agreeing with the possibility. But Rosalie didn't look so convinced, the worry etched into her forehead.

"What happened with Jeff? You said it was an accident?" she asked.

"He was taking me home," I said, "and a car ran us off the road. And then the guy shot at us."

"Someone shot at you? Who?"

"I don't know. Could've been Dan Franklin. Or Will Parker. Or Martin Sanderson. Take your pick."

"What are you talking about? Will? Dan?" Rosalie's worry turned into confusion. "What's going on?"

"That's what I'd like to know," I said.

"How well do you know the men your husband worked with?" Tim asked, turning into cop mode.

Rosalie's eyes settled on the wall behind Tim as she shrugged. "Well, I work with Dan, so I know him pretty well."

"How well?" Tim asked.

Her lips pressed together in a grim line for a second, then, "Not that well, if that's what you're implying. Lou thought the same thing." Rosalie's fingers went to her eye, where the remnants of the bruise remained. The gesture didn't get past Tim, whose expression softened.

"Your husband did that," he said matter-of-factly. "Dan Franklin must have known about that. Do you think that would have given him a reason to harm your husband?"

Rosalie frowned. "I'm not sure what you're getting at."

"Did Franklin feel he had to avenge your honor or something? Did he feel he had to save you? Would he have killed your husband to do that?"

"It wasn't like that," she said.

"So tell me what it was like," Tim said, more gently now.

Rosalie hung her head and brushed a lock of hair off her forehead and behind her ear. "They all told me to leave him," she whispered. "But I couldn't."

I opened my mouth to ask why not, but Tim shot me a look and I stopped.

"I understand that, but would Franklin have taken matters into his own hands?"

She raised her eyes to Tim's face, a small, sad smile tugging at her lips. "Lou was very intimidating. Even with men."

"So you don't think Franklin killed him? I mean, your husband got run down by a car. That's not exactly a face-to-face confrontation that he could control." Something had changed in Tim's expression; the cop was gone. My brother, the one who protected me, had taken his place, but this time, I could see he was feeling protective toward Rosalie.

I started to get a little worried. Rosalie may have been a victim of domestic abuse, but it was clear she knew how to use her feminine wiles, so to speak, to bring a man over to her side. And a thought began to germinate. What if Franklin *had* run down Lou Marino, but she was the one who put the idea into his head? What if she had said some things at work that would have made him think about it? She couldn't have been blind to how he felt about her, and maybe she wanted to see how far he'd go to save her. What if she was the mastermind behind her husband's death?

Personally, I wouldn't blame her. And there probably wasn't a jury in the world that would convict her. Dr. Colin Bixby had tended to her injuries in the hospital. There were records that could prove years-long abuse.

Maybe Ray Lucci's death had been the impetus. And Will Parker's claim that a red convertible had tried to run him down. And then Lou got mugged. Maybe that was for real, and then she'd figured another attempt on his life would be more believable. She'd turned on the charm with Franklin, got him to feel sorry for her, and—*bam!*—he runs down Lou Marino.

Okay, so I was getting a little carried away. None of that would explain why he would go after Jeff and me. Unless that was a total non sequitur. Nothing at all to do with Lou Marino. And what about Ray Lucci and that clip cord and my car?

"Do you think Franklin could have killed Ray Lucci?" I asked Rosalie, without waiting to find out whether she thought he'd killed her husband.

Rosalie looked at the floor. After a few seconds of hesitation, she said firmly, "Dan Franklin did not kill Ray Lucci." As though she knew that for a fact. And if she did . . .

"So who did?" Tim prodded, picking up on this, too.

She blinked several times and shrugged. "Why ask me?"

"Because I think you know something," Tim said. "What is it? What do you know about Ray Lucci's murder?"

"I—I don't know what you're talking about," she insisted.

For a split second, I wondered whether she'd killed Lucci. But she must weigh a hundred pounds soaking wet, and Lucci was a big guy. Well, not so big he couldn't fit in my trunk, but it would've been really difficult for Rosalie to have strangled him and then stuffed him in my car.

But she knew something. I was willing to bet on it. And in Vegas, bets are everything.

"If you know something, it would be best to tell us," Tim said softly.

Rosalie sighed as she wrung her hands in front of her, her jaw tight. She was debating what she should say. I opened my mouth to ask another question, but Tim gave a short head shake and a glare, so I closed it again. He knew what he was doing. Me—well, I was just along for the ride.

Rosalie finally nodded. "Okay," she said, her eyes locked with Tim's. "I do know something, and I guess it doesn't really matter now. Lou's dead."

As she paused, I wanted to scream, "Out with it!" but I didn't think it would go over well. I forced myself to be patient.

Finally, when I thought I couldn't stand it another minute, she spoke.

"Lou killed Ray Lucci."

Chapter 58

"**W**hy?" Tim asked.

Me—I wanted to know how she knew, but he didn't seem bothered by that at the moment.

"They got into an argument. Ray tried to kill him. He had a knife; Lou got all cut up."

"So the story about the muggers—" I said.

"Wasn't true," Rosalie admitted. "The cuts he had were from the fight he had with Ray. He couldn't tell anyone where he really got them."

"But he told *you*," Tim said.

Her lips quivered for a second, and then she whispered, "I was there."

Tim and I exchanged a look before Tim said, "I think you should tell us what happened."

We were still standing in her foyer, next to the table with the candles. The scent was starting to get to me, and I reached out and took Tim's arm to steady myself.

"Come on in," Rosalie said, leading the way into the living room. She gave a glance back at me, assessing my scrubs and tweed jacket. So I wasn't ready for the runway. Not as though I didn't know that.

I plopped down in a plush armchair, but as soon as I hit the seat, it was as if a million little daggers stabbed me in my back. I winced. Tim noticed.

"Are you okay?"

I blinked a few times to keep from crying. "I'm fine," I said, not wanting to miss this.

Rosalie settled herself on the sofa, pulling her bathrobe close and crossing her arms in front of her chest. She had a sort of waifish look about her: long dark tresses cascading over her shoulders, large smoky eyes, and almost transparently white skin. I could see why men would want to protect her. Or overpower her.

She was quiet a few minutes, her eyes focused on the floor, her fingers fiddling with the sash on her bathrobe. Finally, she lifted her face and sighed. "I went over to the chapel that day, you know, to see my dad and Sylvia get married. I knew they were in the car and it wouldn't be a normal type of wedding, but I was happy for him. Sylvia's wonderful." For a second, Rosalie's face lit up with the memory, and then it faded. "When I got there, I thought I'd surprise Lou, too. So I went to the dressing room to see him. But he was really angry. He thought I was checking up on him. I tried to tell him I was there for my father, but he didn't believe me." She cast her eyes down into her lap. "He hit me."

I was pretty sure where this was going. "Ray Lucci saw him do that, didn't he?" I asked.

"Ray walked in right when Lou hit me," Rosalie said, her voice still slightly more than a whisper. "Ray pulled me aside, asked if I was okay; I said he shouldn't worry about me; he said something about how he hadn't planned it this way, but circumstances called for it. He had a knife in a sort of sheath under his jacket, and he pulled it out. I screamed for him to stop, hoping someone would hear and come help, but no one came, and he nicked Lou a few times. But Lou knows how to throw a punch," she said wryly, touching her eye again, "and he flattened Ray. At that point, I knew I couldn't stop him. I just watched as he strangled him."

Rosalie stopped, her eyes wide.

"Lou told me I couldn't say anything. That if I did, the cops would come after me as some sort of accomplice. And then he'd have to kill me, too."

"Accessory," Tim corrected. "He lied to you, Rosalie. If you'd told the police what you witnessed, they would've been able to protect you from him."

I could feel her fear, though. It was alive in this room, probably lurking under the sofa, the chair I was sitting in. She'd lived in fear of Lou Marino, and it wouldn't have been too hard for him to convince her to keep quiet.

We all jumped when Tim's cell phone started ringing. He took it off his belt, glanced at the caller ID, and stood, walking out of sight, down the hall and into the kitchen. I could hear him murmuring, but I couldn't make out the words.

Rosalie shifted on the sofa, pulled her feet up underneath her. It looked as close to a fetal position as she could get into while sitting up.

"You really think I won't get into trouble?" she asked softly.

I'd been trying to eavesdrop on Tim, so when she spoke, it caught me by surprise.

As did another thought I had. Something about her story didn't add up. Something was off. I couldn't put my finger on it, though. My head was all jumbled up like a jigsaw puzzle that had too many pieces missing.

Before I could question her, though, Tim strode back into the room, clipping his phone back to his belt. He cocked his head at me.

"We've got to go."

I stood up, a little too quickly, because the little daggers were back. It had been okay while I was sitting, but too long in one position seemed to exacerbate the situation.

Tim didn't seem to notice this time, however. He nodded at Rosalie.

"I'll be back, probably with another detective, to take your statement. Make sure you don't go anywhere." It was not a request.

Rosalie, who was plainly very susceptible to direct orders from men, nodded meekly. But as Tim started to turn, she said, "What if my father calls? Shall I tell him you're looking for Sylvia?"

Tim's jaw tensed. "That would be a good idea," he said curtly. "Come on," he said to me.

I shrugged at Rosalie as I followed my brother out the

front door and to the Impala. He held the door open, but it was clear if I didn't get in quickly he might leave me here.

"What's the hurry?" I asked when we were both settled and he started the engine.

"That was Flanigan. He's over at that wedding chapel."

"That's Amore? Why?"

"Someone's shooting at the cars driving up."

Chapter 59

I had a vision of a bloody Dean Martin in a torn tuxedo waving a gun around, taking potshots at unsuspecting brides and grooms. Now *that* would make an interesting horror movie. Probably would be a blockbuster.

"Is it Dan Franklin?" I asked. Maybe all the killing had finally gotten to him.

"No one knows. The shots are coming from inside."

"How?"

"Through the drive-up window."

"Has he hit anyone?"

"Not so far, but Flanigan doesn't want to waste time. He's got the cavalry out there."

We made our way back down Charleston, past all the strip malls and the Terrible's, and turned down Las Vegas Boulevard. The lights at Fremont Street, flashing every which way to entice late night revelers, were bright enough to warrant sunglasses.

As we passed Murder Ink, I saw a light on.

I grabbed Tim's arm. "Stop," I said.

"What?"

"Someone's in Murder Ink. We know it's not Jeff."

"We don't really have time for this. Doesn't he have a security service?"

"I don't know. But I feel like something's wrong."

Tim gave a heavy sigh that indicated I was being a royal pain in his butt, but he eased the car over against the curb and cut the engine.

"You stay here," he instructed.

"No way," I said, opening my door at the same time he opened his. "This isn't a place where I want to be alone at this hour."

He couldn't argue with logic, so he agreed and I followed him across the street to Murder Ink. We peered into the front window and saw that the light was coming from the back room. Tim put his arm out and said, "Stay behind me."

We went around to the side alley and around the back. The smell from the Dumpster back here was overwhelming, and I put my hand up against my nose.

"What are they dumping back here?" Tim muttered.

"It's the Chinese take-out place," I said, indicating the screen door and the clanking of pots and pans inside.

Murder Ink's back door was ajar.

Tim pushed the door in slowly. We could hear rustling, as if someone was going through papers, and then something fell with a thud.

Tim's hand was on his gun at his hip, ready to pull it out if necessary. I made sure I stayed behind him, but the curiosity was killing me. Who was in there?

In a smooth move, Tim shoved the door open, and we both bounded inside.

Sylvia looked up, frowning, as she held a box of baby wipes.

"You're not supposed to come through the back way," she admonished, as if it were every day someone broke in through the back door.

I took a deep breath, relieved it was her. "You're okay," I said.

"Why wouldn't I be, dear?" she asked. "Except Jeff left this place a mess. Where is he, anyway? I thought he was with you." She cocked her head toward Tim. "What's he doing here?"

"Where's Bernie?" I asked, not answering her questions.

Her mouth set in a firm line. "He brought me home, but I couldn't just sit around. I've got insomnia, you know."

I didn't know, and it didn't seem relevant right now.

She was still talking. "Bernie said the Gremlin was in the shop, but I found it in the carport like usual, but he'd covered it over with a tarp. I drove that over here."

I'd seen a car in the alley, but it hadn't registered. Unusual, because it's such an unusual-looking car.

"Where's Jeff? I thought he was with you," Sylvia said, indicating me.

Tim and I exchanged a look. She noticed.

"What's going on? Where's my son?"

I sighed. "He's in the hospital. There was an accident."

All the color drained out of her face, and it was almost as if her tattoos went black and white for a second. She dropped down into the swivel chair next to her, all her defiance gone.

"Is he okay?"

I nodded. "He's in surgery."

"What happened?"

I couldn't sugarcoat it. I told her what happened out in the desert.

She took some deep breaths, then pushed herself out of the chair. "I need to go to the hospital."

I looked at Tim. "Why don't you head over to That's Amore, and I can take Sylvia to the hospital. We can take the Gremlin."

Tim mulled this proposal. "That sounds like a plan."

"That's Amore?" Sylvia looked from me to Tim and back to me again.

"Someone's over there shooting at cars," I said.

"What on earth for?"

"We have no idea," I said. "Where did Bernie go?"

"I have no idea," she said, echoing me. "And I don't care." She stuck her chin out defiantly.

"What's wrong?"

"You know," Sylvia said cryptically.

"No, I don't know. Why don't you tell me?"

"*You* found the receipt." She said it as if I was some sort of idiot for not knowing this by osmosis.

Receipt? Oh, right. The bank receipt. "What about it?"

"The man stole ten thousand dollars from me. I made him bring me home because I wouldn't go home with him. I'm getting a divorce."

"Ten thousand dollars?" I asked.

She made a face at me. "You knew about it," she said accusingly. "You asked me about it when you came to Rosalie's earlier. But I didn't take that money out of the bank. Bernie did. I should never have gotten a joint account."

"Did you ask him about it?" Tim asked. He'd been in the background, but now he stepped forward, interested in what Sylvia was saying.

"Sure, I did. He said he needed it for a new car or something. He wanted to surprise me. I didn't want any new car. I've got my Gremlin. Although on the way over here, I realized it might need some fixing after all. There was an awful scraping sound."

A thought flashed through my brain.

It couldn't be.

But maybe it was.

I took a step toward the door.

Tim was on the same wavelength. He was already outside.

"What's going on?" Sylvia called from behind us.

Tim jogged up the alleyway. I discovered my body was really starting to rebel against any sort of movement whatsoever. A soak in a hot tub was what I needed about now, but the adrenaline was pushing me forward anyway.

Tim was leaning down over the hood of the Gremlin. When I approached, he straightened up and said, "This car definitely hit something."

"Or someone?" I asked, remembering that the car that killed Lou Marino was blue. Or maybe an odd shade of purple.

Chapter 60

Sylvia stood with her hands on her hips. "Someone?" she asked. "Who did it hit?" And as it sunk in, she gave a little "Oh!" then asked, "You don't think someone used this car to kill Lou?"

Tim and I exchanged a look. I knew what he was thinking. The same thing I was. Bernie wanted to get rid of the car. Had he killed his son-in-law with it? He'd have had a good reason.

"It was under a tarp, you said?" Tim asked.

"That's right."

Even though Sylvia said she was washing her hands of her new husband and that he'd stolen ten grand from her, I didn't want to believe it. How could a cute little old deli owner do such things? Maybe we were wrong. I hoped we were wrong.

He shook his head. "You can't use this car. You both have to come with me. I'm going to send someone over here to check the car out. Impound it."

"Do I need to use Jeff's car? I hate that thing," Sylvia said.

I didn't really want to tell her that Jeff's car was pretty much totaled.

"Come on," Tim urged.

Sylvia put on a fleece pullover and locked up the shop, and we went around the side of the building between Murder Ink and Goodfellas Bail Bonds. When we got to the

Impala, Sylvia climbed in the back. I tried to argue with her, but she said she was little and not to worry.

"Do you really think Jeff will be all right?" Sylvia asked when we were on the road.

"He'll be fine. I know he will." I was trying to convince myself as much as Sylvia. She leaned forward and patted my shoulder, sending waves of pain through my neck. I tried not to wince. She was just trying to comfort me.

The scene around the wedding chapel was crazy: flashing blue and red lights from the cruisers; spotlights sending pools of light across the white stucco, making it look less washed out somehow; cops scurrying about, most wearing bulletproof vests outside their shirts. I glanced over at Tim, bare chested underneath his button-down shirt. I'd already seen a friend shot tonight; I didn't want to make another visit to the hospital because Tim got wounded.

Tim parked the car behind a couple of cruisers near the sawhorses that had been set up along the entrance to the chapel's driveway. The chapel looked deserted—dark and quiet—despite all the activity outside.

"Stay here," Tim instructed as he climbed out of the Impala.

"Why do men think they can tell us what to do?" Sylvia asked.

"Because they do," I said.

"Well, I don't want to just sit here," Sylvia said. "Let's go."

I wasn't quite sure I wanted to this time. Had something finally snapped? Had my curiosity been sated by everything that had happened? Had I finally become a normal person, who doesn't stick her nose into things that are best left to the police?

Sister Mary Eucharista was telling me I was having a breakthrough.

Sylvia, on the other hand, was pushing open the back door and climbing out, slamming the door behind her. She took a few steps toward the chaos, then turned and beckoned me to follow. When I shook my head, she shrugged and continued on. I watched her through the windshield.

Maybe this was what it was like on a movie set, except this was all real. I watched as Tim approached Flanigan, who held a bullhorn. They had a few words; then a uniform came up to Tim and handed him a vest. I sighed with relief. Good. Now at least Tim would be protected. Except, of course, if he got shot in the head or something awful like that.

I kicked myself for even thinking that.

Sylvia had approached Tim and Flanigan, who didn't look happy she was there.

My cell phone startled me. I reached inside my bag and pulled it out, not recognizing the number on the screen.

"Yes?" I asked tentatively as I flipped it open and held it to my ear.

"Brett? It's Colin."

Bixby. My heart started to flutter, but not in a good way. Rather, in a nervous way. While I wanted him to call me about Jeff, I wanted good news. I wasn't sure I could handle it if it wasn't. I swallowed hard, then tried to make my voice sound normal as I asked, "Oh, hi. Do you have news about Jeff?"

"He's out of surgery, and everything went well."

I smiled involuntarily and took a deep breath. I blinked a couple of times to keep from crying. Seemed good news *and* bad would make me cry today.

Bixby was still talking. "The bullet lodged itself in his neck, but they got it out, and they think he'll have a full recovery. He'll need some physical therapy for a while."

For the first time it dawned on me that he'd been shot in his right shoulder. He was right handed.

"Do you think he'll be able to tattoo?" I asked.

Colin was quiet a second. "I'm not sure. That'll be up to the physical therapist to see what sort of motion he'll have at first."

"Is he awake now?"

"No, he's still in recovery. The anesthesia should wear off in a little while."

"I'll be bringing his mother over there," I said, glancing back up, but Sylvia was now nowhere in sight.

"I thought you were going home," he said. "You should be, you know. You got banged up pretty bad. You need to heal."

Yeah, yeah, yeah, was what I wanted to say, but it would have been way too sarcastic, and he wouldn't have understood, since he had no idea what was going on, and I didn't think this was the time to enlighten him.

Flanigan was shouting something through the bullhorn, but I couldn't make it out. It was facing the wrong direction, so the sound was distorted.

"What's that?" Bixby asked.

"Nothing," I said. "TV."

"Awfully loud."

He was buying it.

Flanigan was saying something else now.

"Listen, Bixby, I've got to go," I said. "Will you be around later, when I bring Sylvia over to see Jeff?"

"I'm heading home, but I'll call you in the morning. See how you're doing."

"Mmm," I said, not really paying attention. "See you, then," I said, flipping the phone shut, my attention on what was going on beyond the windshield.

Flanigan held the bullhorn at his side. The building stayed as quiet as it was when we first got here. I began to wonder whether anyone was inside at all. I hadn't heard any gunshots.

I leaned back in my seat, closing my eyes. I still held the cell phone; it was smooth like the rocks I used to skim across the river at home in Jersey. I felt myself dozing off, despite more shouting from outside my little cocoon. I didn't have the energy to open my eyes to see what was going on.

I felt the cold air sweep across my body as my door opened, but because I was half-asleep I thought it was just part of the dream I was having.

But when I was yanked out of the car, an arm wrapped

itself around my neck; my eyes snapped open, and I struggled to breathe.

I felt the cold metal against the side of my head.

"Come with me quietly. I don't want to have to hurt you."

Chapter 61

I couldn't move to see who it was. The voice was low, deep, not one I recognized.

He dragged me backward a few feet, then shifted his arm a little. It gave me a chance to ask, "What do you want from me?"

"Just a little insurance for now."

I was able to twist my head a little, not without a lot of pain, and I saw him. Will Parker.

I must have looked surprised, because he chuckled and said, "You're a nosy bitch. I knew you knew it was me all along."

He loosened his grip slightly, and I shifted. I could see the torn tuxedo. So it had been Parker out there shooting at us.

"You did steal Joel's clip cord, didn't you?" I asked with a lot more bravado than I felt. But as I thought about how Ray Lucci was killed, it dawned on me that Rosalie had already told me Lou had done it. Two people couldn't have killed one man.

And then I realized what it had been about her story that didn't jibe.

She said she'd gone over to the wedding chapel when Bernie and Sylvia were getting married, to see the wedding. Lou had gotten angry, hit her, and Ray Lucci cut him up. It was then that Lou killed Ray, Rosalie said.

But he couldn't have. Ray wasn't killed until later, because he'd stolen my car. His fingerprints were all over it.

Rosalie had lied. Lou Marino hadn't killed Ray Lucci. Will Parker had. Later in the day, and then he'd returned my car to the parking garage as if it had never been gone.

"Rosalie's protecting you," I said. "She told me Lou killed Lucci. But it was you all along. It doesn't matter now if she says Lou killed him because Lou's dead."

"No thanks to Lucci," he said bitterly.

I started putting it all together. That ten thousand dollars in Lucci's locker. The ten thousand dollars Bernie took from Sylvia. And something that Rosalie said: how Lucci had told Lou that cutting him wasn't how he'd planned it.

Maybe that part of Rosalie's story was true. Everything except Lou killing Lucci.

"Bernie paid Lucci to kill Lou, didn't he?" I asked. "So what happened? How did you end up killing Lucci instead? Why?"

His grip got tighter, and he lifted me up a little, until I was almost off my feet. "He cut him up, but he didn't kill him. He had all that money, and he hadn't done it yet. Lou kept hitting her, and Lucci was dragging his feet." The anguish in his voice was palpable. It was clear how he felt about Rosalie.

"So you took matters into your own hands? Anyway, why didn't Bernie pay you instead to kill Lou? You were the one in love with her."

"That's exactly why I couldn't do it," Parker said, taking the bait, his voice a low growl. The gun had moved from my temple down to my neck now. "Lucci was the ex-con. If he got caught, no biggie."

No biggie to him and Bernie, perhaps, but it was a biggie to Sylvia.

"Why do you think I know all this already?" I asked.

"You can't keep your nose out of anything. When I surprised you at the chapel, I knew you'd been looking in the lockers. I knew you'd found it."

"Found what?"

He sighed. "I'm so tired of you playing stupid. Pretending to buy the crap about how a girl got rough with me but telling me the whole time about how your brother, the cop, was there. I didn't get why you hadn't told him yet, except you were on a power trip. I knew it was only a matter of time, though."

This guy was living in his own little fantasy world. I didn't want to let on that I'd just figured everything out. I'd have loved to know what it was I'd supposedly found in his locker. I hadn't even gotten to his locker. I'd seen Dan Franklin's university ID, and that was it.

"That's enough talking. We've got to go for a ride."

Parker spun me around and shoved me in front of him, his arm still wrapped tight around my chest, so my arms were pinned to my sides. The gun hovered somewhere near my ear. I wanted to scream, but he'd already shot Jeff, so he probably wouldn't have any scruples about shooting me, too.

He weaved me through a couple of cars. The Love Shack was across the street, and we were headed in that direction, away from the police and the lights in front of That's Amore.

"How did you get out?" I asked. "Out of the chapel back there?"

He chuckled, the rumbling vibrating against my ear. "I was gone before the cops got there. Those couples were convinced, though, that I was still in there and told the cops that."

Great. No one would be looking here, across the parking lot and then across the street. He'd taken his arm away from my chest but held on to my upper arm, the gun stuck in the center of my back, where my Celtic cross tattoo was. He was walking so close to me that no one would be able to see the gun or that I was being forced to go.

"How's your friend?" he asked.

"Fighting for his life," I said, trying to choke back a sob. I hadn't signed on for any of this, and I was making promises to Sister Mary Eucharista that I would never get involved in this sort of thing ever again as long as she let me live.

The bigger-than-life Elvis hovered overhead, the Love Shack sign flashing its neon. Anyone watching us would think we were just another couple going in to get married.

I needed to stall for more time.

"So I think I know what happened," I said. "Bernie paid Lucci to kill his son-in-law, who was beating up his daughter. You didn't think Lucci worked fast enough; you had some sort of fight—that's where those bruises on your hand came from—you ended up killing him and putting him in my trunk; then you sat back and waited until the time was right to kill Lou." I paused. "How did you know where to return my car after you killed Lucci?"

"I was with him when he stole it."

Okay, that made sense in a weird sort of way. "So how come your prints weren't found in the car, but Lucci's were?"

He snorted. "Gloves."

People wear gloves only when they know they're going to have to cover something up. "You stole the clip cord; you had gloves; you were waiting for that moment, weren't you?" I asked.

"Always be prepared, right?" His voice was so cold it sent shivers down my spine.

"Lucci didn't really try to run you down, did he?"

"I wish you'd stop with the stupid act."

He was giving me a lot of credit.

I had another question. "Why the rat?"

"I hated that rat."

"Dan said Lucci killed it."

"I did. And I figured what better way to send off Dean Martin than with a rat. Rat Pack, right?" He chuckled at his own joke.

"But you didn't kill Lou, did you?"

He stopped laughing, and he shoved the gun hard into my back. "What do you mean?"

"Bernie killed him. With the Gremlin. But you still wanted money, didn't you? It wasn't enough to have Rosalie. That's why you had him meet you at Murder Ink. To try to get money out of him."

He wasn't arguing with me, so I figured I was on the right track. I wished I had a tape recorder or something so I could prove all this to Tim later. If I had the chance.

We were going toward the door of the Love Shack now. It was a twenty-four-hour wedding chapel, and it bled light out onto the parking lot. If he was going to kill me, it seemed pretty risky to do it here.

And then I remembered Martin Sanderson.

"You're driving Sanderson's car," I said. "Why?"

"It's my car," he said. "Martin doesn't know I switched the plates."

He wouldn't be telling me all this if he was going to let me live.

Maybe I could yank myself away from him. Try to kick up backward and get him in the groin or the shin. Spin around and push him away and run.

As I was going through scenarios in my head, I didn't hear the roar of the engine until it was almost upon us.

The car made the decision for me.

Will Parker threw me aside as the Impala sideswiped him, throwing him up over the hood in a total déjà vu moment.

Chapter 62

I'd lost my balance and ended up on the ground. When I rolled slightly to get up, I saw the gun near my feet. I stood and picked it up. It was big, like that Smith & Wesson that came in the mail for Ray Lucci. Had Lucci been waiting for the gun to kill Lou? Is that why it took so long that Parker felt he had to take matters into his own hands?

"Dear, are you all right?" Sylvia climbed out of the Impala and came toward me. She took the gun out of my hand as though it weighed next to nothing and went over to Will Parker, who lay on the ground, his leg twitching slightly.

Sylvia pointed the gun at him.

"Who do you think you are?" she demanded.

Her white hair was piled on top of her head and held in place with those little butterfly clips; she wore cotton pants and a fleece pullover. If it weren't for the big gun locked between her hands, she'd look like someone's grandmother on her way back from book group or knitting club.

Movement caught my eye. I turned to see Tim running across the intersection, his face grim.

When he caught sight of Sylvia holding the gun on Will Parker, he stopped short, and a big grin crossed his face. He hid it quickly, though, and strode over to her, putting his hand over hers and carefully taking the gun. He tossed a "How are you?" back at me.

I nodded to indicate I was okay.

"What do you think you're doing?" Tim demanded of

Sylvia as he leaned down and turned Parker over, slapping handcuffs on his wrists.

"I tried to tell you, but you weren't paying attention," Sylvia said. "I saw him"—she cocked her head at Parker—"taking Brett over here and it didn't look like anything friendly. Someone had to do something,"

"That's the last time I leave my keys in the car," Tim muttered, pulling Parker to his feet.

"If you didn't keep the keys in the car, then who knows what would've happened to your sister," Sylvia said sharply. She was almost a foot shorter than he was, but she looked a lot taller as she stood with her hands on her hips, admonishing him.

I stifled a chuckle.

Parker glared at me. "It's your word against mine," he growled.

Tim shoved him. "Somehow I think her word is worth more," he said.

A cruiser skidded to a stop behind the Impala, and Tim opened the back door and pushed Parker in, closing it behind him. He turned to me.

"Hate to tell you, but we've got to take a statement."

Story of my life.

I don't know how I did it, but I managed to get myself to the shop by eleven the next morning. I was sitting with my coffee and a bagel when Bitsy and Joel came in. They were laughing about something as they pushed the door open, but when they saw me, their faces froze.

"What happened to you?" Bitsy demanded, her voice stern, although I could tell I was totally off the hook for abandoning everyone yesterday.

Joel came over and gently touched my face. "Sweetheart, you look terrible."

"Thanks," I said, making a face at him. I'd looked in the mirror exactly once that morning and decided I wouldn't do that for the rest of the day.

I'd spent most of the night at the hospital with Sylvia,

waiting for Jeff to wake up. When he did, he gave me a small smile and raised his eyebrows as he assessed my bruises and scrubs, but he didn't say anything. They wouldn't let me stay, because I wasn't family. Tim took me home after I gave my statement about Parker, and I got exactly two hours of sleep. But at least I'd gotten another shower and I could put on clean clothes.

"I'm sorry about yesterday," I said. "I went out for chocolate, and the next thing I knew, I was riding the Monorail and going to Summerlin and getting shot at. And Jeff's in the hospital, and Will Parker tried to kill me a second time and—"

"Jeff? What's wrong with Jeff?" Joel asked, concern etched in a frown across his forehead.

"Parker shot him after he ran us off the road. But he's okay," I added. "He's out of surgery, and they say he's going to be fine."

Bitsy held her hand up. "Stop. You know you have to tell us everything from the beginning, but you've got a client coming in about two minutes. Is that enough time?"

I rolled my eyes. "Not nearly enough."

As I spoke, my client came in. I was a little worried I'd be too tired, but turns out there's a little thing called auto-pilot. I didn't want to tell the client that I could do this in my sleep, because I practically was.

Bitsy plied me with more coffee after my client left, and I went over the story piece by piece. She and Joel and Ace, who'd come in while I was with my client, hung on every word and didn't even interrupt.

I'd gotten pretty much all of it right. When Tim took me home to get a little sleep, he told me Rosalie admitted she and Parker had had an affair; she was protecting Parker by telling me that Lou killed Lucci. Bernie admitted— after the blood type found on the Gremlin matched Lou Marino's—that he'd contracted to have his daughter's husband killed, and when it didn't work out, he took matters into his own hands.

And the thing that Parker thought I found in the locker

room? The reason why he'd tried to run me and Bitsy down at the university and then Tim and me in the parking garage? And why he'd shot at Jeff and me?

A love letter from Rosalie.

"Are you sure?" I asked for the umpteenth time.

Jeff sat in my chair, in my room at The Painted Lady. His shirt was off, showcasing his tattoos. My eyes lingered on the Day of the Dead tattoo that he'd designed himself—a skeleton in a big sombrero, playing a guitar—before moving up to the ugly red wound that was still healing near his clavicle.

"I know you think I'm good-looking, Kavanaugh, but let's get to it," he quipped. He'd been out of the hospital for two weeks. So far we hadn't talked about anything that had happened. I tried, but every time I did, he changed the subject. Like now.

"Bitsy says you're having dinner with that Dr. Sexy tonight."

I rolled my eyes at him. "That's not really your business." I'd had a long conversation with Colin Bixby and asked him why he'd pointed me in the direction of Dan Franklin, who clearly had only an unrequited relationship with Rosalie. But the rumor around the university lab, however, had them having a heated relationship, and Bixby felt Franklin was suspect.

"Bitsy says you have a hard time with commitment," Jeff was saying. "But I don't think so."

I frowned. What would Jeff Coleman know about that? I secretly thought Bitsy was right. I'd had a series of relationships in the last ten years, and none of them had lasted.

"You don't get it, do you, Kavanaugh?"

"I guess I don't," I said, slipping a new needle into my tattoo machine.

He watched me for a second, then said, "Every time you mark your body, you're making a commitment. A lifelong commitment. One of these days it won't be just a tattoo."

What? Was Jeff Coleman becoming profound? Who knew?

But then he ruined it. "Maybe it'll be Dr. Sexy. Tonight. Should I tell your brother not to wait up?" He winked.

I dipped the needle in black ink. Despite his attempt to distract me, the question remained. "Are you sure?" I asked again, the machine poised.

Jeff pointed to a small space of bare skin just above where his wound was. "Right there. And I've never been so sure in my life."

"You and Sylvia have talked about it?"

"That's between me and her, Kavanaugh. Don't worry your little head about it."

But I did worry about it. This wasn't just another tattoo.

I sighed and pressed the foot pedal, and the machine began to whir. I touched the needle to his skin.

There was no stencil. I didn't need one.

It took fifteen minutes.

I wiped the last of the ink and blood away with a soft cloth and took my foot off the pedal. I handed him the small mirror so he could see it.

Jeff took the mirror and gazed at the tattoo.

"You know, Kavanaugh, you could have a good career for yourself if you play your cards right."

I turned to put the machine on the shelf.

I felt his hand on the back of my neck. "Thanks," he whispered, all teasing gone now.

I didn't turn around. I didn't want him to see that I'd teared up. I nodded as I heard him slide off the chair. I reached over and grabbed a tube of ointment.

He stood, shrugging on his shirt.

"You better put this on first," I said, indicating the salve.

He grinned and winked. "You do it."

I rolled my eyes at him, ran my fingers through the ointment, and touched it to the new tattoo, red around the edges, slightly inflamed.

"That's Amore."

Read on for an excerpt from
Karen E. Olson's next Tattoo Shop Mystery

Ink Flamingos

Coming in June 2011 from Obsidian

The picture of the flamingo tattoo was on the blog an hour before they found the body. In retrospect, I probably should've called the cops immediately.

I was working on an elaborate tattoo of a heart wrapped in the American flag when Joel Sloane, one of my tattooists, stuck his head through the door. At The Painted Lady, where we do only custom ink, we've got four private rooms for tattooing, unlike street shops, which merely have stations out in the open.

"Brett," Joel said, nodding to my client, "sorry, but you have to see this."

I set my tattoo machine down on the counter and slipped off the blue latex gloves as I rose. "I'll be a minute," I told my client as I followed Joel toward the staff room. "What is it?" I asked his back.

Bitsy Hendricks, our shop manager, was standing in front of the small TV set in the corner of the staff room. When we came in, she whirled around, her eyes wide.

She pointed at the TV. Red and blue flashing lights lit up the screen, which was filled with a sea of police cruisers and at least one ambulance. Something bad had happened.

At first I was relieved it was a crime scene I wasn't witnessing personally. I'd gotten into a few situations in the last several months that had had me up close and personal with dead bodies, and I hoped that was all behind me now.

Until I saw the picture of Daisy Carmichael on the screen, the reporter's voice-over telling me that her body had been found in a hotel room.

My knees buckled a little, and Joel's arm snaked around my shoulders.

"Are they sure it's her?" I asked no one in particular. My voice sounded far away, like I was talking into a tunnel.

"Yes," Bitsy said flatly. "It's on every channel." And in case I didn't believe her, she aimed the remote at the set and clicked through all the local channels.

She was right. It was on every channel.

"Did they say what happened?" I asked.

"No, just that they found her body."

"Who found her?" I couldn't help myself. My curiosity was too strong.

"Think they said the room service guy."

As she spoke, a gurney rolled into view on the screen, a white sheet over what could have only been a body. I caught my breath.

Joel tightened his grip on my shoulder, and he put his other hand on Bitsy's.

Daisy, or Dee as she was known to her fans, was the lead singer of the band the Flamingos. They were a bit like the Go-Go's or the Bangles, but with a definite edge to their videos despite the wholesome pop sound. It wasn't Lady Gaga edgy, but more of an early-1980s punk look. Daisy, which was the name I knew her by, had come in to The Painted Lady two years ago for the first time. She'd stumbled onto it by accident as she window-shopped at the Venetian Grand Canal Shoppes, the upscale stores that surrounded my shop. While tattoo shops weren't exactly strangers to Las Vegas, aka Sin City, this location was the result of a little blackmail by the former owner, Flip Armstrong. My clientele was a little more high-class because of it, and dropping Daisy's name now and then didn't hurt, either. When she'd first stepped foot through the door, the Flamingos was just a dream. A YouTube-video discovery and two years later, they were at the top of the charts.

None of us had ever seen Daisy Carmichael socially. We'd never had dinner or drinks or even lunch with her. But she had come only here for her tattoos, and since she'd been here so frequently, we felt as though we had known her forever. Despite the edgy persona she portrayed to the public, Daisy was just a girl from Gardiner, Maine, a quiet little town where everything was within walking distance.

". . . an overnight sensation on YouTube," the reporter was saying about the Flamingos as a video of the band playing at the Bellagio on New Year's Eve just weeks ago lit up the screen.

That's right. They'd performed at the Bellagio. I frowned as I thought about it.

"She didn't call for an appointment in December?" I asked Bitsy, who kept track of all our appointments and schedules.

She flipped back her blond bob and narrowed her eyes at me. She knew what I was after.

"She didn't call. But we can't expect her to get a tattoo every time she's here," Bitsy said.

Okay, I could buy that. But I was thinking about that picture of the flamingo tattoo on that blog.

Since I'd had a little time to kill earlier, I'd been playing around on the Internet when I found a blog called Skin Deep—not very original—by clicking on a link from another one.

Skin Deep's latest post featured a tattoo of a flamingo. It was beautiful: long black lines with reds and pinks and oranges. It was one of the best I'd ever designed.

Except when I'd tattooed it on Daisy, there had been no colors.

I had scrolled up to the "About Me" section and read that blogger Ainsley Wainwright admired body art and the history of scarification and felt compelled to take photographs of tattoos seen on the Vegas Strip and post them so everyone could see their beauty. Other blogs were similar, but most added the stories surrounding the tattoos and where the person had gotten them. Skin Deep just showcased the art and let that tell the story. Too bad. I could've used the publicity. Or at least a link to The Painted Lady's Web site.

"When was she last here?" I asked Bitsy. I tried to think of the last tattoo I had given her. A tree branch that wove its way around her arm from her wrist to her shoulder.

"October," Bitsy said without consulting the appointment book. She had a memory like the proverbial steel trap.

Since I'd designed her first tattoo, every time she was in town, Daisy would have another one done. I'd done ten so far. The flamingo was number eight. There hadn't been any color the last two times she'd come in.

So sometime between October and now—it was the second week of February—Daisy had had another tattooist do that color.

"What's wrong, Brett?" Joel asked.

I went over to the light table, where my laptop lay. I booted it up, hooked up to the Internet, and found Skin Deep. I pointed to the picture of the flamingo tattoo. I noticed that the picture had been posted just a little more than an hour earlier.

Joel peered over my shoulder at the computer screen.

"When did she come back for the colors, Brett?" he asked.

I shook my head, puzzled. "She didn't. She can't have color. She's allergic to the dye, so she's got only black tattoos."

"So maybe it's not her. Maybe it's not yours," he suggested, plopping down next to me, his hefty frame testing the boundaries of the chair.

"It's mine," I said, pointing to the four flowers in the tip of the wing. "She wanted one for each of her bandmates. Who else could this be?"

I mulled the picture of the tattoo. I *knew* this was Daisy.

"Is the blogger Ainsley a woman?" Joel asked, startling me out of my thoughts. I'd almost forgotten he was there, if you could forget that a man weighing about three hundred pounds was sitting next to you.

I shrugged. "Have no idea. Could be a man, too, I guess. It's sort of androgynous name."

"So would she"—Joel indicated the flamingo—"have gone elsewhere to get the color done?"

My ego wished that she hadn't. But clearly, she had. I peered more closely at the photograph. The tattoo hadn't started to get infected. If it had, it would have looked like a boil or a bad burn, perhaps even oozing. Maybe she wasn't even really allergic. She'd told me she'd had a reaction to the red dye in an ibuprofen tablet several years ago, which was how her doctors had found out about the allergy. She said that to be on the safe side, she'd prefer to just have black tattoos.

Daisy was a canvas of black lines and curves, which made her tattoos stand out more than others, I thought.

Maybe she'd been in another tattoo shop in another city and the artist had talked her into adding the color. It was possible. It was also possible to get organic inks. I'd suggested that to her, but she'd rejected the idea. Maybe someone else had been more convincing.

I heard Bruce Springsteen singing "Born to Run." Glancing around the staff room, I spotted my messenger bag slung over the back of a chair. I grabbed it and pulled my cell phone out, flipping it open after noting the caller ID.

"Hey, Tim," I said. My brother, Tim Kavanaugh, was a Las Vegas police detective. I had a bad feeling about this.

"You hear about Dee Carmichael?" He didn't mince words.

"Watching it on TV right now. What happened?"

"That's what I'd like to ask you."

I stopped breathing for a second. "What do you mean?"

"We've got a witness who says she saw a tall redhead leaving the hotel room about two hours ago." He paused, and even if my mouth hadn't felt as though it were filled with sand, I knew he wasn't done yet. I waited as I curled one of my own red locks around my finger.

"We found some ink pots and tattoo needles in the trash."

Also Available from

Karen E. Olson

The Missing Ink

A Tattoo Shop Mystery

Brett Kavanaugh is a tattoo artist and owner of
an elite tattoo parlor in Las Vegas. When
someone calls to make an appointment to
get a tattoo of her fiancé's name embedded
in a heart, Brett takes the job but the girl
never shows. The next thing Brett knows, the
police are looking for her client, and the name
she wanted on the tattoo isn't
her fiancé's...

**Available wherever books are sold or at
penguin.com**

OM0003

Also Available from
Karen E. Olson

Pretty In Ink
A Tattoo Shop Mystery

Brett Kavanaugh is a tattoo artist and owner of
Vegas's hottest tattoo shop, The Painted Lady.
And in her spare time, she does some sleuthing.
After Brett and company ink Sin City's newest
drag queens, they're invited to opening night at
the strip's glamorous Nylon and Tattoos show—
which ends in disaster when a stranger with a
Queen of Hearts tattoo fatally injures Britney
Brassieres with a champagne cork. And when
another drag queen is found poisoned, it looks
like someone's targeting Vegas's
fabulous femmes...